"While it is a brilliant rom-com it also has a deeper more serious side that deals with anxiety and the resulting actions from this are dealt with sensitively and give a full explanation. I liked this added touch, that raised an already easy to read book into a memorable book for me.

   If you want something slightly different from the run of the mill Chick-Lits give this a go."

— ALISON DREW

"Fun, romantic and charming!"

— RAE READS

"*Stuck with Me* is your ideal holiday read whether that's laying on a sun lounger topping up your tan reading it, or reading it on your way to your holiday destination."

— THE WRITING GARNET

"What a great book... There were moments in this book that I literally laughed out loud. Then there were moments that just kind of warm your heart..."

— NICOLE LOCKYER - AUTHOR

"I gave this book 5 stars because it is a well written book but also because it made me laugh and cry while I was reading it. Well done Cassandra. Another brilliant book."

— GWEN SAMSON

STUCK WITH ME

A ROMANTIC COMEDY SET IN MAURITIUS

CASSANDRA PIAT

ISLANDGIRL PUBLISHING

ISBN 978-99949-0-389-4

Edited by KT Editing Services, United Kingdom
Cover design by Sue Traynor, United Kingdom
Printed by Imatech Ltd, Mauritius

For Claire...

PROLOGUE

MOLLY

Present day
Departure Lounge, Perth International Airport

"*O*UCH!"

I jumped in my seat, swivelling in horror towards the stranger sitting next to me. "Oh my God! Please tell me I didn't just pinch you!"

His scowl was quickly replaced by a chuckle when he saw the look on my face. "If you wanted to get my attention, you could have just talked to me you know."

"I'm so sorry, not to mention totally embarrassed, but I was actually meant to be pinching myself," I said, feeling like a fool.

"And pinching yourself is something you do for fun?"

"No!" I exclaimed, my face flushing. "I won this trip in a photo competition and I guess I'm having a hard time believing that it's actually real. I mean, just imagine – me,

1

Molly Malahan, from Perth, Western Australia, flying off to Mauritius! Totally surreal."

"Well, Molly Malahan from Perth, Western Australia, I duly confirm that you're not dreaming," he said solemnly, stroking his arm and wincing.

I hid my face behind my hands and groaned in embarrassment.

"I'm only kidding, it didn't hurt," he said, laughing. "Well not much anyway . . ." he added teasingly.

He was friendly and easy to talk to, so we chatted until I finally heard my flight being called.

"Oooh, that's me!" I exclaimed, jumping up in a flash as he watched me, looking amused.

"The plane won't leave without you, you know?" he said, grinning.

I beamed back at him. "Well, I'm not taking any chances!" I chuckled as I waved over my shoulder and practically ran to Gate 3 where we were boarding.

I stepped onto the plane and as I looked around me, my face broke into an ear-splitting grin. I was finally on my way. I glanced at my boarding pass and made my way down the aisle to row fifteen. After putting my bag into the overhead compartment, I slid into the window seat, sighing contentedly.

I was gazing out the window when I felt someone hovering over me. I turned to see a tall, extremely good-looking guy scowling down at me. Although I was rather taken aback by his less-than-friendly expression, I pretended not to notice and greeted him with a welcoming smile.

He grunted what I guessed was a greeting in reply and turned his attention to the overhead compartment, putting his bag inside without another word. I peeked up at him out of the corner of my eye. He looked extremely familiar. Had I met him before? I had no idea. He was in his mid-twenties with short jet-black hair, bushy black eyebrows framing a pair of silver-blue eyes, high cheekbones and a chiselled jawline housing a five o'clock shadow. He was catch-your-breath sexy. As his sullen gaze met mine again, it finally registered.

"Oh my God! You're—", I exclaimed, before stopping in mid-sentence when I realised how impossible that was. I mean, as if Ian Somerhalder, the actor from *The Vampire Diaries*, would have been travelling in economy class.

"No, I'm not!" he snapped, slamming the overhead compartment shut. "So don't bother telling me how much you love Damon, what a great couple Damon and Elena make and blah, blah, blah."

I stared at him in surprise. Okay, so he wasn't Ian Somerhalder – but whoever he was, he needed to lighten up *big time*.

"Erm . . . well, no. Actually, I was just going to tell you that your fly's undone!" I said, pointing to his trousers. *There! Take that, you grumpy hulk of gorgeousness.*

His head swung down, and just as quickly jerked back up again. "How *droll*," he drawled sarcastically, as he – and his perfectly well-zipped-up trousers – slid into the seat next to me.

I chuckled happily at my joke and pulled out the inflight magazine. I flipped through it, trying not to pay attention to my broody neighbour who seemed to be having trouble fitting his tall, Adonis body into his seat. When he finally sat still, I couldn't stop myself from stealing another look his way and was startled to see that he was observing me.

"What's with all the colours?" he asked, raising a disapproving eyebrow at me.

"What colours?"

He waved his hand dismissively in my general direction. "You!"

I bit down a smile and looked down at my fuchsia, purple, turquoise and white striped t-shirt, fuchsia jeans and purple sandals.

"I love being colourful. It makes me feel good," I said, smiling brightly.

"Bit sore on the eyes though," he grumbled, looking away.

I laughed, finding his unfriendliness disconcerting, but amusing. "You really should try colours, you know – I'm sure it would give you a better disposition."

"Sure it would. Not to mention the fact that I would look downright sexy in skinny pink jeans," he said, poker-faced.

Oh wow, had the guy made a joke? Hard to tell. Without another word, he grabbed a book from his bag, flicked through it until he found the page he was looking for, and began to read.

Oh well, guess I've been dismissed, I thought, amused. I snuggled down into my seat, deciding to leave him alone. Before long, I began to feel restless and couldn't stop myself from flashing a sideways glance at him. He was reading, brows furrowed.

"Can I ask you something?" I asked, despite my earlier resolve.

"No," he replied rudely, his eyes not leaving his book.

"Fine." I shrugged. "But I've got to say that for someone who's heading to one of the most beautiful destinations in the world, you sure don't look happy."

He scowled, but said nothing.

"I'm Molly, by the way," I remarked, realising that we hadn't introduced ourselves.

He seemed to hesitate a moment before his eyes darted briefly my way. "I'm Adam."

"Well, it's lovely to meet you too, Adam," I said, arching a teasing eyebrow.

He threw me one of his looks and I forced down the urge

to laugh. I knew I should leave him alone, but I couldn't resist teasing him some more.

"Good book?" I asked with mock innocence, leaning over to see the title. I was able to glimpse the author's name before he pulled it to his chest with a loud, exasperated sigh.

"Are you going to talk to me all the way to Mauritius?"

I guffawed. He was *so* rude. "I'm just trying to be nice and neighbourly. After all, we have a long flight ahead of us."

"Well, I'm not much of a talker."

"You aren't?" I quipped, trying to keep a straight face.

He gave me a withering look and turned away without a word.

"Ok-*ay* . . . I guess I'd better leave you to it then, huh?" I smiled to myself and decided to give the guy a break and let him be. Just because I was bursting with excitement didn't mean that everyone else had to be.

I watched Perth disappear beneath us as the plane soared into the sky. Once airborne, I took out my iPod and put on my favourite playlist. The first song hadn't even ended when I felt his eyes burning into me.

"What now?" I asked, turning to him with a sigh as I pressed pause.

"You're *singing*!"

"I am?" I replied with a chortle.

He shook his head in exasperation and went back to his book. I grinned and pressed play again, making a conscious effort not to sing aloud anymore. But when I heard "Happy" by Pharrell Williams begin, it was impossible for me to resist goading him again. I waited for the chorus to start, then pulled out my right earphone and stuck it to his ear.

"This one's for you, Adam!" I exclaimed, nudging him with my elbow. "Come on, sing with me!" I egged him on and began singing with gusto – "happy, happy, happy. . . " –

bouncing in rhythm to the song and bumping into his shoulder for effect.

He sat there staring at me, eyes wide and jaw slack, but I kept going, undeterred. I was having too much fun teasing him. When the chorus ended, I finally stopped and beamed up at him. He was still gaping at me and clearly thought I was certifiable. I threw my head back and burst out laughing.

"Do you ever switch it off?" I asked, once I'd calmed down.

"Switch what off?"

"Your basic cheerfulness!" I replied, biting down a smile.

I'm pretty sure I saw a flash of amusement in his eyes, but the look came and went in a blink, so much so that I wondered if I'd only imagined it.

Determined to ignore my unfriendly, albeit hunky, neighbour for the rest of the flight and bask in my I'm-going-to-Mauritius glow, I relaxed into my seat and pressed play again.

ADAM

This was going to be so much harder than I'd imagined. How the hell was I going to play at being broody and unfriendly for seven days with Little Miss Sunshine by my side? She was quite something with her multicoloured clothes, her sense of humour and a smile that lit up her whole face. There was no way I would be able to keep my steely gaze and cantankerousness up if she kept teasing me like that. It didn't help matters in the least that she seemed to find my crankiness entertaining.

I would *never* be able to pull this off. Yet, I *had* to . . .

ADAM

Two weeks earlier . . .

"*A*dam! Get in here!" my boss, Luke, called down the corridor from his office door. I saved the article I was working on and made my way to his office.

"Hey Luke, what's up?" I said, as I sat down opposite him. His desk was a mess, and it was a wonder we could see each other over the stacks of papers, newspapers and magazines covering it.

"Adam," he said, nodding his head in greeting. "I would tell you to sit down, but as you've already made yourself comfortable, I guess there's no point, is there?"

I grinned as he chuckled at his joke. His face then grew serious as he leaned back into his chair, eyes on me.

"So, Adam, I called you in here to tell you that I need you to take over Christine's feature for next month's issue," he said. "Her mother's having a knee operation so she has to head home for a few weeks to look after her."

You have got to be joking! I thought, aghast. Christine worked in the real life features section and I, for my part, was a sports writer. I loved my work and was good at what I did. A sports fan myself, my job fit me to a tee. Nothing beat the atmosphere in the players' locker rooms after a victory or the sheer despair after a defeat, and I loved being a part of it. But touching, emotional real life dramas?!!

"But Luke, I haven't done this kind of work for years," I said, running a hand through my hair.

"I saw your portfolio before I hired you. You've done quite a few real life features, and they were good. You're the best we have – your articles are full of humour, and you're a perceptive and sensitive guy. You'll be perfect for the job."

"Can't John do it?"

John was my colleague and childhood friend. He'd also been my housemate until two weeks ago when we'd had to move out of "our" house because the owners were selling it. We were now both living back at our parents' places, but only until we could find somewhere else to rent.

"No, he can't, he's got enough on his plate as it is. Petra's already in the middle of working on something and Laurent is covering the huge overseas conference in two weeks and will be out of the office a lot. So, that leaves you. There aren't any important games or championships going on, so we'll simply hash up something for the sports section. Now, what I suggest you do is meet with Christine. She already has an idea to run by you."

"Sure thing, Luke," I said, with fake enthusiasm. Let's face it, I would rather be getting my legs and chest waxed than work on this, but I had no choice in the matter.

"You'll be fine, Adam. I know you have it in you. To be honest, it's also a bit of a test as the guy who works freelance for us on international events will be taking on a full-time job in America next year, and we want to take on someone local to replace him," he said, pointing to me.

Me? I stared at him, mouth agape. I'd always dreamt of covering international sports events.

"Seriously?"

He nodded. "You do a good job with this and we'll discuss it again next month. I'll have to run it by the board of directors, but I'll back you up. I think you would be a great candidate for the post."

"I don't know what to say," I said, still in shock. "Thank you."

Luke nodded in acknowledgement before jerking his head towards the door. "Now go and see Christine. You have an article to write!"

As I made my way back to my desk, I was bursting with excitement. I couldn't believe I had a chance of becoming the international sports feature writer for the newspaper. I would get to travel all over the world and be a part of international sporting events. I would also get to meet some of the greatest sports heroes of our time. It would be an amazing challenge and something I'd always aspired to. However, I had to get this feature article done first.

With a deep sigh, I dialled Christine's extension, and she told me to come over right away. Grabbing a notepad and pen, I made my way to her office. With each step I took, the exhilaration I'd felt about the promotion dwindled and was replaced by a feeling of dread.

"Hey, Adam!" she said cheerfully, looking up from her computer.

I threw myself down on the chair opposite her. "How the hell am I going to write a real life article, Christine? I mean, look at me – do I look like a sensitive, perceptive guy made to write touching articles?"

"Well-ll," she said giving me a once-over. "No. You definitely look more like someone who should be on the cover of a magazine."

I rolled my eyes, not amused in the least.

Suddenly I realised that I hadn't asked about her mother. *Nice, Adam!* "I'm sorry to hear about your mum by the way."

"Thanks," she said, smiling. "But she'll be fine. It's not a major operation but she lives alone and will need help getting around for a few weeks."

"That's good to hear. I hope everything goes well," I said, as I leaned back into my chair. It didn't take more than a few seconds for my thoughts to return to the dreaded article and I looked back at her. "Do you honestly think I can do this, Christine?"

"Of course I do. I had a look at your earlier pieces when you worked for *It's Your Life* magazine and they were great. You're funny and sensitive and have a wonderful way with people."

"Stop, you're making me blush," I said, touched by her praise. She wasn't one to lavish compliments when it came to work. She laughed, leaning over and handing me a sheet of paper. I skimmed over it before looking up at her with a frown.

"This is your project. Her name is Molly Malahan. She's twenty-five years old and works as a photographer for Events Xtraordinaire," Christine explained.

"Right. And what's so interesting about her?" I asked, looking down at the sheet again.

"Well, the other day my friend Nicole and I were discussing the fact that some people just seemed fundamentally happy no matter what they faced in life. So we wondered if happiness was a feeling, as in you were either happy or sad, or if it could actually be a choice. That's when she told me about Molly – always has a smile on her face, is never in a bad mood, sees everything positively to the point of being super annoying apparently."

"That's all well and good, but I still don't get it."

"On my way home that day, I thought about our conversation and decided that I should write an article about this Molly girl. I wanted to observe her and see if a) she is a genuinely happy person, b) if she has chosen to be happy or c) if she pretends to be happy."

I still had no idea where she was going with this, and I wished I didn't have to find out.

"The thing is," she went on, "I realised that I wouldn't get the answers I'm after by simply interviewing her."

"No?"

"No. It's too complex for that. I have to see her in everyday life and test her to see how much she can cope with and still keep smiling."

"And how exactly did you plan on doing that?"

"Well, that's the problem. I'm not sure yet," she admitted, grimacing. "I guess you'll have to help me out here, seeing as you'll be the one taking on this article."

"Great," I grumbled.

She grinned, totally impervious to my sulkiness. "Nicole works with Molly and suggested that we hire their company to organise an event for us and make Molly's life a nightmare to see how she copes."

I shook my head. "One night or one day isn't enough time for an article like this. It would have to be something that spreads out over at least a week or two."

"I know, but how the hell are we going to insert ourselves into her life all of a sudden? Do you think we could go and work at Events Xtraordinaire for two weeks, passing ourselves off as trainee photographers or something?"

"Not passing *ourselves* off, passing *me* off!" I exclaimed melodramatically, making her giggle. "Besides, I'm useless at taking photographs and don't know the first thing about cameras. She'd catch on straight away."

"I guess you're right," she said with a sigh. "Don't worry, I'll think of something. Hey! How about you accidentally bump into her and ask her out on a date?" she exclaimed as an afterthought. "Then you could date her over two weeks and test her that way."

"You have *got* to be joking!" I exclaimed incredulously. "I *refuse* to mess with someone's feelings for an article."

Christine rolled her eyes. "Fine. But we have to come up with something. And soon."

"Okay, let's give it until tomorrow morning," I said, getting up to go. Pausing near the doorway, I turned back to her. "For the record, I really hate you for doing this to me."

She laughed good-naturedly as I headed out the door, waving over my shoulder. What had Luke and Christine got me into? How on earth was I going to encroach into this happy Molly's life and find out if she is fundamentally happy, if she's chosen to be happy, or then again, if she's simply pretending to be happy? "Test her" to see how she copes – what does that even mean? I didn't like it. I just didn't like it one bit. I groaned, burying my head in my hands.

The worse thing was that I knew I would have to do this, and do it well, if I wanted to stand a chance at getting that promotion.

2

MOLLY

"*Y*ou look great, sweetheart. Now, please turn your head a little to the side," I said, smiling patiently and wondering how I could possibly be this calm after spending half an hour photographing Zoe, a little terror. She'd been a nightmare, but I couldn't help finding her adorable. Needless to say, I'd been hopeless at being stern with her, which obviously hadn't helped, but thankfully we were almost done.

Zoe looked at herself in the mirror, contemplating the dress she'd changed into, and her face scrunched up in distaste. "I don't like this dressth – ith's horrible! I look nothing like a printhesse in it!" she screamed, stamping her foot.

"But you *do* look like a princess," I said, trying to cajole her. "Even prettier than a real one."

She didn't look convinced and I realised that if I wanted to get this photo shoot done, a bit of bribery was essential. I was already dreaming of relaxing in a hot bath with a glass of red wine . . .

"Can I tell you a secret?" I said in a conspiratorial whisper.

"Yesth!" she cried, running towards me, her eyes shining with excitement.

"If you want to become a real princess when you grow up, you have to learn how to smile all the time and be nice to everyone. That's how little girls become princesses. Do you want to give it a try?" I whispered in her ear.

"Yesth, yesth, yesth!" she exclaimed, jumping up and down in delight.

I went on to tell her what to do, and it worked like magic. She sat when I told her to sit, smiled when I told her to smile and was the most adorable little princess ever. I wished I'd thought of it sooner. I finally snapped the last shot and sighed with relief.

I loved my work, but it could be exhausting at times. I was privileged to do the work I did as I got to share in the most special moments of people's lives. They allowed me into their world for a few hours, and it was magical. I love catching that exact moment when the groom sets eyes on the bride as she walks into the church; the look of love and emotion passing between the parents as their daughter says her vows; the look of pure delight on a child's face when opening a present, or even a burst of laughter between friends – perfect moments made everlasting by me - how can I *not* love my job?

I strolled back to my car, happy to have finished for the day. I thought about stopping off to see my mum on my way home but didn't have the energy to see her after the day I'd had. People often tell me that I've always got a smile on my face, and it's true that I always try to focus on the positive side of every situation, but even I have my limits . . . and

handling my mum requires all the happy vibes I possess.
photo shoot with little Zoe had exhausted me, and I really
wanted to go home.

Home is a small three-bedroomed house I share with
Zach, one of my best friends, in Mount Pleasant, not far
from the Swan River. I love our house – it's a mixture of Ikea
(bright colours = me) and vintage chic (Zach) and is super
cosy, colourful and homey with big comfy sofas full of multicoloured cushions in various sizes and colours, photos in a
mix-and-match of frames on the walls, a big antique mirror
in the dining room, candles everywhere and a super-funky
kitchen.

Zach and I share the same passion: photography. The
only difference is that I'm fascinated by people, whereas he is
more into nature. He is a photographer for *National
Geographic* and travels all over the world. Unfortunately, this
means he's away a lot, but I'm happy for him because he loves
his work. When he's around, we spend hours talking shop
and dissecting our photos, discussing the angle of light and
the size of the aperture and exposure for each one. We
converted the third bedroom into a photo studio, with a
corner for developing our prints when we use our old
cameras. The walls of the studio are covered from top to
bottom with a selection of our favourite photos, a mix of
nature and people, and the effect is breathtaking.

Zach, Anna – my other best friend – and I have been
friends since junior high. We were in the school's arts
programme and while Zach and I went on to study photography, Anna went into events management. After graduation,
Anna opened the small events management firm I work at
and employed me as their photographer. We both love
working together and are passionate about what we do.

I put my bag down on the table before heading to the
bathroom to run my much-awaited bath. I poured a good

dose of bath salts into the water before going back to the kitchen to get a glass of wine. As I sank into the warm water, I sighed, feeling my whole body relax. What more could a girl want?

I thought of the wedding shoot I had the following day at King's Park. It was such a beautiful spot with Perth, South Perth, and the Swan River in the background. I was really looking forward to it. I loved weddings. Although I hadn't given my heart out to anyone since I was seventeen, preferring to play it safe, I was a real romantic at heart and hoped that one day someone would sweep me off my feet . . .

3

ADAM

"*A*dam, get in here right now!" Christine hollered over the phone the next day. "I've found the solution!"

I groaned and made my way to her office. I didn't want to do this article and wished they'd leave me alone in the sports department.

"Sit down, sit down!" she said, motioning towards the chair impatiently. "I'm so excited I could pee in my pants!"

"Please don't!" I said gravely, making her laugh.

"So here it is – my friend Nicole's boyfriend owns a travel agency and the agency was given two free tickets and one week's accommodation to – get this . . . *Mauritius!*"

"Yes, so . . ." I frowned. I didn't see how that had anything to do with me.

"Well, it seems that no one at the agency can take time off at the moment and the ticket is only valid for another two weeks, so Nicole offered them to me. Since I can't go either – *ta-daaa . . .*" she said with delight, brandishing two airplane tickets at me. "They're all yours! Two tickets and seven days all-expenses-paid at the Le Panache Beach Resort in Mauritius! Isn't that genius?"

I frowned again, still not following her.

"Don't you get it? It's perfect. You'll take Molly with you and you'll have a week to get to know her and test her out and get everything you need for the article!"

I finally understood where she was going with this and my mouth fell to the floor.

"You're kidding, right?"

"No! Of course I'm not. It's brilliant – if I do say so myself."

I stared at her in disbelief. "And how exactly do you suggest I go about it with this Molly girl I've never met before? Should I pop over to her office, introduce myself, and in the same breath invite her to come and spend a week with me in Mauritius?" I asked, my voice laced with sarcasm. "Yep, I can definitely see how that would work!"

"Oh, don't be such a killjoy," Christine snapped, scowling at me. "Nicole will pretend that she'd entered one of Molly's photos in an alleged competition run by the agency, and that Molly had won, the prize being a trip to Mauritius for a week."

It was my turn to scowl at her.

"Before you say anything, she's already chosen the photo and planned all the details. Molly is apparently the least suspicious person around and won't doubt a thing."

"Fine," I said, with a long-suffering sigh. "And how do we explain that I'm going with her?"

"She won't know. You'll happen to be sitting next to her on the plane and then be in the same hotel, with a room next door to hers," she explained, eyes sparkling with delight.

"I still don't get how she'll suddenly want to spend every last minute with me," I said, not at all convinced this would work.

Christine arched a teasing eyebrow and grinned.

I rolled my eyes and stood up. Jamming my hands into my pockets, I walked towards the window and stared outside. What had she got me into?

"You'll have to sign up to any activity she chooses and find yourself everywhere she is, and basically become the bane of her existence."

I turned around and scowled at her as I sat back down. How on earth was I going to pull this off? I might have inherited Ian Somerhalder's looks, but I was by no means an actor.

"Just remember this conversation, how annoyed you are, how you're all broody and scowling – and pretty much act that way all week," Christine said with a big smile.

"Fine!" I finally retorted. "It's not like I have much choice in the matter anyway." I grabbed one of the tickets and a hotel voucher from the desk. "When do we leave?"

Next Monday, it seemed.

One week . . . one week to devise my strategy. Maybe I could go and take a crash course in acting. I didn't even know what this Molly Sunshine person looked like. What if she was a complete toad? Then again, I didn't have to date the girl or marry her, I simply had to annoy her and stalk her. *Great! Just great,* I muttered under my breath as I walked back to my office, threw myself on my chair and stared into space as I thought about the mess I found myself in. I couldn't believe this was happening.

A few minutes later, John strolled past and poked his head into my office. Seeing the look on my face, he frowned.

"Why so glum, mate?" he asked, leaning his tall frame against the door and crossing his arms over his large chest.

"I've been given an assignment from hell!"

His eyes widened because I wasn't one to complain about the assignments I was sent on.

"That sounds pretty bad. Want to tell me about it?" he asked, walking in and sitting down opposite me. I gave him a rundown of the situation and he listened in silence, but his amusement was reflected in his hazel eyes.

As his lips twitched, I stopped short. "It's *not* funny!"

"Come on, it kind of is," he replied, laughing. I scowled at him, unamused. "Oh relax, will you? Besides, you haven't told me how you plan on meeting this Molly girl yet."

"Well, I was getting to that before you so rudely interrupted me with your laughter!"

He struggled to put on a straight face and said, "Okay, no more laughing. I promise."

I narrowed my eyes at him in warning, before carrying on. "I'll be going to Mauritius and spending a week there – with her."

"*Whoa!* Hang on a sec there!" John exclaimed, holding up his palm. "Do you mean to tell me that you're pulling that face because you have to go to *Mauritius* for a week?"

"Yes! It's not as if I'll get to relax and enjoy myself. I have to spend it with a girl I've never met before and spend the week harassing her!"

"But it's a tropical island, Adam – sun, sand and sea, and lots of gorgeous locals!"

"Are you really that dense or are you doing it to annoy me?"

He chuckled. "I don't understand why you're so upset. Look at it as an adventure. You're off on an all-expenses-paid trip to Mauritius for goodness' sake!"

After John left, I sat staring out the window for a while, lost in thought. Although I could see where he was coming from, I couldn't muster up any excitement because, any way I looked at it, the bottom line was that I would have to harass a stranger for a week and pretend to be someone I'm not. As if that wasn't bad enough, there was also the possibility of a promotion hanging in the balance . . . If I messed this up, I would lose the chance of getting the job of my dreams.

4

MOLLY

J was sitting at my desk going through the photos of my shoot with little Zoe when Nicole, one of my colleagues, walked into my office with a huge smile on her face.

"I have some amazing news for you, Molly!" she said, sounding excited.

"You do?"

"Yes!" she exclaimed, waving a piece of paper in front of me. "You've won a trip to Mauritius!"

"I've *what?*"

"You heard me! You've won a trip to Mauritius!" she repeated, putting a voucher down in front of me. I glanced at it briefly before staring back at her, my eyes popping out of their sockets.

"Seriously?"

She nodded. "Yep! Seven days in a five-star resort!"

"But *how*? What? I mean . . ." I stuttered, unable to form a coherent sentence.

She laughed and explained that she'd entered one of my wedding photographs in a competition organised by her boyfriend's travel agency, and that I'd won. I couldn't believe it. I'd never won anything in my life – except for a painting set in a drawing competition in fourth grade. But this! An all-expenses-paid trip to *Mauritius*! I screeched in delight, jumping into her arms and hugging her. I felt her tense up a little because we weren't exactly – or at all – close, but I didn't care, I was *so* excited. I told her I would check with Anna to see when I would be free to go and would let her know.

"About that . . ." she said, grimacing. "There is one teeny problem. It's one of those special deals and you have to leave next Monday. It's not negotiable."

"Oh no," I replied, my smile fading. "It might be a bit too short notice then."

"Of course not! You can't miss this chance," Nicole exclaimed. "We'll cover for you here and if there are any photo shoots, we'll hire a freelance photographer to replace you next week. We do that when we have too much work on, so we can do it now too."

I went straight to Anna's office and told her the news.

"*Oh my God!*" she shrieked, jumping into my arms and hugging me tightly. "That's amazing! Of course you have to go. This is a chance of a lifetime."

"I *knoooow*!" I squealed, jumping up and down in her arms. "I'm so excited!"

After work, I drove to my mum's place to tell her the news. I didn't particularly want to go because, my mum being my mum, I knew that she wouldn't be very enthusiastic and would put a damper on things. However, she needed to know as soon as possible so she could mentally prepare herself for my departure.

As I pulled into her driveway, I took a deep breath and psyched myself up – like I always have to do – before going in.

My dad died when I was nine years old and I don't remember him much. All I know is that he never smiled or laughed and that I often felt worried when he was around. My mum had forever been trying to cheer him up and make him smile, but she'd seldom managed. I hadn't understood why he was always so sad, and for a while I even thought it was my fault. But as I grew up, I realised that he suffered from depression. My mum tried to compensate by being over-positive and over-enthusiastic about everything – I guess to try to make life at home less gloomy for us all. But it clearly took a lot out of her, because when he died in a car accident, she seemed to just sag with exhaustion and she became the shadow of the woman she had once been.

I hadn't understood the change in her, and although I'd done everything I could to try to make her smile, I hadn't often succeeded. It had made me miserable. Then one day, when I was twelve, I was sent to see the school psychologist. She was lovely and made me see that I wasn't to blame for my mum's behaviour. She also explained that I didn't have to be like my mum and dad, and that I could keep smiling and laughing if I chose to. So that day, I promised my twelve-year-old self that I would never be like my parents and I would do everything in my power to be happy and look at the good side of things. Although it hasn't always been easy, I've more or less managed to stick to my decision, despite the pain of living with a depressed and anxious mother.

"Why on earth do you want to go there?" my mum exclaimed, when I told her the news. "It's so dangerous to take the plane nowadays, there are so many crashes, and not to mention terrorists!"

I spent my whole visit comforting her and convincing her that it was exciting and fun and that I would be fine, and more importantly, that she would be fine without me.

It was a relief to finally be home. I pushed the door open and switched on the lights. Everything was quiet, which meant that Zach was either working late again or sleeping over at his girl-of-the-moment's place. He didn't have time for a relationship because he was away so much, but that didn't stop him from always having some girl or other on his arm when he was around. I loved teasing him about his sluttish ways, but knew that he was a real softie at heart.

I pulled a wine glass out of the kitchen cabinet, filled it to the brim and headed to the sofa where I settled myself down with a huge sigh. I took a sip of wine, closing my eyes and savouring the taste as it slid down my throat. I somehow always felt so vulnerable after seeing my mum. I took another deep breath. *Positive thoughts, Molly,* I urged myself. As I began to relax, it suddenly registered that I was off to *Mauritius.* My face broke into an ear-splitting grin as I cried out to the empty room, "I'm off to Mauritius on Monday! *Woo-hoo-oo!"*

I bounced off the sofa, spilling half my glass of wine over the floor. "Oops!" I giggled, deciding to ignore the mess for now, and began dancing around the room, chanting at the top of my lungs, *'I'm going to Mauritius, I'm going to Mauritius.'* Suddenly I froze. Zach was standing in the open doorway with a huge grin on his face, and next to him stood a gorgeous brunette, looking at me, mouth agape.

"You okay there, Mol? You don't look too . . . er . . . sober," he said, raising a teasing eyebrow.

"I'm not drunk!" I exclaimed. "I'm just very excited!"

"That, I can see." He walked into the room. "And may I ask why?"

"*I won a trip to Mauritius!*" I screeched, running towards him and jumping into his arms. The brunette watched us silently, eyes wide.

Zach hugged me back and chuckled. "That's amazing! How—"

"I know! *Totally* amazing," I replied, cutting him off as I pulled away from him. I opened my mouth to tell him about the competition when a thought crossed my mind.

Zach looked bemused as my mouth opened and closed. "What's wrong?"

"Oh *nooo*! I don't think I've got a decent bikini! I can't go to Mauritius without a great bikini." I turned on my heels and ran off. Zach's laughter followed me to my room, making me laugh too. I'm pretty sure the gorgeous brunette rolled her eyes my way, but I *so* didn't care, because I was going to Mauritius – *and she wasn't*!

5

ADAM

Present day

I'd been standing in the plane's matchbox toilet for the past ten minutes practising my scowls and dark looks in the mirror, but I had to get out before they sent someone to check if I was partaking in the Mile High Club thing, or if I had died or something.

Okay, Adam, you can do this! I took a deep breath and finally pulled open the toilet door. I made my way back to my seat and as I approached, I saw that Little Miss Sunshine had her headphones on and was watching a movie. I slumped into my seat and was flipping through the selection of movies when Molly burst out laughing. I spun towards her, fixing a scowl on my face. Obviously sensing my eyes boring into her, she turned to me, her face alight with humour.

"You've got to watch this. It's *Two Weeks Notice* with Hugh Grant and Sandra Bullock."

"*Urrgh*," I said with a shudder. "Don't mind if I don't."

She rolled her eyes with a laugh before turning back to her screen, totally unperturbed by my unfriendliness. Getting back to the task at hand, I scrolled through the list of movies once more, but nothing piqued my interest. I was way too distracted to concentrate on a film anyway. My mind was racing, and I couldn't help worrying about the upcoming week with Molly.

I snuck a look at her. She was pretty cute with long, chestnut hair falling in gentle waves down her back, a cute little nose and a surprisingly sexy mouth. I'm not quite sure what was sexy about it, maybe her lips being a little pulpier than I would have expected. Her large almond-shaped eyes, unguarded and expressive, were a striking shade of green and were framed by long eyelashes. She had a sort of natural, unknowing beauty, and there was just something about her that made me want to keep looking . . .

As she laughed aloud again, I nudged her. "You're doing it again."

"Sorry, what was that?" she asked, pulling one of her headphones off.

"You're laughing aloud again! It's really annoying."

She looked a bit taken aback, but then just laughed good-naturedly. "I'm sorry, but I can't help it – Hugh Grant cracks me up!"

I shook my head with faked irritation. She grinned and put her headphones back into place. She was incredible. If I'd been in her shoes, I would have told me where to stick my bad mood ages ago.

Oh jeepers. This was *so* not going the way I had imagined.

6

MOLLY

*T*he poor thing was still being a complete grump. This time, it seemed that I was laughing too loudly. *As if!* I glanced his way and saw that he was scowling at his screen. It was a wonder he didn't have huge crease lines on his forehead with the amount of scowling he did. A real shame too with the looks he had. He still hadn't smiled once since we took off, although I'm pretty sure I saw his lips twitching earlier – probably wishful thinking on my part.

As the air hostesses came to serve dinner, I realised I was starving because I'd been far too excited to eat before leaving.

"Mmm . . . that smells wonderful," I said, smiling at the air hostess as she handed me my tray.

Adam scoffed next to me. "I just know you're going to tell me that there's nothing more delicious than airplane food, aren't you?"

"Well, it does smell pretty good," I retorted cheerfully, as I pulled off the aluminium cover and dug in.

When I flashed him a sideways glance a few minutes later, he hadn't started eating yet and was staring at the food with distaste. He must have sensed that I was watching him because all of a sudden he jammed a forkful of chicken into his mouth and exclaimed theatrically, *"Mmm . . . ooohhh . . . just heavenly,"* and rolled his eyes upwards as if he were in ecstasy.

I burst out laughing. "There you go! That's the spirit!"

He gaped at me. "Are you for real?"

I laughed even harder. For some reason, the grumpier he became, the more hilarious I thought he was. I'd never met anyone so cranky before and somehow I got the impression that it wasn't just a one-off or the male equivalent of PMS, but that it was simply the way he was. How sad was that?

We carried on eating our meal in silence for a while, but in the end I couldn't resist baiting him again and nudged him playfully. "Delicious, isn't it?" I said with mock innocence. He furrowed his brows menacingly before turning away. I giggled happily to myself. This was turning out to be such fun.

However, after dinner I gave up trying to make conversation and settled down to watch the rest of the movie. I snuggled happily into my seat and decided to ignore Mr Grumpy Dumpy.

By the time the movie ended, the lights had been dimmed and I decided to try to get some sleep. I took off my headphones, switched off my screen and tried to find a comfortable position. I'd just shifted positions for the third time when I heard an exasperated sigh coming from my right-hand side. No need to ask who it was. I lifted my gaze and found him scowling at me once again.

"What?" I asked, rolling my eyes.

"Are you quite done moving there?" he grumbled. "You're getting on my nerves jittering around like that!"

"My-oh-my, looks like someone forgot to take their happy pill this morning," I quipped, cocking my head as I held his gaze.

"Looks like you, on the other hand, took a few too many!" he shot back with a scowl.

I lost it again. I couldn't help it. He threw me a dirty look, obviously not amused that I had taken it as a joke.

"Can I go to sleep now?" I asked.

"Just stop moving around, whatever you do!" he groused, turning back to his screen.

"Yeah, yeah," I muttered before snuggling into my seat again, making a special effort not to move too much, and fell into a peaceful snooze. I dreamt of coconut trees and sandy beaches with turquoise blue seas . . . and there was definitely no sign of Mr Grumpy Dumpy anywhere on the beach.

I woke up to the sound of the breakfast trolleys being pushed along the aisle. Adam was still fast asleep and it surprised me how relaxed he looked. My gaze lingered over him for a minute . . . he sure was gorgeous.

As the trolleys approached us, an air hostess prodded Adam gently. He opened one eye and stared at her in confusion. As he took in the beautiful lady in front of him, his face broke into a lopsided smile. *Oh my goodness, Adam had just smiled!* I gasped in surprise and his head spun towards me, the smile dying on his lips as he straightened up. Oh well, I guess it's just *me* he doesn't like then.

I stared outside the window as I drank my coffee, wishing that Adam had been friendlier because I was bursting with excitement at the prospect of spending a week in a luxury hotel in Mauritius and desperately wanted to talk about it.

Adam's sullen voice broke me out of my reverie as he muttered, "This coffee tastes like muddy water."

I looked at his surly expression. "Oh, and that would be because you've tasted muddy water before?"

He shot me one of his withering looks and I rolled my eyes in response. I seemed to be doing a lot of that where he was concerned.

Half an hour later, the pilot informed us that we were starting our descent and would be landing in Mauritius shortly. I squealed in delight as I saw the coastline appear and grabbed Adam's arm.

"Look! Look! Look!" I shrieked, pointing out the window to the endless stretch of white sandy beaches and blue sea. Adam looked at me as if I had grown two heads but glanced outside for a second, before turning away without a word. Oh well, his loss, I thought as I carried on staring dreamily out the window. When the plane hit the tarmac and began careering down the runway, I felt the familiar fear grip me and without realising what I was doing, I grabbed Adam's hand and squeezed the life out of it. I'd always been terrified of landings, fearing that the brakes wouldn't take and we'd go crashing into a million pieces. Finally, after what seemed like hours but was in fact a few seconds, the plane stopped. I exhaled loudly – we were safe.

Adam jerked his hand out of my grip, scowling.

"I'm not much of a hand-holder," he muttered, grimacing, as he wiped his hand on his trousers. I guffawed at the look of disgust on his face, but felt my face flush nevertheless.

"Sorry about that. I have a bit of a thing about landings."

"You don't say." He raised a disapproving eyebrow at me.

Oh my word, the man desperately needed a hug. I wondered how he would react if I suddenly gave him a huge bear hug. I chuckled just imagining his reaction. He stared at me once more, clearly wondering why I was laughing to myself like a crazy woman, then shook his head and got up to remove his bag from the overhead cabinet. I was truly surprised when he handed mine over to me. So there *was* some kindness in there somewhere. I smiled and thanked him, but of course he ignored both my thanks and my smile and stared ahead.

Once inside the terminal building, I went through immigration and lost sight of Adam for a while before spotting him again at the baggage carousel. After getting my suitcase, I walked past him and stopped to say goodbye.

"Enjoy your holiday, Adam. It was nice to meet you," I said, smiling wickedly.

He nodded and waved without saying anything, turning back to the conveyor belt.

"Where are you staying?" I asked, before realising that I didn't even care. Oh well, seemed like a good idea at the time.

He turned and stared at me. "At a hotel."

I snorted with laughter. I should have expected that. I honestly couldn't figure out what I thought of him – he was as infuriating as he was funny. One thing was clear: he did not like me. Oh well, can't win them all. Besides, I wouldn't have to see him ever again anyway. I pushed my trolley away, waving over my shoulder, and made my way towards the exit. I walked out of the airport and stopped short, looking around me in awe. OMG! I was in MAURITIUS!

7

ADAM

I heaved a sigh of relief as I watched her multicoloured form walk off. I had no idea how I was going to carry out this assignment successfully. I'd spent most of our seven-and-a-half-hour flight being extremely cranky and unfriendly and she hadn't flinched at any of my remarks, scowls or comments. On the contrary, I seemed to put an even bigger smile on her face if that was at all possible. My face hurt from scowling so much. I was usually a friendly kind of guy and this felt like I was acting in a movie, playing the role of my evil twin.

I made my way to the counter to find out about the transfer bus and was told that the agency had booked a seat for me on the hotel's airport shuttle. After asking for directions, I made my way towards the exit. I groaned inwardly, knowing that if the agency had booked a seat for me, they would also have booked one for Little Miss Sunshine. I didn't have the energy to go back to my acting. I'd already had more than enough for today. As was to be expected, as soon as I stepped onto the bus, I ran straight into her.

"This has to be a bad dream," I grunted, just loudly enough for her to hear.

She laughed good-naturedly, sliding into her seat.

"Oh *please* tell me you're not staying at Le Panache Beach Resort too?"

She looked a bit surprised, but smiled and nodded. "Sure looks like it, Grumpy Dumpy!"

I pursed my lips tightly, fighting down a smile at the well-deserved nickname, then walked to the back of the bus and sat down, relieved to be alone. I relaxed into my seat and closed my eyes. I was actually feeling exhausted after the flight. As we drove out of the airport and sped down the motorway, I opened my eyes and gazed out the window at the endless sugar cane fields. After a while, we turned off and began driving through a few small villages which had a lot of rickety little shops lining both sides of the street. Some were painted in bright trendy colours advertising Coca-Cola, Fanta, Emtel or other brands which I'd never heard of, and they looked amazing, whereas others looked as if they'd been there for hundreds of years and were about to crumble to the ground at any minute. For the most part, there were no pavements so there were people, bicycles, dogs and cars on the road, which undoubtedly made it quite a challenge to drive, and most drivers seemed to spend a lot of time with their hands on their horns. We drove past a 'Speed Zone' sign which sounded quite exciting, as if we were about to enter a special zone where speeding was allowed or where races took place, but it was, in fact, simply to warn drivers there were speed cameras up ahead.

Eventually we found ourselves enclosed in the majestic mountains ranges for a while, before the ocean suddenly appeared and spread out ahead of us. It was stunning. We drove down towards the sea and past a public beach called Flic en Flac – I couldn't help smiling at the name; it had a great ring to it. I sighed happily as I took in the endless extent of translucent blue sea, imagining myself diving into it soon. It was exactly what I needed.

I let everyone get off the bus before walking out myself so that Molly would have enough time to check in. Somehow I preferred waiting until later to see her reaction when she realised that we were room neighbours. She would probably just laugh it off, but I was the one who needed time to prepare myself for *my* reactions and comments.

I strolled around the front of the hotel, admiring the architecture of the buildings, the thatched roofs and the coconut trees everywhere. I could even smell the sea and was suddenly impatient to get to my room, change and head straight to the beach. I walked into the reception area just as Molly was about to leave. I hid behind a pillar, waiting for her to go, and overheard the porter telling her that he would bring her luggage over in five minutes. As I watched her heading off, I suddenly had an idea. I'd just found a way to annoy her big time . . .

As soon as she was out of sight, I walked up to the porter and told him not to worry about Molly's suitcase, that I was with her and would bring her luggage for her.

Once I was given my key, I took both our suitcases and headed to my room, hoping that I wouldn't bump into her on the way. But luck was on my side – there was no sign of her. I quickly opened the door to my room and rolled both our suitcases inside, hiding Molly's in the bathroom.

Our rooms were on the ground floor. Mine had a huge king-sized bed to the left and a little lounge with an L-shaped sofa and a wall-mounted TV to the right. Large sliding doors opened up onto a little veranda on which there was a small round table with two chairs on one side, and two long rattan deck chairs on the other. Every room had its very own private little garden which then gave way to a bigger lawn that eventually led directly to the beach. I could see the sea in the distance. I breathed in deeply and sighed with pleasure. *This is the life*, I thought with a smile.

I walked back inside and threw myself onto the bed. For the first time since finding out about this trip, I felt a little tug of excitement to be in Mauritius. Maybe it wouldn't be too bad after all. I relaxed for a few minutes, just looking out over the turquoise blue sea, watching a yacht slowly sailing past. It was so peaceful. If only I didn't have to pretend to be grouchy, this could really be an amazing holiday. I changed into my board shorts and when I stepped out of my room, I ran into Molly. She stared at me, mouth agape and I glared back at her, pretending to be outraged.

"Are you *stalking* me or something?" I asked with narrowed eyes.

She laughed dryly and nodded. "Oh yeah, I spend my time stalking cranky, unfriendly men who seem to dislike me immensely."

I had to concentrate hard to keep my scowl in place and bite down my laughter.

"Anyway, although I would *love* to keep chatting," she said, "I have to go and sort out a little suitcase problem."

"What problem?" I asked with mock innocence.

"The porter was meant to be bringing my suitcase to my room but he never showed up. I went back to the reception area but he wasn't there. I'm going back now to see if he's returned."

"But wouldn't your suitcase still be at the reception if it wasn't delivered to your room?"

"Apparently not. With my luck, he probably delivered it to another room and, as we speak, some stranger is busy trying on my bras and knickers for size."

Once again I forced down a spurt of laughter and said with nonchalance, "Worse comes to worse, you could always just go straight home."

Her eyes widened for a split second, then she shook her head and laughed good-naturedly.

"Okay, I'd better head back there now." She waved and took off back towards reception. As my eyes followed her, I couldn't help grinning as I wondered how long it would take her to figure out what had happened to her suitcase . . .

8

MOLLY

I couldn't believe that guy. What was his problem? He'd spent the whole flight being unfriendly and blatantly rude and now he was suddenly joking around with me? If only it were funny. It was just bloody infuriating!

The image of the porter telling me with a big smile that my suitcase had been brought to my room by 'ze nice gentleman woo ees stayeeng in room 345 next to you' flashed through my mind again as I opened the mini fridge and grabbed an orange juice. I was tempted to open a bottle of wine, but it was a bit early for that – even though I could undeniably use it. I settled on the veranda with my drink and waited for Mr Funnypots to return so I could get my suitcase back.

Arrghhh! *The cheek of the guy!* I felt like screaming with frustration. I wanted to go for a swim, not be sitting here a prisoner in my room when I had the sea in front of me.

Okay, breathe, I urged myself, knowing that I needed to calm down. *You're in Mauritius. Just look around you and take it all in. Forget about your stupid suitcase, you'll get it back soon enough.*

I gazed out at the magnificent ocean spread out in front of me, aware that my little voice was right. I breathed in deeply a few times and checked if I felt better. Nope, I still wanted to kill him!

Half an hour later, I finally heard Adam's sliding door open and I jumped up as he walked out bare-chested, hair wet, holding a towel. My breath caught in my throat as my eyes wandered over his body and bare chest.

He hung his towel over the chair and suddenly turned to me arrogantly, cocking an eyebrow. "Enjoying the view?"

If it had been anyone else I would probably have been mortified, but I was so annoyed with him that I didn't care he had caught me ogling him.

"It's amazing! They really weren't lying when they said this place was paradisiac," I replied.

He smirked. "Sure. Whatever. Have you got your suitcase back?"

"What do *you* think?"

He furrowed his brows and cocked his head to the side. "You sound . . . angry."

"Where's my suitcase?" I snapped, hands on hips as I stared him down.

He held my gaze unflinchingly for a moment, before rolling his eyes and saying flippantly, "If it's a blue one with a big 'Molly Malahan' label stuck on it, then I'd have to say it's in my bathroom."

I stormed past him into his room before stopping midway and spinning back towards him, arms by my sides, fists clenched.

"I don't get it!" I cried out angrily. "I spent over seven hours sitting next to you on the plane and all I got was the cold shoulder. Not *one* smile, not even a mouth twitch! And *now* you suddenly discover that you have a sense of humour and go all jokey on me?"

He stared at me and something flickered in his eyes – amusement, annoyance; I wasn't sure.

"I didn't do it to make you laugh or to be funny. I did it to get back at you for being so annoying on the flight."

My mouth did an 'O' as my brows snapped together. "*Annoying*? I was just trying to be *friendly*!" I cried in indignation.

"Yeah, exactly – bloody annoying!" he said, giving me one of his disgruntled looks.

I didn't know if I wanted to scream or laugh at this point. He was just *so* . . . I couldn't even find the words to describe him. "Oh, just get out of here will you?" I said, shaking my head and sighing deeply.

"You're in *my* room," he said pointedly, crossing his arms over his chest and leaning against the edge of the sliding door, his gaze fixed on me.

Oops! I bit down a smile, suddenly finding the situation increasingly hilarious. "Fine! I'll get out then."

"You do that."

I pushed my chin up defiantly and stalked past him, making my way back to my room. As I was about to step on my veranda, I realised I'd forgotten my suitcase. A giggle escaped from my lips, but I stifled my laughter and tried to put on an angry face as I turned and marched back into his room. He was still leaning against the door watching me, and I'm pretty sure he looked amused behind all that broody dark-look thing. I stomped to the bathroom, grabbed my suitcase and headed back to my room.

"You're welcome," he called out snootily, which suddenly made me want to turn around and hit him. *Arrrgh!*

I couldn't understand how one minute he annoyed me so much that my hairs stood on end, and then the next minute he made me want to squeal with laughter. *Damn him!*

9

ADAM

I chuckled to myself as I made my way back inside and headed for the shower. The sea had been warm and wonderful, but I hadn't wanted to stay too long because I couldn't help feeling guilty that Molly was stuck without her suitcase. I wasn't used to playing this bad boy role so it would take a bit of getting used to.

Little Miss Sunshine could definitely be irked, that much I had witnessed, I thought, grinning, as I turned on the shower and stepped under the cool water. It had taken all my strength not to burst out laughing at her outrage, especially when she said that she hadn't so much as gotten a 'mouth twitch' from me throughout the seven-and-a-half-hour flight. She sure was a feisty little thing when she got angry. I had to hand it to her though; she didn't stay angry for long. I had seen the mirth in her eyes when she'd stormed back inside to get her suitcase.

I already had quite a few things to say about Molly

Malahan despite the little time we'd spent together. She was definitely an interesting subject, and I was pretty sure that she wouldn't make my job easy, but it might be fun to taunt and tease her a little after all.

I stepped out of the shower, drying myself off before pulling the towel around my waist and heading into my room. I picked up my phone from the bedside table and saw that I'd received a text message from John.

How's it going? Still peeved at being in Mauritius? How's your subject? Is she hot???

I grinned and typed back:

All good here. Subject definitely interesting. Things are looking up.

A few seconds later I heard the ting of a new message.

But is she hot?

I chuckled as I typed the reply.

Not hot, but definitely cute . . .

I decided to leave it at that for now. Putting my phone down, I rummaged through my suitcase, which lay open near my bed, and grabbed a pair of shorts and a t-shirt.

I pulled them on before peeking outside to see if Little Miss Sunshine was out on her veranda again, but everything was closed and there no sign of her anywhere. I wondered what she was up to.

10

MOLLY

This is just heavenly, I thought with a contented sigh. I was lying on a wooden deckchair on the beach, soaking up the sun and gazing in wonder at the sea stretching out for miles on either side of me. A cool breeze caressed my body and brought the wonderful aroma of the sea to me. I inhaled deeply, feeling on top of the world.

Sensing someone approaching, I looked up to see a waiter heading towards me with the fruit cocktail I'd ordered. I grinned in delight, seeing that it was just like in the movies – served in a coconut, with a straw and a cute little red cocktail umbrella sticking out on the side.

Sitting up, I took the coconut from him and thanked him before putting the straw to my lips. It was delicious and I could taste the blend of pineapple, coconut, apple and orange in it. I wished that Anna or Zach were here with me. It's always more fun when you have someone to share things with.

There's always Adam, a little voice inside of me said.

"Yeah, right, good one. Have you *met* Adam?" I answered dryly.

Well, he's pretty hot, the annoying little voice replied.

"He's not hot, he's bloody annoying!" I snapped back. "Now go away and leave me in peace to enjoy my cocktail!"

Pushing thoughts of my broody and suitcase-stealing neighbour aside, I once again focused on my surroundings and noticed a group of guys playing volleyball further down the beach. *That's what I have to do!* Not play volleyball, of course, as I'm hopeless at that, but do other activities, preferably of a non-athletic kind, where I could meet others. I'd noticed while I was checking in that there were quite a few activities and excursions available, and I was pretty sure we could sign up for them at reception. I would head there as soon as I'd finished my cocktail to find out what was on the next day. I was going to make this holiday memorable, I decided with a smile.

Half an hour later, I made my way to the reception desk and asked to be shown the list. Water sports, windsurfing, sailing, kayaking, tennis, golf, scuba diving, snorkelling, glass-bottom-boat excursions . . . and the list went on. There were also a few day excursions from the hotel, such as a day in a town called Quatres Bornes to visit the local market there, or a trip to Casela World of Adventures, among many others. I thought about it for a minute then decided that I would start with the glass-bottom-boat trip the next morning. I wrote my name down and was happy to see that there were at least ten other people already on the list. I spent the rest of the day strolling around the hotel, visiting all the nooks and crannies. It spread out for miles and had three pools, a spa, a gym, a kids' club, tennis courts and a huge golf course. The lawns and gardens were beautifully kept, with pink, purple, white and red bougainvillea bushes everywhere, not to forget endless hibiscus bushes with large red flowers in bloom, and of course the coconut trees which lined the long stretch of beach in front of the hotel. I ended my tour by taking a long walk down the beach, loving the feel of the soft sand between my toes and the sound of the sea gently lapping against the shore.

As night fell, my eyelids began to feel heavy and I realised that in Perth it was already eleven o'clock at night, although it was only seven o'clock here in Mauritius. No wonder I was falling asleep. I ordered room service, not having the energy to go out to dinner. Besides, I didn't relish the thought of eating by myself.

After a delicious seafood linguini, I changed into my pyjamas and got into bed. It was the most amazing bed ever. I bounced up and down on it, giggling gleefully like a five-year-old. The pillows were just perfectly mushy, the sheets super-soft and silky, and the bed could comfortably fit at least four people. I snuggled happily into my sheets and thought about my day. I hadn't bumped into Adam again, which was surprising in a way, but then again the hotel was so huge that he could have been anywhere. Who cares, anyway? I would finally be meeting nice, friendly people the next day; ones who wouldn't steal my suitcase or give me the cold shoulder. I didn't need Adam.

ADAM

"*A* glass-bottom-boat trip? You have got to be kidding me," I grumbled to myself as I left the reception. I headed towards the breakfast buffet area and for once I didn't have to pretend to be pissed off. I was truly annoyed at having to spend half the day in a glass-bottom boat. I was an active kind of guy and this was way too slow for me. I'd managed to stay clear of Merry Molly all day yesterday – which was probably because I'd slept through most of it. Then she hadn't shown up for dinner so I had been free to chill out and enjoy my evening without having to scowl or grumble, which had been a real treat.

I spotted Molly a mile away. Once again, she was dressed in a wide array of bright colours which, funnily enough, suited her to perfection. Suddenly I had a brainwave and knew exactly what I could do to rile her some more . . .

I quickly turned away before she noticed me and headed back to reception. I asked for the activity sheet once more and discreetly crossed both our names off the list for the glass-bottom-boat trip scheduled for ten o'clock. *Adam Wilson, you are a genius!* I congratulated myself as I made my way back towards the restaurant, my bad mood forgotten.

Unfortunately, an annoying little voice inside my head suddenly made itself heard and said disapprovingly, *You can't do that, Adam! What kind of person are you?*

"Oh shut up! It's my job, I have to do this. I want that promotion," I snapped back.

Yeah, well, you suck!'

"Yeah, whatever!" I thought angrily, but felt the guilt overtake me. "Damn it!" I muttered under my breath as I turned and stormed back to reception, yet again asking for the same sheet. The receptionist looked at me with amusement. "Can't make up your mind, sir? Too many choices?"

"Yeah, something like that," I muttered vaguely as I scrolled through the list for the third time. She seemed to be watching me and I hoped she hadn't noticed me crossing out our names earlier.

There was no glass-bottom-boat trip in the afternoon and the one scheduled for the next morning was fully booked. Damn. Now what? I couldn't put us back on today's ten o'clock one because I needed to stick to my plan - it was a perfect way to rile her. I noticed there was a snorkelling trip to the reefs in the afternoon – it would have to do. I put our names down for that, feeling better. Okay, it wasn't glass-bottom boating, but it was even better, if you asked me. I made sure not to write Adam and just put Mr Wilson so that Molly wouldn't know it was me if she came to see the list later. As I scrolled through the other activities, I saw marlin fishing, and simply imagining Molly trying to catch a huge marlin made me laugh out loud and before I could stop myself, I put her name down for it.

Satisfied I had done all I could to remedy the situation, I

headed back to the breakfast buffet area and found her near the fruit table, helping herself to some watermelon.

"Okay, you're on, Adam," I mumbled to myself and headed towards her.

"Didn't your mum tell you that you can't wear *all* the colours of the rainbow at the same time?" I said by way of greeting as I looked her up and down, grimacing.

"Well, hello to you too!" she said brightly. "So nice to see you're in a better mood today!"

My lips twitched but I managed to keep my scowl in place. I ignored her comeback and grabbed a plate to follow on behind her. I noticed that her plate was piled high with food.

"You do know that this is a buffet and that you're allowed to serve yourself as many times as you want, don't you?"

Her mouth curved into a smile. "I guess I'm just lazy. Can't be bothered getting up again once I sit down."

My lips twitched as she turned and walked off. I couldn't help admiring her spunk. It was baffling how unruffled she was by my unfriendliness. I couldn't wait to see how she would react to the glass-bottom-boating prank . . .

MOLLY

I'd managed to calm down somewhat and was lying on a sun lounger on the beach, reading a *Marie Claire* magazine and forcing myself not to have murderous thoughts about Adam. I didn't understand if he was trying to be funny or if he was just being a jerk. The latter, more than likely.

I felt a shadow fall over my body and looked up to see the devil himself. I yanked off my sunglasses and glared at him, refusing to acknowledge how sexy he looked as water trickled down his drool-worthy chest.

He cocked his head to the side, crossed his arms and observed me through furrowed brows. "Hmmm . . ." he finally said, pursing his lips sideways. "Little Miss Sunshine suddenly looks more along the lines of Little Miss Cloudy with a chance of thunderstorms."

Not trusting myself to speak, I turned away without a

word. What was he doing here? Had he come to relish in the fact that he had made me furious with his stupid joke?

He flopped down onto the sun lounger next to me and looked at me again, cocking an eyebrow. "What's the problem?"

"Oh, not much really," I finally replied, my voice oozing with sarcasm as my eyes bored into him. "Seems that *someone* took my name off the glass-bottom-boat trip planned this morning and put me on the marlin fishing excursion instead!"

"And you don't like marlin fishing?" he replied nonchalantly as he brushed a hand through his wet hair.

"That's *not* the point!" I snapped back.

Argh! I could just wring his neck. I took a deep breath to steady my nerves before continuing. "The girl at reception told me she'd seen a guy making changes this morning but she hadn't thought anything of it at the time."

"Strange . . ." he murmured as he stretched his legs out in front of him, putting his arms behind his head and leaning back on them as if he didn't have a care in the world.

How could he lie like this, without any remorse whatsoever? My blood was boiling but I wouldn't give him the satisfaction of seeing me blow up.

"And the funny thing is that she said he looked exactly like . . . Ian Somerhalder!" I said icily, as I glowered at him.

He rolled his head my way for a minute then, shrugging non-committedly, straightened up again and said flippantly, "So that could be anyone, right?"

I slapped my hand on my forehead in frustration. "ARRRGHHH! Just go away, will you!" I couldn't cope with him for a second longer. Who did he think he was anyway? "Besides, why exactly are you here? Did you come to gloat about your little joke? Well now it's done – so just *go*! I'm sure you have other friends to go and see."

"*Friends?* What are you talking about? Haven't you *met* me?" he said, gaping at me, straight-faced.

To my utter disbelief, I felt a bubble of laughter pushing its way up. Why couldn't I stay angry? It was so annoying to never manage to stay angry at people, even when they deserved it – like Adam right now.

He wasn't in the least bit put out by any of this and just leaned back in his chair, looking his usual unfriendly, yet gorgeous, self. Of course, I couldn't *not* notice that he was gorgeous, I mean, just imagine having an Ian Somerhalder lookalike lying there next to you on a sun lounger in Mauritius, bare-chested. Yeah, well, unfortunately although the idea of it is drool-worthy, the actual reality of it is much less appealing because it's pretty difficult to enjoy the looks when the personality is such a disaster.

I suddenly swivelled back towards him. "Why?"

"Why what?" he asked, frowning as he fixed his beautiful silver-blue eyes on me.

"Why did you do it?" I asked, genuinely curious.

"Because glass-bottom-boating is boring."

"You hate me, so what do *you* care if I do something boring or not?"

"I don't hate you," he said, brows furrowed again as his eyes held mine for a minute. "Okay, fine," he finally acknowledged with a sigh, rolling his eyes heavenwards. "Maybe it's true that you tend to get on my nerves a little . . ."

I raised my eyebrows at him, cocking my head.

"Okay, a lot," he amended. "But I'm bored, and for some reason it gives me great pleasure to be the bane of your existence."

I shook my head and sighed heavily. I mean, what did you answer to that? I wasn't used to people being unfriendly and unkind to me. I was generally pretty much liked by everyone and didn't have to counterattack much. I didn't understand the guy, but I didn't want to waste my holiday being stressed out and angry because of him. I hoped that he'd soon find a friend or a girl to pass the time with so that he would leave me alone.

"Why on earth are you in Mauritius anyway? You sure don't seem happy to be here."

"I won the trip in a raffle – so here I am," he said, arms outstretched.

My eyes widened. "Hey, I won this trip too!"

"Well ain't that grand."

"It is, actually – well, except for the part where I am constantly being pestered by a broody, unfriendly man!" I said petulantly, getting up, grabbing my bag and throwing my magazine and sun cream into it before putting it over my shoulder and walking off. I wouldn't let him spoil any more of my day. I was in Mauritius and I was going to enjoy it.

"Hey! Hang on a minute!" I heard him call out as I walked off.

I hesitated, not sure whether I could be bothered listening to what he had to say or not, but in the end curiosity got the better of me. I stopped and turned, taking a few steps back towards him.

"What now?" I sighed.

"For your information: your name is on the snorkelling outing leaving at two o'clock."

"What? You should be sued for messing with me like this! Surely it's a form of harassment? We're strangers after all!"

"Strangers? Are you kidding me! You spent seven and a half hours yapping away at me *and*," he said, grimacing and pointing an accusing finger at me, "you even *held my hand*!"

"Fine. Whatever!" I snapped, glowering at him. I just didn't know how to react anymore. I had no idea if I was grateful or annoyed for what he'd done. Once again I spun around and stormed off, feeling amused, angry, frustrated and confused all at the same time. Who was that guy, and why didn't he leave me alone?

13

ADAM

I arrived at the jetty at a quarter to two and waited for Molly show up. I knew she would freak out when she saw me here. I couldn't exactly pretend that I didn't know she would be here because I was the one who'd put her name down for this. I had no idea what I would say in my defence, but hoped that once I was in my 'role', I'd think of something.

Just before two, I recognised her silhouette approaching the jetty. Her long hair was tied in a low ponytail with a few loose tendrils falling around her face. Her green eyes were hidden behind a pair of bright pink sunglasses which would have looked hideous on anyone else, but suited her perfectly. As she looked down the jetty towards the boats, she suddenly did a double take. Okay, so I guess she'd spotted me. She stared towards me but kept walking, obviously not sure if it was really me or if her eyes were playing tricks on her. When she was finally close enough to be sure, she stopped dead in her tracks, pushed her sunglasses up on her head and levelled her gaze on me suspiciously. This assignment was proving to be much more fun than I'd anticipated, I thought, grinning inwardly.

After a few seconds, she headed purposefully towards me. She was quite something with her fuchsia pink crop top, a slightly transparent fuchsia pink sarong with purple and white tropical flowers on it, her bright pink sunglasses that now sat on her head and a purple sunhat which she held in her hand. And to complete the look, she had a multi-coloured striped tote bag hanging off her shoulder. To say that she was colourful would be the understatement of the year.

As soon as she drew level with me, I threw my hand over my eyes and cried out, "Owww! You have *got* to stop dressing like that. The glare radiating off you is blinding!"

Her mouth opened, then closed, then opened again like a fish and finally, to my huge surprise, she shook her head and laughed.

"Here," she said, thrusting her bright pink sunglasses at me, her eyes dancing with mirth. "You can borrow my sunglasses!"

My look of surprise was genuine. I had *so* not been expecting that. I pushed her sunglasses away with what I hoped was a look of undiluted horror, and she burst into laughter once more.

Suddenly registering the fact that I was also going snorkelling, she put her hands on her hips and stared me down defiantly.

"Snorkelling, Adam?" she said incredulously. "Seriously?"

Thankfully, before I could think of an answer, she went on.

"With all that pent-up anger and general broodiness you should be out skydiving, or rock climbing, or abseiling, or . . .

I don't know . . . boxing, but snorkelling? No way. This is just plain weird," she said, shaking her head.

I pushed down my amusement and kept a straight face. "It's a free country. I can do what I like. And I love snorkelling, although . . . now that *you're* here, it kind of spoils it somewhat."

"Yeah, whatever. You're the one who put my name down for this anyway," she said in a huff.

"I have no idea what went through my head now that I come to think of it," I muttered, just loud enough for her to hear, as I shook my head and sighed.

14

MOLLY

I ignored Adam and walked towards the boat a few metres away, eager to hop on. I wouldn't let Grumpy Dumpy annoy me or ruin this beautiful afternoon. I noticed that there was a blonde woman standing alone on the jetty not far from the boat and wondered if she would be joining us on the snorkelling trip. As I observed her from behind my sunglasses, I couldn't help noticing that she looked a bit sad. I would try to introduce myself if she came on the boat. It would be nice to have someone to talk to. Well, someone friendly anyway. Then again, her husband or boyfriend was probably on his way to join her. I doubted many people travelled alone to places like Mauritius, unless they won trips like Adam and I had. For the life of me, I couldn't understand why Adam was coming on the snorkelling trip. It clearly wasn't his cup of tea and it's not as if he was doing it to be with me. Maybe he was just lonely and thought hanging around with me, even though I annoyed the crap out of him, was better than being alone . . . *Nah*, it was definitely weird.

I snapped out of my reverie and felt someone hovering over me. I looked up to see the blonde lady standing in front of me, smiling shyly.

"Hi."

"Hi," I replied, smiling warmly at her before removing my bag from the bench, motioning for her to sit down. "I'm Molly."

"I'm Samantha," she answered, settling down next to me. "I couldn't help overhearing you and your boyfriend earlier. I guess you guys are fighting, huh?"

I pulled a disgusted face. "Oh my God! He's *not* my boyfriend! We were sitting next to each other on the plane on the way to Mauritius, and now we keep bumping into each other at the hotel. It's safe to say that we don't exactly get along. He is the broodiest human being I've ever had the misfortune to meet!"

"He's pretty gorgeous though, isn't he?" she said, glancing towards him.

"Yeah, I guess, but such a shame about the personality."

She laughed, pulling her eyes away from him. "So, are you here with anyone else then?"

"No, unfortunately not. I won this trip in a photo competition. It's kind of sad not to have anyone to share all this with - well, except for Mr Grumpy Dumpy over there of course!"

She grinned, then suddenly her eyes clouded. "I'm also here alone."

I looked down at her wedding finger. "I can't help noticing that you're wearing a wedding ring - are you newly separated?"

Oh no, what if she was newly widowed? I suddenly thought in horror. *Damn it, Molly! Why can't you ever roll your tongue in your mouth seven times before talking?* I scolded myself mentally.

I clapped my hand over my mouth. "Oh jeepers! I'm so sorry. That's so indiscreet of me!" I cried before she could answer.

She smiled kindly, clearly amused by my embarrassment, and said reassuringly, "Don't worry, it's a fair question." She looked down at her ring for a moment before smiling sadly up at me. "No, we're actually still together, but I did a bit of a runner."

I was trying to work out what she meant by "a runner" when she went on. "I think I was suffering from major burnout and just had enough. I called up the travel agency, booked a trip to Mauritius and hopped on the plane the next day – which was on Monday – leaving him and my mum to deal with everything."

"Oh! Hadn't been expecting that," I said, with a smile.

"I've never done anything like this before, but I felt that if I didn't get away, I'd go crazy. It's been so incredible having these past few days to myself. Of course I'm racked with guilt most of the time and I miss them like crazy, but I had to do this for my sanity, and, in a way, for our marriage."

I nodded and squeezed her hand reassuringly. "Okay then, we'll just have to make sure that you get all the relaxation and fun you need so that your batteries will be fully recharged when you head home to your family."

"I'm so happy to have found someone to talk to – it's pretty weird being all alone when I'm used to being surrounded by people all the time. At home I have a hard time going to the toilet without being disturbed!"

I laughed. "I can't say I have that problem myself, but it does feel lonely to be on holiday by myself, so I'm really glad to have met you too."

The last few passengers finally arrived and joined us on

the boat. Adam was the last one on and, as luck would have it, the only seat left happened to be on my left-hand side, Samantha being on my right.

As Adam sat down, I leaned towards him and said in a loud whisper, "I am seriously starting to worry about your stalking tendencies."

"Why would I torture myself by doing such a thing? I already have a massive headache simply by looking at you!" he retorted, squinting exaggeratingly.

I rolled my eyes and looked at Samantha, who was clearly having trouble hiding her amusement.

"This is Samantha, by the way," I said, remembering my manners, and was relieved that he at least had the grace to turn towards her and mumble "Hi".

The boat was finally on its way and Samantha and I talked easily. She was from South Africa and told me about her life, her children and her husband.

"My problem is that I don't know how to organise myself to keep up with everything that's expected of me. I make a list and I forget it, or I go to the shop to get one thing and come back with ten things but not the thing I had gone for! I remember that it's my turn to do the tennis run, but I forget to pick up one of the kids. I remember that my child has a birthday party, but I forget to buy a present . . . it never ends," she said despairingly.

I couldn't help giggling, despite her weary look.

"I know it probably sounds funny, but it really isn't. I feel like I'm always just one step behind, forever running after my tail. It's exhausting – and depressing."

"Don't be too hard on yourself. I can't imagine what it must be like to have two kids, a husband and a house to manage. I think I'd be worse off than you if I were in your shoes."

She smiled. "You're just being kind. Honestly, I look

around me and there are so many super-mums around handling work, their house and kids and managing perfectly well. But I can't. The other day I went to school to drop off the kids and I forgot to wear shoes! I had to go all the way back home to get a pair and my children were super late. I mean who forgets to wear shoes?"

I burst out laughing and heard Adam heave an exasperated sigh. I turned pointedly back towards him.

"Can't you girls keep it down?" he grumbled. "I came out here to enjoy the peace and quiet of being out on the water and all I can hear is jabber, jabber, jabber – giggle, giggle, giggle."

Samantha and I looked at each other, eyes full of mirth. "Told you," I mouthed and she nodded with a grin.

Just then the boat slowed to a stop and the skipper informed us that we had reached the reef. We excitedly pulled off our clothes, picked up our masks and snorkels and got ready to jump overboard. I turned towards Adam to find him standing there, staring at me with an expression I couldn't quite read in his eyes. He looked a bit dazed.

"Are you alright?" I asked, thinking that he may not be feeling well.

"I'm fine!" he growled, sitting down again and getting his mask and snorkel. "Just readjusting to the lower glare level now that you've undressed."

I rolled my eyes, not bothering to reply, and looked towards Samantha, who was about to jump overboard. The boat suddenly rocked, probably as a result of too many people jumping off at the same time, making me stumble and fall backwards against someone's back or chest. I just had time to hear Adam's familiar voice cry out "ARGHHH!" before I heard him splash heavily into the water below. His fall made the boat rock again and I teetered some more before stumbling backwards, hitting my back against the bench. *Ouch!* That hurt.

I was about to get up to check if Adam was alright when I heard him shout, "Darn it! What is that girl's problem?"

What a jerk! And here I was worrying about him. He'd been about to jump into the water anyway so what was the big deal? What's worse, I was the one who had actually got hurt and would probably end up with a huge bruise. I was suddenly more than fed up with him.

"Will you *shut up?*" I shouted angrily over the edge of the boat.

He looked a bit startled by my outburst, but soon recovered and bellowed, "For your information, *I'm* the one who got knocked into the water by *you*! Not the other way around!"

"Yeah, well get over it! It was an accident, okay?" I bit back angrily as I winced and rubbed my back. I turned away from the edge and sat down again. It didn't hurt too badly, but for some reason Adam's anger and harshness bothered me. I didn't understand why he treated me this way; after all, he barely knew me, and I'd been nothing but friendly to him despite his crabbiness and stupid pranks. I guess he had problems – I didn't know the first thing about him after all. So I couldn't judge him.

Come on, get over it, Molly! I urged myself. *Smile, get into the beautiful water and swim – and all will be well.* I crossed over to the other side of the boat, as far away from Adam as I could get, put a smile on my face and jumped in. The water was heavenly and I soon forgot all about Adam as I lost myself in the majestic underwater life.

15

ADAM

I snorkelled along the reefs, enjoying the feeling of being cut off from the world. At least underwater I didn't have to scowl. There were so many fish of all sizes and colours swimming around the corals and rocks – it was beautiful. I thought back to Molly and couldn't help feeling guilty for lashing out at her for making me fall into the water, especially since I'd wanted to burst out laughing imagining myself flying through the air because little Molly had bumped into me.

Although my suitcase and glass-bottom-boating pranks hadn't kept her angry for long, somehow I felt that this time it would be different. I'd hurt her feelings, so it would be interesting to see how long she would stay angry and hurt, and if it would affect her general happiness for a while.

As I swam along, I tried to stop my thoughts from going in the direction that they clearly wanted to – but in vain. I kept seeing flashes of her earlier on the boat . . . *Oh my, that body!* My breath had caught in my throat when she'd taken off her sarong and stood there in her little pink bikini. She didn't have the body of a supermodel, but she had gorgeous curves, a flat stomach, perfect breasts and olive skin that looked so soft . . . I had been mesmerised. It had taken me by surprise because up to now I'd never thought of her as anything but Molly, my subject. I thought she was cute, but I'd been too absorbed in finding ways to annoy her and getting material for my article to really pay attention. I really didn't want to notice her body or her big green almond-shaped eyes because this was work and I needed to stay focused.

16

MOLLY

*W*e headed back to the mainland after spending almost an hour snorkelling. It had been like a dream. On the way back, Samantha and I chatted excitedly about everything we'd seen, and I noticed that Adam sat quietly a few seats away from us. He hadn't said a word to me since our screaming match earlier, and I didn't try to engage in conversation with him either. Although I was no longer angry with him, somehow I thought it best if we didn't talk. For some reason, Adam + Molly = major disaster. In a way, I felt that he could have apologised for yelling at me like that, but then again, I knew that his anger had been from the shock of falling into the water and I didn't need to take it personally.

Samantha and I made plans to meet for dinner later, and I headed straight back to my room for a shower, after which I planned on spending an hour or two reading on my veranda. I'd had enough sun for the day. I put on a pair of purple, pink and white striped shorts and a short purple crop top and pulled my hair into a messy ponytail before going outside to hang my towel out to dry.

"That's quite a bruise you have there."

I froze at the sound of Adam's deep voice. Oh my goodness, he sounded so sexy. *Molly!* I scolded myself, wondering where on earth that thought had come from. I slowly turned towards him, towel in hand, and saw him lying on one of the rattan deck chairs on his veranda. I nodded in answer to his question, not knowing what to say.

"Do you have some cream to put on that?" he asked, his gentle tone taking me by surprise.

"No, but I'll be fine," I answered before turning back to the chair and hanging my towel over the edge.

Without saying a word, he got up and went back into his room. Oh, okay then. "Well, goodbye to you too," I muttered to myself, feeling both annoyed and amused. I was about to head back inside when I heard him calling me. I turned to see that he was making his way towards me with a tube of cream in his hand. My gaze swept over him and I couldn't help notice his toned chest and his abs . . . *Earth to Molly! Need I remind you AGAIN about his less-than-agreeable personality?* my little inner voice reminded me, and rightly so.

"Here, it's Arnica gel. Put some of this on and your bruise should be gone by tomorrow," he instructed, handing it to me.

"Thanks so much," I said, dumbstruck. I squeezed some gel onto my finger and rubbed it on my bruise as best I could as he stood waiting, his eyes on me.

Before I knew what was happening, he'd moved behind me and began rubbing the gel on my back. I stood stock-still, too stunned to move or talk. Every molecule in my body was on high alert at his touch, and I had to remind myself to breathe. I hoped he couldn't tell the effect he was having on me. *Oh, stop that!* I scolded myself again. *Just because a man hasn't touched you in a while doesn't mean you have to practically self-combust with lust when one finally does.*

"There, that should do it." He screwed the lid back on, and although he still wasn't smiling, his voice was gentle.

"Thank you," I said again, dropping my gaze and feeling uncomfortable for the first time since I'd met him.

He nodded in acknowledgement and without another word, turned and left. I watched him walk off – for the life of me, I couldn't understand the guy. He abruptly stopped in his tracks, turning to face me. "I'm sorry about earlier. I shouldn't have shouted at you like that. It was an accident." Before I could close my gaping mouth and answer, he had taken off again and disappeared inside.

Well, that sure was unexpected, I thought, feeling a bit dazed. I didn't know what to make of him, and unfortunately, he was beginning to intrigue me way too much for my liking. Fully determined not to let Adam take anymore space than he already had in my head – and my holiday – I decided that I would read in my room instead to make sure I didn't bump into him again. I hadn't even read three lines when my thoughts drifted back to him and the feel of his fingers caressing my skin . . . *He was* not *caressing your skin!* my inner voice reminded me. *He was just rubbing some gel on your bruise for goodness' sake.*

I shook my head to clear it of the exquisite memory and forced myself to come back to earth, but I couldn't help thinking that I'd seen another side to Adam – still no smile, but there was definitely a touch of kindness there.

17

ADAM

Oh crikey. What had just happened? Why on earth had I walked up to her and rubbed the gel on her back like that? *Way* too intimate, and it had made my heart race wildly like a stupid teenager. Why was she suddenly having that effect on me? It was Merry Molly for crying out loud. *Stay focused, Adam*, I chided myself. *You're here to do a job.* And it was really important that I do it right.

All the way back on the boat, I'd wanted to go up to her to apologise, but she was having a good time with Samantha and I felt she deserved some peace.

When I'd seen her standing there with the big bruise on her back, I'd felt pretty bad for being so hard on her. So instead of doing what I should have done – staying in my room and carrying on being the bad guy – I'd brought the Arnica gel to put on her bruise. To make matters worse, I'd then rubbed the darn gel on her back *and* said sorry about the boat thing. *Good work,*

Adam. Sure Luke will be patting me on the back for that one! I sighed deeply. I decided to stay indoors for a while as I needed to be me for a few hours – this whole fake bad guy role was exhausting.

I'd have to think of some way to annoy her tonight though because I needed more material for my article. So far she seemed pretty normal to me. Okay, granted, she had a sunny disposition and loved to wear really bright, multi-coloured clothes, but she also got angry like anyone else – she just didn't bear grudges. I wasn't sure there was really more to Molly than that. The whole happiness theory thing seemed a bit far-fetched. Either you're happy or you're not, surely? Some days you are and some days you're not. How can you choose or decide to be happy? It just doesn't seem logical or plausible in my opinion. Some people have happy natures, like Molly, and others are just more pessimistic or bad-tempered.

I think I'd heard Molly making plans to meet Samantha for dinner. They would probably end up at the beach bar afterwards so I'd have to see what I could do to be a nuisance again. I groaned, throwing myself on my bed, not looking forward to it at all.

On my way to dinner, I dropped by the reception area to see what activities Molly had signed up for – or more accurately, had signed *us* up for – the next day. With trepidation I scrolled though the events and could just see myself having to attend a knitting workshop or a ballet class. My finger stopped as I finally spotted her name under Casela World of Adventures. "Great!" I muttered under my breath. I had nothing against nature and adventure parks, per se, but we were in Mauritius, a paradise *island*, and the perfect place for doing everything I loved – diving, surfing, kite-surfing or water skiing – and definitely *not* a place to be strolling through a nature park.

As I scanned the list of names, I noticed that Samantha hadn't signed up. How did she manage to get out of it? I wondered grouchily. *Oh yeah, that's right,* I reminded myself in disgust. *She's not stalking a stranger to write an article! Not to mention doing everything she can to make the said happy stranger unhappy.* I cringed at the thought of what I was doing. How could we journalists do things like this for an article? After all, we weren't talking about objects here, but real people with feelings. Was it as easy as that for us to forget about that and think only of ourselves and what we would get out of it? It would appear so. *Jeepers!* I was such a jerk . . . but I *really* wanted that promotion.

As I arrived at the buffet area, I spotted Samantha and Molly on the terrace having dinner together. They were talking and laughing, looking like they'd been friends forever. I'd known Molly for barely two days and I already knew she was the sort of person with whom you felt at ease right away. I had dinner alone on the other side of the restaurant, not wanting them to see me. I would have to make an appearance after dinner, but I wasn't sure how I would go about it . . .

18

MOLLY

"Any news from home?" I asked Samantha, raising my eyes towards her as I lifted my fork to my mouth. We were sitting outside on the terrace as it was a beautiful night. The stars lit up the sky and we could just make out the waves gently breaking onto the shore.

"Well, I turned my phone on this morning and there were about twenty missed calls and messages from my husband, begging me to talk to him," she said, grimacing. "I feel so guilty, but I'm not ready yet. Being away makes me realise how much I love him and the kids, but I can't handle all the demands they place on me. I have to find a way to lighten my load a little and my husband has to acknowledge that I'm not one of those wonder women who can do it all."

"He has to accept that I'm disorganised, late, forgetful and that I can't juggle everything at the same time and get it right. I want to feel shouldered by him instead of constantly feeling that he's frustrated because I can't do everything he expects me to. He's too demanding . . . and I try so hard to please him, to please the kids, to find time for my friends and family – but it's too much. I can't cope. I feel like I'm always failing somewhere and can't keep going on this way."

I reached for her hand and squeezed it gently. "You really need to tell him all of this, you know."

"I know . . ." she said with a sigh. "I've tried before but he gets upset and feels that I'm criticising him and doesn't seem to understand what I'm trying to say. He's so organised, in control of everything, has lists that he actually follows – instead of losing them like I do! But I need him to accept that I'm not like him and never will be."

"Why don't you write to him? That way he can't interrupt you halfway through to defend himself, he will simply have to read it all the way through. It's ideal since you're far away anyway."

She stayed quiet for a while, staring ahead of her, clearly deep in thought. After a moment, she looked towards me again with a smile. "I think that's a great idea."

"Be sure to tell him everything you feel. I think I read somewhere that the best way to get someone to really listen without feeling attacked is by avoiding to say things like, 'You do this or that, you say this or that, you never,' but rather, 'I feel such and such a way when . . .' – I actually have *no* idea where I read that or heard that, but it sounds like good advice!" I grinned, putting another forkful of the mouth-watering fish into my mouth.

"Yes, we did something like that at our engagement encounter weekend – it's important to bring everything back to yourself and how you feel, rather than attack the other person by saying 'you do this, you do that'."

Every time she spoke of her husband, I could see the love she felt for him reflected in her eyes, and her kids were clearly her pride and joy so I truly hoped she would be able to work things out.

I felt sorry for her because I knew it wasn't given to everyone to be organised. I, on the other hand, had learnt to be organised very early in life because I pretty much had to run the house for my mum when she'd been depressed. I'd had to make sure she paid the bills, that there was food in the fridge, that the dishes were washed and that we had clean clothes to wear. Luckily my dad's family had been quite well off so we'd never had money problems. Now Mum works as a freelance translator and copywriter, which is great as it keeps her busy and gets a bit of money coming in, not to mention she can do it from home.

Samantha and I spent the rest of dinner chilling out and enjoying each other's company like long-lost friends. It was lovely to have someone to talk and laugh with.

After dinner we headed to the beach bar for drinks. As we approached, I noticed Adam sitting on a bar stool, his back to us, talking to the barman. I nudged Samantha and pointed towards him.

She grinned. "Oh my, he's even gorgeous from the back. Hmmm, check out those biceps – and that butt."

I giggled and took her arm, pulling her in the other direction. I didn't want to see Adam tonight.

"Grab a table while I get us some drinks," she said, turning towards the bar. "Shall we try out one of the local tropical cocktails?"

"Sounds perfect." I looked around, noticed a couple leaving a table on the deck by the beach and made my way to it. I sat down and pulled out my phone, wanting to see if Anna had texted me. I scrolled through my messages, lost in thought, and jolted in surprise when I felt someone's hand on my shoulder.

"How's your back?" Adam said from behind me. Even

when he was trying to be nice – like now – he sounded annoyed.

"Much better, thanks to your magical cream," I answered, twisting slightly in my seat and smiling at him over my shoulder.

"Good," he said with a nod.

My eyes followed him as he made his way around the table and went to lean on a wooden pillar just opposite me. I tried to stop myself from noticing how his white t-shirt stretched over his muscular torso and the way his jeans hung off his waist, but it was hard . . . He was so sexy! *Oh shut up!* I scolded my inner goddess or whoever it was that was putting these thoughts into my head. *It's just Adam, for heaven's sake –* grouchy, annoying, snarky and not-particularly-nice Adam.

He stood there silently, sipping his beer, his eyes scanning the bar area. When I realised that he had no intention of talking to me, I couldn't help asking, "What is it about me that you dislike so much?"

He stared at me, blinking a few times, before looking away without a word.

"So, what is it?"

"What is what?" he snapped, throwing his head back and downing the last of his beer.

"What is it about me that annoys you so much?" I repeated.

"Never said you annoyed me," he answered curtly, leaning down and putting his glass on the table.

"Right. Ever heard the phrase 'actions speak louder than words'?"

His gaze flicked briefly towards me and I'm pretty sure he seemed amused, but he looked away before I could be certain.

"It's just strange, because, present company excluded, people usually like me," I said.

"Yeah, me too," he replied, straight-faced.

I snorted with surprised laughter. "Oh well, there's definitely no accounting for taste, is there?"

He narrowed his eyes at me before looking away as I laughed again. I had no idea why he didn't leave, but he stayed there, leaning against the pillar, arms crossed, eyes looking around. I turned towards the bar, hoping to see that Samantha was on her way back so that she could save me from Mr McGrumps, but she seemed to have started a conversation with a couple sitting next to her. Great, just great. I groaned inwardly.

After standing there in silence for a while, Adam sighed loudly. I glanced towards him, observing his broody demeanour. "And you're still here – *why?*"

"Wouldn't be very gentlemanly of me to leave you here all alone would it?"

"And when exactly did you evolve from being a caveman to a gentleman?" I said snidely, quite proud of myself for giving him some of his own back.

His eyebrows shot up, then he threw me one of his dirty looks.

I, of course, began giggling, which completely spoiled the whole badass attitude I'd been going for.

Adam looked away into the distance again, probably also hoping to see Samantha heading back so that he could leave. As I observed him, his eyes suddenly lit up with what seemed like excitement. Not possible, surely. I looked around to see what had caught his eye but couldn't see anything out of the ordinary. When I turned back, Adam was making his way back to the bar.

Obviously sensing my eyes on him, he waved over his shoulder. *The cheek of him!* Couldn't he at least say goodbye? "Good riddance," I muttered under my breath as I grabbed my phone and sent a text message to Anna:

Mauritius amazing. The company – not so much.

ADAM

*T*here he was! My next "let's peeve Molly off" plan. He was perfect, I thought happily as I pushed myself off the wooden pillar and walked off without saying goodbye. I was really acting like a caveman, I thought guiltily. To make up for it, I waved airily over my shoulder, hoping that she was watching me. She was proving to be quite a rival in the snarky remarks department and it was getting to be painful to stop myself from laughing. Christine had been right about her positive nature and happy-go-lucky attitude, but she hadn't warned me about her feistiness and her sense of humour.

"Hey there," I said with a big smile as I reached him, sliding onto the bar stool next to him.

He turned towards me and his googly eyes almost popped out of their sockets as his mouth fell to the floor. *Oh no.* I groaned inwardly – a Somerhalder fan.

"Well blow me down! A-are you Ian Somerhalder?" he stuttered, holding his palm over his heart.

"No, I'm Adam. And you are . . . ?"

"Henry," he said, still staring at me wide-eyed. "Henry Darlinton."

"Great to meet you, Henry," I said, giving him a pat on the back. "Okay, how about you stop staring at me like that now? I swear I'm not Ian Somerhalder."

"But you look just like him," he said in wonder, pushing his thick, round black-rimmed glasses back up his long nose.

"I know. But if you look closely, I'm much younger and *way* more handsome than him ," I said with a wink.

He laughed. Or at least I think it was a laugh. Sounded like a horse neighing or some sort of animal sound. *Oh my word, this was going to be even better than I thought!*

"So here's the thing," I said, laying my hand on his shoulder. "I need you to do something for me."

"You do?" he replied, eyes wide behind his glasses.

I nodded, wondering if he would go along with it.

"O-kay . . ."

"You see that lovely girl with the long wavy hair and multicoloured clothes sitting all alone at the table over there," I said, pointing towards Molly.

He followed the direction of my finger and, spotting Molly, he nodded.

"Well, I was just talking to her a few minutes ago and she told me that she was feeling a bit lonely. She actually noticed you standing near the bar and said that she'd love it if a guy like you chatted her up."

He beamed happily, pushing his glasses up his nose again.

"So how about it, huh?" I grinned, patting him on the back encouragingly.

"Well, if the lady wants me, wouldn't want to disappoint her now, would I?"

As he began neighing or snorting again, I grinned happily. He was so perfect. From his large round glasses and googly eyes to his long pointy nose, awful laugh and terrible sense of style (loose brown corduroy trousers worn really high above his waist, a red shirt with a chequered sleeveless sweater and pointy shiny brown shoes) - *brilliant*.

"Good on ya, Henry," I said with a lopsided smile, then nudged my head in Molly's direction. "Now go for it – she's waiting for you. Oh yes, nearly forgot. She's shy and won't want to seem overly interested, but don't let that stop you. She loves it when guys are really forward and persistent."

Oh my word, Molly would hate this so much, but boy would I love this, I thought, chuckling to myself.

"Mustn't keep the lady waiting then, must I?" he said, picking up his glass of beer from the bar before turning and heading towards her. I watched him as he meandered through the tables and couldn't stop myself from laughing. I ordered another beer and settled on the bar stool, preparing myself for the show.

20

MOLLY

*a*s I waited for Anna to reply, I sent a quick message to my mum telling her I was having a wonderful time and that I hoped she was well. I'd forced myself not to think about her too much because it made me anxious. I wanted to relax and forget about it all. She replied straight away telling me that she was okay and happy to know I was having a good time. I let out a sigh of relief.

Just as I leaned forward to put my phone on the table, I heard it ting again with a new message. I looked down and smiled, seeing that it was from Anna this time.

Tell me more about "the company not so good" part?

I grinned and leaned back into my chair. How on earth did one sum up Adam in a text message? I wondered.

Suddenly I felt someone's eyes on me and glanced up to

see a tall, thin man with huge, thick, round black-framed glasses and a long pointy nose baring all his teeth at me.

"What's a lovely lady like yourself doing sitting here all on your own?" he said with a strange smirk. His accent was rather posh, definitely British. Without giving me the time to answer, he went on. "Well, it's your lucky night because I'm here now, your very own knight in shining armour!" he said, ending with a flourish before snorting, literally, with laughter. He sounded exactly like a pig snorting, or was it a horse neighing? Crikey, it was hilarious. I put my hand in front of my mouth but couldn't stop a giggle from escaping. I felt awful, but realised with relief that he thought that I was laughing at his joke and he was, in fact, delighted.

"I'm Henry. And you are?" he asked, still smiling widely as he pushed his large round glasses up his nose.

"Molly," I said, smiling politely.

"Oh my giddy aunt!" he said with a chuckle. "You Americans have the silliest names!"

"I'm actually Australian." I grinned.

"You are? Oh, you poor thing."

I laughed, but had no idea if he was joking or not. I wasn't really sure what to say and didn't want to seem rude.

Where on earth was Samantha? I really wished she would hurry back, but she was still chatting to the couple and had clearly forgotten all about me. I moaned inwardly before shaking myself up and deciding to give the guy a chance.

"Are you enjoying your holiday?"

"I am now," he replied, wiggling his eyebrows suggestively, which made his huge glasses bounce funnily up and down his long nose. He actually reminded me of Steve Urkel in *Family Matters*, except that he didn't have the high-pitched voice and the suspenders.

Once again at a loss for words, I looked towards the bar,

desperately hoping to catch Samantha's eye, but no such luck.

To my horror, he pulled out the chair opposite me and sat down. "You don't mind, do you?"

I shook my head. What else could I say?

"Didn't think you would," he said, snorting again. Suddenly, his face grew serious and he leaned forward over the table, his eyes fixed on me. I swallowed hard, feeling increasingly uncomfortable. "I'm known for *feeling* things, you know, having a *gut feeling,* and tonight my gut tells me that you fancy the pants off me! Am I right, or am I right?"

My mouth fell to the floor and my eyes popped out like a champagne cork. I sure hadn't been expecting *that!* And how on earth could he be so forward and so cocky?

"Er . . . um . . . " I stuttered, having no idea what to say.

He was beaming confidently, his eyes still fixed on me. "Don't be shy, I think you're pretty cute too. Not exactly my type, but cute nonetheless," he said, as he took a sip of beer and observed me over the rim of his glass. I let out a nervous giggle, not believing the cheek of him. But being me, I had a hard time being rude or unkind to anyone (except maybe Adam), so I didn't say anything. Suddenly, he reached over the table and took my hand in his. I froze. I badly wanted to snatch my hand away, but didn't want to hurt his feelings. I couldn't help feeling sorry for him because looking the way he did, he probably wasn't very popular with the girls. Although, come to think of it, he definitely seemed very sure of himself. I gently removed my hand out of his grasp.

"I'm sorry, but I'm not really comfortable with this. We've only just met," I said, squirming.

"He told me you were shy," he said, smiling indulgently at me. I frowned, wondering what he was talking about, but before I could ask him, he leaned forward again and said in a conspiratorial whisper, "Don't be shy. I like you too, so let's get straight to the good stuff . . . I'm leaving tomorrow so we mustn't waste any precious time, must we now?"

Oh no, my eyes were doing their popping out thing again and my mouth was back wiping the floor. He seemed to think that I had the hots for him after spending, what, three minutes, talking to me.

"I'm really sorry, but I don't understand what's going on here," I said, deciding that honesty was the best policy in times like these.

He bared all his teeth at me again. "Well, you're lonely and I'm available – you fancy me and I think I could definitely fancy you, so all is good, is it not?" he said with that British accent of his, as he once again tried to take my hand.

I pulled away quickly and stared at him incredulously. Why on *earth* did he think I fancied him? I didn't get it. Oh crikey, where was Samantha, I thought despondently, looking back towards the bar. *Damn it!* She was now talking to Adam. Are you kidding me? I tried to catch her eye, but she was deep in conversation. Adam, on the other hand, looked towards me and caught my eye. He wiggled his eyebrows at me, nudging his head towards Henry. He looked amused, damn him. I mouthed "help" but of course he ignored me and his mouth curled up into a half-smile as he picked up his drink and cocked it towards me in a "cheers" salute. *Oh my goodness, he was enjoying this!*

"I know women are intimidated by me because I'm rather dashing, but just relax, Molly, I'm a good man," Henry was saying as I turned back towards him.

I burst out laughing – surely he couldn't be serious? As I took in the genuine look of surprise on his face, I realised that he had in fact been dead serious. *Oh my goodness!*

"I'm so sorry. I tend to burst out laughing for no reason when I'm nervous," I said rather lamely by way of excuse, not wanting to hurt his feelings.

"That's perfectly alright. I understand. Now, how about you and I go for a lovely walk on the beach?"

Oh no. What was I supposed to say now?

"Just the two of us, hand in hand . . . what could be more perfect?" he purred, leaning towards me and taking my hand again. This time I wasn't fast enough and he held on tightly. My heart raced and my face flushed in embarrassment. I was so hopeless in situations like this, always wanting to please everyone and be nice.

"So how about it?" he asked again, squeezing my hand gently and trying to get me to look into his googly eyes. Oh lordy, I was being chatted up by Steve Urkel.

He tugged on my hand and started to stand up, wanting to pull me up with him.

"Er . . . no! I can't!" I cried out as I pulled my hand out of his, knowing that the only way out of this without hurting his feelings was to lie. "I'm waiting for . . . er . . . my boyfriend!"

He stopped short. "Boyfriend? But he told me you were alone and lonely," he said, clearly perplexed, pushing his glasses up his nose again.

"Who did?" I asked, frowning. It was the second time that he had mentioned a "he".

He pointed towards the bar. "Your friend over there."

"My friend?" I replied dumbly, swivelling in my chair to see who he was pointing at. "Who?"

"I can't remember his name, but it's the guy that looks like Ian Somerhalder."

"Adam? Are you kidding me! *Adam* told you that?" I shrieked in outrage, spinning back towards Henry, my eyes wild.

He nodded. "He said you were shy and that you fancied me so I had to be pushy and forward with you," Henry explained, his eyes avoiding mine as he fidgeted with his glass. Poor guy.

"The little s—!" I hissed through clenched teeth, pushing my chair out noisily as I got up. "I'm going to tell him *exactly* what I think about his stupid joke."

I stormed off and was already halfway to the bar when I realised that I was probably reacting exactly the way he'd been hoping I would. I stopped dead in my tracks. "No! You know what?" I said out loud, turning on my heels and heading back towards Henry, who was staring at me in bewilderment. I went around the table and stood next to his chair, extending my hand out to him. "Best way to get mad is to get even. So take my hand and let's go for that walk!"

Henry looked unsure and glanced towards Adam then back at me again, before his face broke into a big smile. He took my hand and pulled himself up. "Okay, let's do this."

We walked out of the bar, arm in arm, and made our way towards the beach. I looked over my shoulder and saw Adam staring at us, mouth agape. I threw him a triumphant smile over my shoulder before turning back to Henry.

"This is so exciting! I feel like a total badass," Henry said, looking down at me with a big grin, making me laugh. We began chatting, now both totally relaxed, and I found out that although he wasn't a looker, he had a lot of charm. I just loved his British sense of humour and we spent a wonderful evening together – and I'd managed to get even with Adam.

21

ADAM

I woke up with a headache and decided to order room service for breakfast. I lay back against my pillows and grinned stupidly into my cup of coffee, thinking back to how Molly had got the better of me last night. The look of triumph on her face when she'd looked over her shoulder as she walked off with Mr Googly Eyes was priceless. At first I was completely dumbstruck that my little plan had backfired, but then I looked at Henry again and knew there was no way in the world that she could fancy him. I wasn't one to think that looks were the only important thing when judging someone, but with his looks she would have needed a bit of time before deciding that his personality overpowered his geeky bespectacled look. That's when I knew that she had in fact played me over. Henry must have spilled the beans one way or the other, and instead of coming to rant and rave or punch me in the face like I expected – and certainly deserved – she'd decided to play along and fool me into believing that my little plan had back-fired. I shook my head in wonder. She just never ceased to surprise me. But one thing was sure: there was never a dull moment with her.

The trip to Casela World of Adventures Park was at ten o'clock, so I had an hour and a half to relax in bed. I couldn't help enjoying the sheer pleasure of lazing between the sheets. The weather was once again beautiful, although I'd been woken up by the sound of torrential rain during the night. It had been surprising as the sky had been full of stars when I'd headed back to my room after dinner, and then suddenly the sky was falling down on us. The sun was now out again, although there were a few clouds on the horizon. I had yet to see a cloudless sky in Mauritius, unlike in Perth where we had never-ending pure blue skies in summer.

At five to ten I made my way to the reception area and, as I approached, Molly turned and saw me. Her brows snapped together and she glowered at me. I stopped short, arching my eyebrow.

"Really?" she said, walking up to me.

"You obviously can't stay away, can you? It's actually getting to be pretty annoying, you know," I said, crossing my arms over my chest and giving her one of my looks.

She sighed loudly, then asked impatiently, "Do you ever get up on the right foot?"

"Nope. Always put my left foot first," I replied, poker-faced, and walked off towards the others, but not before seeing her hand fly to her mouth to hide her laughter. I couldn't help grinning and wondered when she would bring up Henry. I didn't have to wait long.

"So, I met someone last night," she said, coming up behind me.

I turned to her. "And what a catch he was."

Her mouth fell open in shock. "That's so mean."

"Well I'm sorry but the guy looked just like Steve Urkel in *Family Matters*!"

She giggled, obviously having seen the resemblance too, but then the smile fell off her face and, crossing her arms, she fixed me with those beautiful eyes of hers. She did not look happy.

"What you did last night was plain callous. Fair enough, you wanted to annoy me, and you succeeded. But what about poor Henry? You made him look like a fool, and he didn't deserve that."

I looked away, knowing it was true. I had no right to use him and make a fool out of him simply to serve my purpose. I was deeply ashamed of myself, but of course I couldn't tell Molly that. So instead I glared at her and said coldly, "Oh lighten up, it was just a joke. Not my fault you have no sense of humour."

"*You?* Talking about a sense of humour?" she bit back.

I walked off feeling really cranky and knew that my bad mood and scowls would be for real today. Molly wasn't the only one who didn't like me very much right now . . .

MOLLY

*A*dam had gone to sit at the back of the bus and I settled in the front seat. I wanted to stay as far away from him as possible. I had no idea what his problem was and why he was always broody, unfriendly and bad-tempered, but then again, it wasn't my concern. I just didn't understand why he wanted to play tricks on me and annoy me, but I guess he was bored and that I was an easy target.

When we arrived at Casela World of Aventures Park, we were given a map and shown the various activities available. There were so many things to see and do, but what caught my eye was the quad ride – I absolutely loved quad bikes. I hesitated for a moment because it was a bit expensive, but then decided to go for it. The guide told us that we would be leaving in half an hour and showed us where we were to meet him.

As I had half an hour to kill, I decided to go to the aviary walk-through as it wasn't far from the entrance. I admired the ponds I passed on the way which were full of fish, swans and ducks. Huge trees provided a canopy over the ponds, protecting us from the sun. It was beautiful and really peaceful, and I could imagine myself settling down on one of the benches with a good book.

Once inside the aviary, I was mesmerised by the huge multicoloured parrots and wide range of other birds who roamed free within the large aviary. Some flew around, some stayed in their nests and others perched on the trees. I jumped as three large parrots suddenly skimmed over my head. I laughed at myself and watched them make their way at high speed all around the aviary, flying low. I was surprised when my eyes fell on Adam further ahead. He was looking in fascination at the parrots as they whizzed over his head. He must have felt my eyes on him because he suddenly looked my way and our eyes locked. "Bloody parrots almost bit my head off!" he grumbled before walking away. I sighed in exasperation and called out to him, "I'm sure they have support groups for people like you, you know."

He stopped in his tracks, looking over his shoulder with a frown. "Support groups?

"Like Alcoholics Anonymous or AA, except in your case it would be MGA!"

I could see his mind ticking over, trying to work out what the letters stood for as I marched up to him. "Mega Grumps Anonymous!" I barked into his face. "Or TDA – Totally Depressing Anonymous! Or wait, even better, MPITAA – Major Pain in the Arse Anonymous!"

The look on his face was priceless – mouth around the floor somewhere, eyes wide. I stomped off, fighting down a burst of laughter.

"You, on the other hand, really need to go to YTYSH

Anonymous!" he called out a few seconds later. I grinned but kept walking, knowing that it would infuriate him if I ignored him. I could sense him upping his pace behind me as he swiftly closed the distance between us.

"You Think You're So Hilarious Anonymous," he said snidely, before storming past me.

I burst into laughter and could have sworn that he was smiling when he overtook me, but clearly he had no intention of letting me witness it. I didn't get it. I mean, if he wanted to smile or laugh, why didn't he just do it? Why did I feel like he often stopped himself or turned away so that I wouldn't notice?

Adam suddenly stopped abruptly and turned towards me, hands on hips and bearing his customary scowl. "WAYFM?"

"Huh?" I replied dumbly then wanted to kick myself for reacting.

"Why are you following me?" he said, shaking his head and rolling his eyes at me in a "duh, it's so obvious" way.

I bit down a burst of laughter. I loved his sense of humour, although I still couldn't figure out if it was intentional or not.

"JGSW!" I said proudly, following him.

He stopped, but didn't look back.

"Just going same way," I said, imitating his tone before overtaking him again.

Once again, I'm sure I saw a ghost of a smile on his lips, but it was gone before I could be sure. I followed him for a moment but then stopped short when I reached the restaurant. I stood mesmerised by the panoramic view. It reached out over the mountain ranges and all along the west coast. What an amazing spot for a restaurant. I wished Samantha had come, we could have had lunch here. I finally took off again and noticed Adam heading to the left towards the monkeys. I took a right and headed down towards the quad area.

I strolled past beautiful ponds, larger this time with an abundance of birds such as pink flamingos on the banks and in the water. I passed a little animal farm where I could see deer, ducks, rabbits, baby goats and other farm animals. I spotted a hippo enclosure and went to have a look. The enclosure was large and there were a few hippos grazing happily. I laughed as I read the sign on the fence: "Do not stand, climb or lean on the fences. If you fall, animals could eat you and that might make them sick".

I finally spotted the quads up ahead. When I reached the group, the guide smiled and greeted me. "We were waiting for you. I hope you're happy to share a quad because unfortunately we have a full session today. You can each take turns driving so that you share in the excitement."

I smiled back. "No problem, I don't mind being driven."

"Good! Because I sure in hell don't intend to get on behind you!" I heard Adam's familiar voice grumble behind me. *No way.*

I spun around and there he was. "No!" I cried incredulously before I could stop myself. What was he doing here? I hadn't even noticed him heading here or signing up for the ride in the first place.

"Looks like it," he said with a half-shrug, sounding as enthusiastic as I felt.

I groaned. This could not be happening!

"Tell me about it," he grumbled into my ear.

I sighed, I had no choice but to go along with it because I didn't want to make a scene in front of everyone. They were already staring at us, clearly wondering what was going on. I would have to grin and bear it and make the most of it. It was only a quad ride – besides, we wouldn't have to talk, so it should be just about bearable.

We each got assigned our quads and headed towards them. Adam climbed on and got settled before telling me to hop on. I climbed up, feeling as excited as a kid going on her first motorbike ride. I loved motorbikes and quads; riding them gave me such a sense of freedom.

"Here goes," he said, switching the ignition on before turning to me and motioning towards his sides. "I think you need to hold on."

Grinning wickedly behind him, I threw my arms around him and wrapped them tightly around his chest, pressing myself against his back. He wiggled around a little, trying to get me to loosen my hold, but I held on firmly, fighting the urge to giggle hysterically.

Finally, he sighed noisily, clearly exasperated, and grumbled, "I said *hold on* not *squeeze to death*."

"Oops! My bad," I said, removing my arms from around him, chuckling happily at my joke. He turned to look at me and as realisation dawned, he gave me a withering look, making me laugh even harder.

We finally took off, following the guide as we meandered our way through the nature park. I loved feeling the wind blowing through my hair – it was exhilarating. We spotted giraffes, lions, zebras, rhinos, and deer. I pointed and screeched excitedly every time I saw something, but was met with nothing more than an unenthusiastic nod or grunt from Adam each time. For some reason the more it happened, the more it made me giggle.

The scenery was to die for. The Black River Gorges on our right were majestic and contrasted beautifully with the blue sky overhead – which was slowly filling up with clouds. The weather in Mauritius never ceased to amaze me – it was like going through four seasons in one day. You woke up and it was sunny, hardly a cloud in the sky and no wind. Then later the wind would pick up and a few clouds would start appearing, then in the afternoon the clouds would get heavier and often at night it would rain.

As we made our way up the mountain, the road began to twist and turn quite sharply and I began to feel uneasy. I tightened my hold on Adam, and this time I wasn't trying to be funny. I leaned my head against his strong back to feel more secure and as I got a whiff of his scent, I couldn't help inhaling deeply, wanting more. *Molly Malahan!* my inner voice mocked. I felt ridiculous, but darn it, he smelled so . . . irresistible – clean and fresh and so masculine. He slowed down slightly and threw a glance over his shoulder.

"Are you *smelling* me?" he shouted incredulously over the noise and I felt myself turn crimson.

Suddenly realising that he was looking back at me and not at the winding cliff we were driving on, my embarrassment was replaced by sheer terror.

"LOOK IN FRONT OF YOU!" I screamed, squeezing him even more tightly as I imagined us plunging down the edge of the mountain. I felt his shoulders heave in exasperation but he turned back to the road.

"I CAN'T BREATHE! You're crushing me to death here!" he hollered over his shoulder, before wriggling in his seat, trying to get me to loosen my hold.

"I'm sorry," I shouted into his back. I hadn't realised how tightly I'd been holding on to him and, feeling extremely foolish, I loosened my grip and mumbled, "I don't like heights too much."

He glanced back at me, probably to ask me to repeat what I'd said, but as soon as he saw the look on my face, he slowed down completely.

"Is this better?" he called out over his shoulder.

"Y-yes. Thanks," I replied, completely stunned by his reaction.

We carried on up the mountain paths, seeing more

zebras, monkeys and plenty of deer. We stopped off at a view point from which the view was amazing and extended way past the Black River Gorges and up to Le Morne Mountain. The ocean and the coastline were spectacular in the background. It was such a beautiful island. I took out my camera and went snap-happy. I took dozens and dozens of photos from every angle, not wanting to miss a single spot of the magnificent panorama spread out in front of me. Adam sauntered up to me and stood there silently, alternating between looking at the view and observing me as I snapped away excitedly.

After a few minutes, he pointed towards the view and said poker-faced, "I think you missed a spot *just there.*"

I rolled my eyes but I couldn't help giggling, because I knew I had gone a bit overboard with my snap-happiness today.

I was about to put my camera away when Francoise, a lady on one of the other quads, came up to me and kindly offered to take a photo of the two of us. Before Adam could say anything, I passed her my camera and stood next to him, smiling widely. Knowing that he was probably scowling made me grin all the more.

"There you go," she said, handing me my camera with a smile. I thanked her and looked at the photo. I was standing with a huge smile on my face, while Adam stood sideways next to me, arms crossed, scowling down at me. It was hilarious and represented us so beautifully. I passed the camera to Adam, telling him to have a look. He grumbled, but took it, before glancing briefly at the photo. "The sky's really blue," he said, deadpan, handing me back the camera before strolling off.

I burst out laughing, my eyes following him as he strutted off. He was so "manly" with his long and muscular legs, his sexy butt, his large shoulders . . . *Drool alert!* my annoying little voice teased, snapping me out of my reverie. I quickly pushed all thoughts of sexy Adam away, reminding myself – again – that his personality, on the other hand, sucked, and walked back to the quad as if I hadn't just been lusting after his body.

We finally took off again and to my astonishment, when we reached the plains which were pretty flat, Adam asked me if I wanted to drive. I didn't have to be asked twice and settled myself happily into the driver's seat.

I stormed off, full of confidence, and was surprised to feel Adam tense up behind me.

"RELAX!" I shouted, laughing into the wind. "I've done this before."

A few minutes later, he suddenly exclaimed, "Slow down, there's a pothole ahead, go to the left a bit."

I did as I was told although I'd seen the pothole and knew what to do. Two seconds later, he cried out, "Watch out, there's a pretty low branch up ahead on the right", soon followed by, "Whoa, slow down, there's a turn up ahead!", "Watch out, another pothole", and finally, "Molly, be careful, you're going to hit the tree!"

Having had more than I could take, I slammed on the brakes, causing Adam to bang hard against my back.

"Owww," he groaned, rubbing his chest. "What was that for?"

Without a word, I climbed off the quad and glowered at him, hands on my hips. "You are the *worst* back-seat driver I have *ever* had the misfortune to meet!"

His eyebrows shot up and he gaped at me in surprise. It was the first time I'd lost my temper like this. *Yeah, well, take that, Mr McBloody Broody!* I thought angrily as he continued to stare at me, which only made my blood boil even more.

"And *stop* gaping at me like that!"

His eyes danced with amusement as he looked at me, but

I wasn't in the mood for the sudden appearance of his Dr Jekyll side. I gestured for him to move forward into the driver's seat, then walked behind him, giving him a little push forward to help him along – not that it had any effect on his huge bulk.

"What are you waiting for? Just move forward and drive!" I snapped, pushing him again, but it was like trying to move a wall.

"No," he said, shaking his head and crossing his arms, totally unruffled by my anger. "Don't feel like driving."

I shot him a killer glare and stormed back to the front of the quad, crossing my arms angrily. "Fine, we'll stay here then, because I sure as hell am *not* driving with you behind me ever again!"

"Sure," he said, shrugging nonchalantly, making me want to stamp my feet and have a full-on tantrum – but I glared at him instead, determined to stand my ground. He casually climbed off the bike and stretched, looking like he didn't have a care in the world. Argh! He was so flippin' infuriating – I wished I could . . . *Could what? Hit him? Kiss him?*

Oh shut up, will you? I mentally snapped at the annoying little voice in my head, which was making itself heard once more. I really wasn't in the mood for her snarky commentary. As if I could hit this big hulk of a man, and as for kissing him – why on earth would I want to kiss such an annoying, grumpy, pain-in-the-arse Neanderthal?

Because he's gorgeous, funny, infuriating, total scrumptious . . . it replied teasingly. And while my inner voice and I were debating Adam's scrumptiousness, he stood there watching me, waiting.

"Come on, Molly," he cajoled. "Just get on and drive."

Still too annoyed to even contemplate giving in to him, I turned and started walking away from him.

"I promise I won't say another word until we get back," he

added softly. The gentleness of his tone caught me completely off guard and I stopped dead in my tracks. I turned slowly and studied him through narrowed eyes, wondering what to do next. I knew I was acting like a child – not that I would ever admit that to Adam, of course – and decided to get a grip. I sighed heavily and walked back to the quad.

I settled down in the driver's seat and couldn't stop myself from muttering, "And men have the cheek of saying that women are the worst back-seat drivers."

"Now who's being cranky?" Adam said with unconcealed amusement.

Trust him to choose now, when I'm furious, to reveal he has a sense of humour.

"Well, at least I have a very good reason to be! You're just bad-tempered all the time for no reason at all."

Ignoring my retort, he cocked an eyebrow at me and asked, "Are we off then?"

I held his gaze for a minute then let out a long sigh.

"Fine. But not *one* word, you hear me? Not *one*," I said, pointing my finger at him in warning.

"Not one." He nodded solemnly, making me want to laugh all of a sudden, but there was no way I would give him the satisfaction. Without another word, he hopped back on and we were finally on our way again. He kept his promise until the last bend in the road; I was going a bit fast but was in full control, when suddenly he cried out, "OH MY GOD!"

I slowed down to a stop, turned towards him and looked daggers at him.

"That wasn't a *word*! That was a *prayer*!" he cried melodramatically.

I huffed, repressing a smile, and could feel him grinning into my back, as strange as that may seem. Once again, I wondered why he refused to smile or laugh *with* me. He was so exasperating, but there was something about him . . . I had actually loved feeling him pressed behind me, his hands holding onto my waist. It had felt so intimate somehow. I sighed. I didn't like the direction that my thoughts were beginning to take . . . no, I didn't like it one bit.

23

ADAM

I watched Molly walk up the stairs towards the animal farm and couldn't stop myself from chuckling. I'd been so close to losing it so many times all morning and had no idea how I'd managed to keep it together. I'd felt bad for a while about the whole Henry thing but then when she began with her anonymous support group thing, all I wanted to do was laugh.

She'd been amazing driving the quad – so sure of herself and clearly loving it. She'd been so cute when she'd jumped off, furious with me. She was quite spectacular when she got angry, not to forget, absolutely beautiful . . .

When it was finally time for us to leave, I made my way towards the bus, wondering how Molly would react towards me after our quad ride. To my great surprise, her face broke into a huge grin as I approached. I cocked an eyebrow at her, keeping a straight face, but I was sure she could see the mirth shining in my eyes. I honestly hadn't had this much fun with a girl in a very long time.

We finally made it back to the hotel and I headed straight to my room, changed and went for a quick swim in the pool. I then stayed in my room until dinner and began writing my article. I received a message from John asking me how it was going, and I replied briefly that things were quite complicated, but fun. He also asked how my subject was. I wasn't sure what to reply and ended up just writing: *Still cute – and very feisty.*

At half past seven, I made my way to the dinner buffet. I was starving as we'd only eaten a sandwich at Casela and not much else since. I sat down to eat and saw Samantha and Molly arrive. Samantha waved as they walked past me and I nodded a 'Hi' in return. I almost smiled but caught myself in the nick of time. Molly ignored me, which made me chuckle into my plate.

After dinner, I headed to the bar to get a drink and stayed to chat to the barman for a while. I didn't know anyone else as I had been so busy scheming and plotting things against Molly that I hadn't had time for anything else. I made sure that the girls couldn't see me because I was sick of scowling and wanted to just be "me" again for a while.

The band soon started playing and they announced the first song as a Mauritian sega dance, inviting us all to join them to learn the traditional creole dance. I saw Molly and Samantha heading excitedly to the dance floor and watched in amusement as they attempted to learn the moves. The music was actually super catchy and the dance itself involved a lot of hip swaying and twirling. As Molly began getting into the swing of it, I became mesmerised as she swayed her hips in rhythm to the music . . . I'm sure my mouth fell open at some point, and I wouldn't be surprised if I even drooled. I was shaken back to reality when I heard the barman say in his stilted English, "She good. Nice moves," motioning towards Molly. I nodded, grinning at him and giving him a thumbs up. I was still staring at her when she looked towards me and caught my eye, motioning for me to come. I shook my head and mouthed "No way" and she stuck her tongue out at me. "Very mature," I mouthed in reply and grinned. Realising what I'd done, I turned away quickly, but not before catching the look of surprise on her face. Damn. She'd seen me smile. *Scowl, Adam, scowl. Be angry, be mean, be bad-tempered!* I mentally reminded myself.

Two seconds later I felt a tug on my arm and turned to see Molly standing there, eyes sparkling. My scowl was back in place and I was determined that this time it would not budge.

"Come and dance!" she said, bouncing excitedly in front of me in time to the music.

"No. Absolutely not," I answered, shoving my hands in my pockets. "I don't like dancing."

"Yeah, yeah, of course you don't. But I really think it might help to remove that huge stick that seems to be wedged up your bottom."

My eyes popped out at the cheek of her, and I bit down a bark of laughter. "I am *not* stuck-up!"

I honestly was the least stuck-up person I knew, but it was true that I had been acting like a pompous jerk towards her.

"Excuse me, but you are by far the most pompous person I have ever met!" she said, her eyes shining with amused exasperation. "You've got to learn to relax a little."

"I'm perfectly relaxed, thank you very much."

She opened her eyes wide to show how ridiculous she felt my statement was, then shrugged and said flippantly, "I'm only trying to help."

"Do I look like I *want* your help?"

"Hmmm . . ." she said, giving me a once over, her eyes full of mischief. "Actually, no. I can't say that you look much like you *want* my help – but, by God, do you look like you *need* it!"

I quickly turned away, desperately fighting down a burst of laughter, and took a sip of my almost empty glass of beer to give me time to refocus. When I turned back towards her, she was standing there, hands on hips, looking mighty pleased with herself and clearly waiting for me to say something.

"So? Are you ready?" she asked, nudging her thumb towards the dance floor.

"What part of 'No' don't you understand?" I replied sarcastically. "The N or the O?"

"Oh stop being so lily-livered!"

I grimaced. "Lily-livered? What kind of word is that?"

"It means stop being such a coward!" she exclaimed, tugging at my elbow.

I shook my head and muttered, "Lily-livered? Me, lily-livered? What next?"

"Well prove it!"

Before I could stop myself, I had put my glass down, bounced off the stool and grabbed her hand. "Fine. You're on."

24

MOLLY

*O*h blimey. I hadn't expected him to agree. I just wanted to give him a bit of his own back by annoying him, but it had backfired and I now found myself being pulled towards the dance floor by my very own Broodonis.

The music had switched from sega to rock 'n' roll, and the band were playing "By The Rivers Of Babylon" by Boney M. Adam began expertly throwing me into twists and turns. I was happy to find that I was following his lead quite easily and we soon found ourselves taking over the dance floor. People actually stopped to look at us as he pulled me over and around his shoulder and twirled me in, out and around. His eyes shone and although his brow was furrowed in concentration, his mouth was relaxed and upturned for once. It was the first time I'd seen him like this, and he was even more gorgeous than usual. When the song ended we both stood there for a moment, looking at each other, breathing heavily. I felt exhilarated and my face broke into a huge grin. To my surprise, the corner of his mouth lifted up to the side in reply. Was he actually half-smiling at me? I couldn't believe it, but I was too excited about the dance to dwell on it.

"Wow! You sure can dance!" I exclaimed as I brushed away a few strands of hair that had escaped from my ponytail and were now stuck to my sweaty face.

He shrugged non-committedly, wiping a few beads of sweat off his own forehead with the back of his hand.

"It was amazing. I felt like I was a professional dancer," I continued, still bursting with adrenalin.

He raked his hand through his hair. "Yeah, well, let's not get too carried away, shall we?"

"Guys, that was amazing!" Samantha cried enthusiastically as she reached us on the edge of the dance floor. "Where did you learn to dance like that?" she said, turning to Adam.

"I took ballet classes when I was young," he replied, deadpan, making Samantha and I break into peals of laughter. Slipping his hands into his back pockets, he looked at us, shaking his head and rolling his eyes.

"What about me? Didn't I look like a pro up there too?" I asked Samantha with a grin.

"Of course you did! You were both great!"

"See, I told you I was dancing like a pro," I said, nudging Adam teasingly.

"Whatever you say," he answered, sounding bored and once again rolling his eyes upwards.

"You know, Adam," I said, looking at him through narrowed eyes. "With all that eye-rolling you're doing, it's lucky you're not Anastasia Steele and I'm not Christian Grey, otherwise I'd definitely have to put you over my knees and spank you mighty often!"

His eyebrows shot up and Samantha and I giggled.

"And why are you assuming I know what you're talking about?" he asked petulantly when we'd stopped laughing.

"Well it sure looks like you did," I retorted, tilting my head and quirking an eyebrow at him smugly.

"Okay fine, but it's only because my ex-girlfriend loved those books and for some reason seemed convinced that I was interested in hearing every last detail of the story."

I glanced at Samantha and gesturing towards Adam with my thumb, I said incredulously, "Did you hear that, Samantha? He's actually had a girlfriend before!"

For a split second, I saw the twinkle of suppressed laughter in his eyes before he furrowed his brow again.

"And why exactly should that be surprising?"

"Oh, you know . . ." I said, giving a half-shrug. "Can't be easy keeping up with all that cheerfulness!"

Samantha snorted next to me and I bit my lip to keep myself from joining her. Adam's eyes bored into me as he crossed his arms over his chest.

"Hmmm . . ." he said, pressing his lips together, narrowing his eyes at me and rubbing his chin with his thumb and fore-finger. "You know, I may not be Christian Grey, but I can still throw you over my knees and spank you."

Samantha and I looked at each other, eyes wide, and broke into fits of laughter.

After a moment, Adam cleared his throat loudly. "O-*kayyy*, all this laughter is a bit too much for me, so if you'll excuse me, ladies, I think I'll go back to the bar now."

We waved him off, still laughing. Once again he had managed to annoy me, surprise me and make me laugh. I had even gotten a smile from him, I thought, grinning happily, but I had to admit that he remained a complete enigma to me.

25

ADAM

I decided that I would go deep-sea diving today. I'd been dying to do it since I'd arrived, and today I would finally do it. It would allow me to relax, and besides, it would do me a world of good to stay away from Molly for a day. I was starting to have too many disturbing thoughts about her: her body, her eyes, her smile . . . I desperately needed to take a beat. Besides, I was pretty sure I'd heard Molly mentioning something about going to the markets with Samantha today, so either way, it worked out perfectly.

I'd just finished getting dressed when I heard someone pounding on my door. I wondered who it could possibly be and was surprised to find Molly standing there, looking rather annoyed.

"Oh dear, wake up on the wrong foot did we?" I teased, as I leaned lazily against the doorframe. Her beautiful green eyes narrowed, obviously not finding me amusing in the least. I pressed my lips together and desperately attempted not to smile as I waited for her to speak.

"Samantha just told me that she wouldn't be able to come to the Quatre Bornes markets with me today because she's too hungover. I can't go alone and I really, *really* want to go!"

"Well, why don't you just go tomorrow?"

"I wanted to. But market day is only on Thursdays, so it has to be today!" she wailed.

"O-*kay*, but without meaning to sound dense – what have I got to do with this?"

She sighed heavily and looked down at her hands. My eyes widened as I suddenly knew what she was about to ask me. *No way, Molly Sunshine!* But then she looked up at me with pleading eyes. Oh damn.

"*Please* come with me, Adam. You're the only other person I know."

I shook my head, not quite believing that she'd asked me that. "*Me?* Come to the markets with *you?* To do what exactly?"

"Shop!" she exclaimed, her face breaking into a big grin. "Pretty please, Adam! Don't you want to visit a new town and see how Mauritians live? The markets are full of local crafts and it'll be a great cultural experience too. I'll help you choose fantastic presents for your family – and even all your girlfriends," she added mischievously.

"And why on earth would I say yes to such a horrific proposition?"

She giggled and looked up at me again, batting her eyelashes. "*Pleeease.*"

"But what I don't get is why you would choose to spend the day with someone you find grumpy and pompous!"

She laughed again and I had a sudden desire to hug her. "Beggars can't be choosers, Grumpipots!" she teased, her eyes sparkling with mirth.

"That's really sad," I said gravely, making her giggle some more. As I looked at her, I realised that there was nothing I would rather do than spend the day with her; even going diving paled in comparison. *What was happening to me? I hated shopping!*

"Okay, fine! You win. But on one condition . . ."

"Yay!" she screeched, jumping into my arms, taking me by surprise. "Thank you, Grumpy Dumpy!

"One condition," I repeated sternly, raising my pointer finger.

"Sure. Anything."

"Take off whatever it is you're wearing right now and put on the least colourful clothes you own. My head will hurt if I have to spend the day with you looking like that," I said, waving my hand in her general direction and grimacing. She actually looked really pretty in her short multicoloured tie-dye dress, but I had to find something to rile her with.

She looked down at her dress in surprise and then shrugged. "Deal."

Oh no. What on earth had I got myself into? Why hadn't I said no? How was I going to spend another whole day being negative and broody when I had this beautiful, funny and delightful creature by my side? Life wasn't playing fair with me.

26

MOLLY

I went back to my room, smiling broadly. I couldn't believe Grumpy Dumpy had agreed to come with me. I also couldn't believe that I'd actually *wanted* to ask him to come – and not to mention, how excited I was at the thought of spending the day with the scowling master of all times. I didn't want to dwell on it too much and concentrated on finding the least colourful thing I had in my wardrobe. I spotted my long, white summer dress and grinned happily to myself. It would be perfect for Adam. I usually wore it with a bright belt and colourful accessories, but not today. Today I would go for the all-white look, I thought with a grin. I put my hair up in a ponytail and put on a simple silver pair of loop earrings and white lace-up sandals. Perfectly boring, Adam would love it.

Half an hour later, I knocked jauntily on Adam's door, chirping gaily, "It's time to *go-o!*"

He opened the door, forehead furrowed. Oh dear, what

was I going to do with him? His eyes then widened in surprise as he took in my new look. I smiled mischievously and held the sides of my dress, turning around to show him the full look. "You like?" I asked, batting my eyelashes at him for the second time today.

"No," he answered as he walked out. "But at least I don't have to wear my sunglasses all day," he added, closing the door behind him. I grinned, amused as usual by his less-than-friendly comebacks.

I settled myself happily in a window seat in the minibus that was taking us to Quatre Bornes and couldn't stop myself from grinning as Adam slumped down unenthusiastically by my side. We fell into a comfortable silence as I gazed out the window at the endless extents of sugar cane fields and the majestic mountain ranges as we headed inland. After a while the countryside gave way to small villages, until finally we entered the town of Quatre Bornes. There were shops on both sides of the road, food stalls, motorbikes and scooters, bicycles, stray dogs and so many people everywhere. It was so vibrant, full of colours and life. All sorts of unfamiliar smells wafted past us as we drove slowly into town. I glanced at Adam and noticed that he was as mesmerised as I was.

"Blimey!" he exclaimed, still staring out the window. "And there I was thinking *you* were colourful!"

I laughed as I watched Indian ladies walking past in their gorgeous saris in deep shades of red, yellow or green, with splashes of gold. Some were dressed as if they were going out on the town, they looked stunning. There was such a mixture of races, it was fascinating. Creoles, Chinese, Muslims, Indians, Europeans, tourists – so many people everywhere.

We finally drew up outside the markets, which were, in fact, a huge area covered by what seemed to be precariously laid-out tin roofs. The guide told us that we were free to roam around and he'd be back to pick us up in two hours to go to the Bagatelle Shopping Mall.

Adam's head spun towards me. "Bagatelle Shopping Mall? *No way!* That was *not* part of the deal!"

"Keep your pants on, honey bunch! We'll just take a taxi back to the hotel when we've finished here."

"*Honey bunch?*" he echoed, cocking an eyebrow at me, his eyes definitely brimming with contained laughter.

I giggled. I had no idea where that had come from. He was the last person on earth who fitted the endearment honey bunch.

"I wouldn't mind going to Bagatelle actually," I said, deciding not to comment on the honey bunch thing. "It's a relatively new shopping mall which apparently has great shops, cinemas, restaurants and pubs. So how about it?"

He gave me a dark look. "Absolutely *no way!*"

"Okay, fair enough," I said, knowing how guys hated shopping. I nudged him excitedly. "Let's hit the markets then!"

He groaned. "Please tell me this is all a bad dream and that I am about to wake up."

I burst out laughing. "You'll love it – just follow me."

I had no idea why he had agreed to come, but despite him being his usual annoyingly broody self, I was happy to have company. We walked towards the market place, which seemed to be divided into two or three long aisles running from one end of the market place to the other and parallel to each other. The stalls were packed one next to the other, back to back from one aisle to the next, and consisted of one or two tables per stall, with clothes (for the most part) piled high on them and lots of hangers hazardously hung up all around the stall. There wasn't much room to walk as there were so many people around. It was loud and so different from anything I'd seen before – it was fascinating.

Adam, on the other hand, stopped short as we arrived at the entrance.

"I am *not* going in there!" he cried, pointing inside. "It's packed like sardines!"

"Oh stop being such a killjoy!" I said, pushing him forward.

"I am not a killjoy, but this is . . . I can't even find words to describe it!" he exclaimed, throwing his hands in the air. As I took in his huge frame, I could understand his reluctance at going into the jam-packed markets, but there was no way I was letting him get out of this.

We pushed our way delicately down the aisle through the crowds as the vendors all tried to draw us into their stalls as we walked past. "Shirts at Rs 100! Great price, great quality!" or "Dresses for only Rs 200 – all sizes, colours and styles", "T-shirts, made in Mauritius – best price!". It was a bit over-whelming, but great fun.

"Look at those!" I exclaimed, pointing to a stand with colourful shirts with big hibiscus flowers on them. "It's so Mauritius – I just have to get one for Zach."

"First of all, they look Hawaiian to me, and second of all, you cannot buy a shirt like that for Jack or anyone else for that matter!"

"His name's Zach."

"That's what I said."

"And why on earth not?" I asked, still looking through the pile of shirts.

"If you really don't know, ask *him*!" he cried, motioning towards the vendor.

"Fine!" I snapped, turning to the vendor with a smile. "Sir, do you think this would be a nice shirt to buy for a man?"

"Yes, of corse. It loveely. Vary beeuteeful, so colourful weef ze big flowers on it," he answered enthusiastically with an accent which was either French or Indian or a bit of both.

I turned happily towards Adam, but my smile faltered when I saw him raise an eyebrow at me and shrug in an I-told-you-so way. I was puzzled. "But he just said—"

Adam cut me off. "That it was loveely, vary beeuteeful and so colourful weef ze big flowers on it – my point exactly!"

"I don't get it," I said, genuinely confused. It sounded positive to me, but Adam didn't seem to think so.

"Is Jack gay?" he asked me, eyebrow raised.

"His name's *Zach*. And no, he's not gay," I cried in frustration.

"Well there you have it then! You just can't buy a *loveely, vary beeuteeful, so colourful shirt weef ze big flowers* on it for a straight guy!" he said determinedly, before turning and walking off, leaving me standing there staring at him mouth, agape.

What the?

27

ADAM

She stomped angrily behind me. "You are *such* a bore!"

My head spun back in surprise at her tone and I glared at her, although I just wanted to laugh. "I am *not* a bore. I just have good taste and don't happen to think that colourful shirts with flowers are very masculine."

"Yeah, right. Here, why don't you buy this lovely white shirt here?" she said, pushing a white shirt in my face. "So exciting and different."

My lips twitched dangerously as I put the shirt down. "Are you done?" I asked in amused derision.

She glared at me for a moment, her eyes glowing with anger, then suddenly her expression softened and a large grin spread over her face, and she nodded. We began making our way down the aisle again. I wished I could tell her that I liked wearing colours too – okay, maybe not quite as colourful as hers, but my wardrobe was definitely not full of black and grey clothes, and I actually had a Hawaiian shirt in there somewhere.

She stopped short at one of the stalls, making me bump into her.

"Owww!" I groaned exaggeratedly and heard her giggle. I couldn't help biting down a smile; her laughter was so contagious.

"Look at these t-shirts! Aren't they great?" she said in delight, holding one with the Mauritian dodo bird, a local emblem, sega dancing on the beach. They *were* actually cool, with dodo birds in typically Mauritian scenes – the dodo around a campfire on the beach, the dodo going fishing, the dodo golfing, the dodo lying in a hammock, etc.

"Yes, and I'm sure Jackson would much prefer one of these as opposed to the flowery shirts back there!"

"Who's Jackson?" she asked, looking at me with a frown.

"Your housemate," I answered, rolling my eyes.

Her forehead creased in irritation, then suddenly all her features relaxed and she burst out laughing.

"You're doing it on purpose!" she cried out, pointing an accusing finger at me.

"Doing what?" I asked with wide-eyed innocence.

But she was onto me and punched me playfully on the arm. "Oh my goodness! Were you consciously cracking a funny there, Mr Grumpy Dumpy?"

"As if," I replied wryly, before turning away to stop myself from grinning back at her. This was just hopeless. I was a pathetic actor and it was impossible to stay grouchy with Molly. I was going to go crazy here and article or no article, I didn't see how I would be able to keep this charade up all week.

"Look at this one, it's great," she said, showing me one with the dodo holding a bottle of the Mauritian Phoenix beer with the slogan *No Problem in Mauritius* written under it. I loved it, and it would be a perfect gift for John.

We soon found out that the designs didn't come in all sizes and colours. It was extremely amusing because I asked for a white *No Problem in Mauritius* t-shirt in large, and after looking through the piles for a while, the vendor finally handed me a blue t-shirt with the same design, but in medium. He then explained that he didn't have one in large but that it didn't matter as it was the same thing and would probably fit. When I mentioned that I'd asked for a white one, he said flippantly, "I not 'ave white, but ze blue is good also."

I felt Molly's shoulders shake with silent laughter beside me and I leaned over and whispered in her ear, "Why bother choosing sizes and colours, huh?"

Molly stifled a giggle and asked for a red t-shirt with the dodo sega dancing on the beach in small. He came back and handed her a red t-shirt but with the dodo fishing design. "I 'ave no more sega on beach but this one just ze same".

We glanced at each other again, my mouth breaking into a lopsided grin while I tried to stop myself from howling with laughter.

"Why bother choosing a design either, huh?" I muttered under my breath, just loud enough for her to hear. She slapped her hand over her mouth and snorted, as the vendor looked on, bemused.

It took us ages to get the t-shirts we wanted as he never seemed to have quite the size or colour we asked for in the design we chose, so we had to choose another design or colour in the size we needed.

When we were ready to pay, Molly began bartering with the vendor, who she now called by name, Sanjeev, trying to get him to reduce the price for us as we were buying eight t-shirts. "Okay, I give you good price Mister becose you are veev zis loveely lady."

Molly grinned proudly at me, nudging me playfully in the ribs. "See how great I am at this bartering business? You should try it, it's fun," she said, then stopped, cocked her head to the side and gave me a once over, before adding with a grin, "Then again, somehow I don't think it would work as well if you did it . . ."

I smirked and turned away before breaking out into a full-blown grin. I was so fed up with this stupid assignment, I would burst if I had to stop myself from smiling and laughing for much longer.

We carried on down the various aisles, going up and down, pushing through the crowds. It was exhausting, and after an hour I'd had more than enough, but Molly was having none of it.

Another half hour went by in which time Molly managed to get me to buy a lovely tablecloth for my mum, sarongs for my three sisters, and a shirt for my dad. She also bought all sorts of colourful sarongs, t-shirts, blouses, skirts, and multi-coloured baskets woven in Mauritius for everyone she knew. Finally, I'd really had more than enough of shopping for a day – make that a year – and told her that we were leaving right away. She sulked for all of thirty seconds, before grinning and telling me that I was right, that enough was enough. I heaved a huge sigh of relief as we headed back outside.

"I'm starving," she said as we reached the street. She looked around us for a second, then pointed to our left. "Look at the food stall over there. Shall we try it out?"

"Sure." I was always happy to try out local foods, and I was also starving. We made our way to the stall and asked what they were selling. "*Gateaux piments*," the man replied with a strong accent – once again it was hard to tell whether it was French, Indian or Creole. "Deleecious but hot hot!" he added with a toothy grin. The people were all so friendly here and you really got the impression that the saying "No problem in Mauritius" was their general attitude.

"So, are you game?" Molly grinned mischievously at me.

"Wherever there's adventure and excitement – I'm in!" I said flatly, in my best Eeyore impersonation.

She looked at me, her eyes wide with amusement, and slapped me playfully on the arm. I headed to the rickety stall, chuckling to myself, and bought us a paper cone full of *gateaux piments* and samosas and my stomach rumbled at the smell. Molly took one of the *gateaux piments* from the cone and handed it to me before getting one for herself.

"Okay, on the count of three, we both put it in our mouths – no spitting out. This is a cultural experience!" she said, her eyes sparkling.

I raised a teasing eyebrow. "You do realise that we have absolutely no idea what we are about to eat, don't you?"

"Yep!"

"Okay, you're on!" I said, holding it up to my mouth.

On the count of three we both popped our *gateau piment* into our mouths, eyes on each other. They were slightly spicy but delicious.

"Umm, sho good . . ." Molly said, her mouth full.

It seemed that they were some sort of chilli balls made of dough and spices. We happily began ploughing through the whole bag until Molly bit into one that had a huge red chilli in it and she became as red as the chilli, hyperventilating with the heat of it, jumping up and down and waving her hand in front of her mouth as tears poured down her face. I couldn't help laughing at her but she was in too much pain to notice that I was finally laughing. I ran across the road to a little shop and bought her a bottle of water and some dry bread, and that seemed to finally calm her down.

"Oh my gosh! I must have eaten a whole red chilli or

something. It was awful," she wailed, wiping her wet face with the back of her hand and taking deep breaths. "Think I'll go easy on those next time."

Still hungry, I noticed another food stall up ahead to our left and headed there to see what they were selling. They were *dhol puris*, a type of flatbread which looked a lot like tortillas, but the guy told me were primarily made with yellow peas (dhol) and flour, and a little cumin and saffron, water and oil and then filled with a special *rougaille* sauce (onions and tomatoes cooked together) or yellow split beans, chutneys and pickled vegetables. Molly asked the seller if they had chilli anywhere in them.

"You like it hot, Miss?" he asked with a toothy grin.

"No! No, no, no, no. I don't. Not hot for me!" she exclaimed, wide-eyed, shaking her head vigorously, making me chuckle quietly behind my hand.

We bought a few pairs of *dhol puris* and spotting a bench in what looked like the gardens of the Municipal Council of Quatre Bornes on the other side of the road, we made our way there. The *dhol puris* were actually delicious and just melted in the mouth. I went back to get a few more and we ate in companionable silence.

"I wish I could have filmed you having your chilli ball crisis," I blurted out with barely concealed amusement. "It was truly a classic moment."

"Do you thrive on seeing people suffer?"

I looked away to hide my smile, then turned back and shrugged. "Not really, but I do know a funny moment when I see one, and you jumping up and down, red-faced, with tears running down your cheeks was definitely one of them."

Her mouth opened and closed, then she just shook her head and chuckled quietly. We sat in silence watching the world go by. There was so much traffic and so many people everywhere. It was fascinating, and a world away from life in Perth.

"I really need the toilet," Molly suddenly said, grimacing.

I looked around, then pointed to a tiny bush a little further off and said, "There's a bush over there – go for it."

"Are you going to look, though?" she asked cheekily, catching me off guard as I fought down a bark of laughter. Not trusting myself to speak without laughing, I just rolled my eyes and said nothing.

"That's it, I'm twenty-five years old and I'm going to pee in my pants!" she cried dramatically.

"Relax. There's a KFC over there. There will definitely be toilets in there." I pointed to the other side of the road.

She practically made us sprint to KFC, and I let her go in while I waited outside with our bags. It was almost a quarter past one and it was more than time to head back to the hotel. I looked around but couldn't see any taxis around. This clearly wasn't New York with its never-ending yellow taxis or even London with its black taxis, but we would just have to ask someone where we could find one. What was our hotel called again? Darn it, I actually had no idea. I hadn't done the booking and hadn't paid attention and could absolutely not remember the name. I'm sure Molly would, though, I thought gratefully, just as she burst through the door looking relieved.

"Okay, Molly Sunshine, this is all the excitement I can take for a day. It's time to head back to the hotel but there don't seem to be any taxis around," I grumbled, looking up and down the street. "Maybe they don't exist in Quatre Bornes."

"Stop being so melodramatic – of course there do! I'll go ask someone."

She's so damn cute, I thought, watching her walk off with her long wavy hair swinging back and forth in her ponytail as she headed towards an old man. Her smile illuminated her face as she spoke to him. He looked at her with a toothless grin and pointed to the right, explaining something to her. She nodded and smiled before waving and heading back to me.

"Oh Adam, he was *so* cute. Did you see his smile? He didn't have any teeth!" she exclaimed, putting her hand on my arm, her eyes shining up at me. I couldn't help loving the intimacy of the gesture and it sent a shiver all through my body.

"I'm just thrilled to know that you find him hot, but can we get back to the taxi situation now please?"

She giggled. "I actually didn't understand a word he said, so I can't promise anything," she said, twisting her lips comically. "But I *think* he said 'taxi zat way'!" She pointed up ahead to the left.

"Okay, lead the way," I said with a ghost of a smile. "What's our hotel called again?"

She stopped dead in her tracks, her little brows furrowed in concentration, and I waited for her to answer. Suddenly, her hand flew to her mouth and she looked towards me in horror. "I have *no* idea."

"No way!" I exclaimed incredulously. "Do you at least have a vague idea of what it may sound like?"

"I really don't know. Maybe something like Lapana or Lapna Beach Resort?"

"That does actually sound familiar. What's that big public beach just before the hotel? Fit in Flac? Or is it Flipping Flat, or Flic Flac—" I suddenly stopped in my stride as I realised that Molly was laughing riotously behind me. I turned and scowled at her.

"I'm sorry, but it just sounds so ridiculous! Fit in Flac, Flipping Flat, Flic Flac or hey, why not Fit and Fat?" She laughed. "Wait! I've got it, I've got it! It's actually Flippin' Fat!"

I turned away to hide my grin but I'm sure she'd caught on by now that I was hiding my amusement. It was no secret to me that I was failing dismally at my role as Grumpy Dumpy. I just hoped I hadn't blown my cover completely.

"Well, however funny it sounds we still have to find our way back to this flippin' place," I said, making her giggle again.

"Alright," she said seriously when she had finally calmed down. "So, to sum up the situation: we know that our hotel is called something like Lapana Beach Resort and that it's found near a public beach called Flic Flac, Flipping Flat or Fit in Flac right?"

I nodded, trying not to smirk. She looked at me and spurted with laughter. "We're in deep trouble!"

We finally decided to try our luck, hoping that the taxi drivers would understand where we needed to go. We followed the man's directions to the taxi stand but it was quite some way up and it took us ages to get there because Molly kept stopping in front of every second shop window to show me some great dress or bag or local craft (all super bright and multicoloured, of course).

Finally, we got to the taxi stand, which was thankfully pretty full of taxis, and we approached the closest one.

"Okay, Molly, you're on," I said, motioning for her to go ahead.

She grinned up at me and led the way towards him. "Ex-cu-se me, do you sp-eak En-gl-ish?"

"He's not dumb, you know. You don't have to speak so s-l-o-w-l-y," I whispered in her ear.

She glared at me and hissed "Smartass!" before turning her smile back to the taxi driver. I grinned, loving her feistiness.

He smiled at her. "Yes, I do. You vant me to take you vhere?"

"Well, um, there is one small problem," she said, scrunching up her nose cutely. "We can't really remember the name of our hotel."

"Oh dear, I cannot tell you that zees 'as 'appened before," the taxi driver replied with a grin. "But maybe you can tell me vhere it eez and I can guess?"

"Well we know that it sounds something like Lapana Beach Resort and there's a public beach near it that's called Flipping Flat or Flic Flac or Flic and Fat."

The driver threw his head back and bellowed with laughter. "Zat eez so funny. You are probeebly speaking of Le Panache Beach Resort near Flic en Flac."

"Yes, yes, yes!" Molly screeched, jumping up and down and grabbing my arm. "That's it! I remember now. Can you take us there please?"

"Yes, of course. It eez only about half ze hour from 'ere," he replied with a big smile.

Relieved to finally be heading back to the hotel, I relaxed into the back seat next to Molly. We had just driven off when I noticed the driver staring at me in the rear-view mirror. Recognising the signs, I groaned inwardly, waiting for the question to come.

"Are you ze famousse actor on ze television?" he asked, still looking at me. "You look veree ze same as actor I saw in film ze ozer day."

"No, I'm not an actor actually, but apparently I look like Ian Somerhalder from the Vampire Diaries and Lost."

"Ah, yes, yes, zat's ze one," he said, nodding. "My vife zink ee's veree 'andsome. Me I am a man, so I not know!" He laughed.

I chuckled but said nothing. I could feel Molly's eyes on me. The driver glanced at me again briefly, looking disappointed. I got that a lot too when people realised I wasn't Ian, they all got that disappointed look.

"Ahh, zat's a peety. I 'aven't 'ad a famousse actor in my taxi before," he said, sighing. "No matter, I veell still tell my vife zat a man who looked just like a famousse actor came in Ravi's taxi!" He laughed again.

We then fell into a comfortable silence for a few minutes before he started chatting to us, asking questions about our stay and telling us about his life. He was very talkative, and I loved hearing his broken English.

Twenty minutes into the drive, I suddenly realised that I was really bursting for a pee and there was no way I could wait for us to get to the hotel. Thank God for the endless sugar cane fields, I thought to myself, before leaning towards Ravi. "I'm sorry, Ravi, but I have a serious call for nature."

He nodded and to my great surprise replied, "Yes, we 'ave so much vonderful nature in Mauritius. Just look at ze mounteens and ze sugar cane fields . . ."

"Er . . . um . . ." I said, amused, trying to interrupt his talk on nature, but he was on a roll.

"You know we 'ave many indeegenous plants and treez in Mauritius – you must go visit our forests and parks. So much nature, yes . . ."

I didn't want to hurt his feelings by cutting him off because he seemed so proud of his island, so I waited patiently for him to finish while Molly shook with silent laughter by my side.

"That's great," I said, when he finally stopped talking. "But what I meant was that I have a serious *call for nature.*"

He smiled. "Yes, ven you see so much beauty it is like a calling, yes? Just look at ze mounteens on ze left. Ave you ever seen somezing so beeuteeful?" he said happily.

Suddenly realising that he probably had no idea what the expression "call for nature" meant, and that I wouldn't be able to hold on for much longer, I blurted out loudly, "I'm sorry, Ravi, but I really need to pee!"

He glanced back at me, eyes wide, looking really surprised at the desperation in my voice.

"But of course, I vill stop rite away. Vy didn't you tell me sooner?" he asked, clearly perplexed.

Molly guffawed behind her hand as Ravi slowly pulled up on the side of the road. As soon as the car came to a halt, I jumped out and raced off into the cane fields.

MOLLY

"*P*oor man! Vy didn't he tell me before?" Ravi said, shaking his head as we watched Adam sprint off into the sugar cane fields.

I shrugged, concentrating really hard to stop myself from laughing hysterically.

Finally, Adam ran back to the car and fell in, looking relieved. "Thanks, Ravi, I feel so much better now."

I laughed at his obvious relief and he turned to me and gave me a wink. My eyes bugged out and my mouth fell open. It was the end of the world as I'd known it – Adam had just winked at me! He pretended not to notice my gobs-macked expression and just turned back to the driver and picked up where they had left off. It just didn't add up – not that anything much about Adam did anyway. I leant my head against the window and watched the countryside speed past us. I was too tired to talk so I let Adam chat to Ravi. Come to think of it, he was being unusually friendly.

Thoughts of my day with Adam kept popping into my head: Adam trying on purple and pink straw hats asking me, straight-faced, if I thought they would look good on his mum and sisters, me and Adam eating the *gateaux piments*, Adam telling me to go pee behind the bush . . . I just couldn't help smiling to myself. Despite his non-stop grouchiness, he still managed to be a lot of fun and I was glad that he'd come with me. I still had no idea why he'd agreed to accompany me, but whatever his reasons, I was grateful.

When we saw the sign indicating Flic en Flac, Adam and I looked at each other and I burst out laughing. To my absolute astonishment, his face broke into a lopsided grin. OMG! First a wink and now a smile! As I felt my heart race wildly, I realised that maybe it was safer if he just kept scowling at me after all.

When we returned to the hotel, we headed straight to our rooms, both exhausted. It was already half past three.

"Thanks so much for coming with me, Adam," I said with a smile as we reached my door. "It was fun."

He looked at me and raised an eyebrow. "You called that *fun?*"

I grinned and nodded. He turned towards his door, throwing me a quick wave over his shoulder.

Once inside, I fell onto the bed gratefully. Gazing out through the sliding doors, I hesitated between sleeping or going for a swim. Opting for a swim, I changed into my bikini, grabbed my towel and headed down to the beach. The water was wonderfully warm and as I swam, my mind once again drifted back to our day at the markets. I had loved seeing a side of the *real* Mauritius, its culture and traditions. And Adam . . . I dived under the water to stop my thoughts from going there again. I didn't want to think about him right now. I finally went back to my room for a much-needed nap. I hadn't seen Samantha at all and wondered if her husband had written back to her. I decided that I'd go and find her as soon as I got up.

I woke up as the sun was starting to set. I walked to the beach and sat down, gazing in awe at the magnificent sunset. There were a few clouds on the horizon but it made it all the more beautiful. I ordered a glass of *Miravel* Sauvignon Blanc, which was delicious, and happily lay on a deck chair, enjoying the view. As it grew dark, I went off to look for Samantha and found her reading in the lounge area.

"Hi, you!" I said, dropping down in the sofa opposite her.

"Hi, yourself!" she said, smiling up at me as she put her book down on the side table. "So how was it? I'm so sorry for letting you down – I haven't had a hangover like that in years. It was awful," she groaned.

"Poor you. Pity you didn't come though because it was a fascinating experience."

I told her about Quatre Bornes and the markets, the smells, the crowds, the diversity of the population, the traffic and then I mentioned Adam. Her eyes widened in surprise at the sound of his name and she put her palm up to stop me. "Wait, wait, wait!"

"What's the matter?"

"Adam? As in Adam Somerhalder McGrumpy?" she asked incredulously.

I nodded sheepishly.

"How? *Why?*" she exclaimed, sitting up straight in her armchair.

"Well . . ." I said, fidgeting with my bracelet, looking anywhere but at her. "I asked – no, actually, to be honest – I *begged* him to come with me." I grimaced, looking through my eyelashes at her. She gaped at me, shaking her head. "I didn't want to go alone, okay? And I don't know anyone else here."

"Fair enough," she acknowledged with a smile. "So how did it go? Is he thawing out a bit?"

"Well, it's strange because I can't stop laughing when I'm with him. The thing is, I don't know if he actually makes jokes or if he's just totally weird in a funny kind of way. Sometimes I catch him hiding a grin or I see a hint of a smile on his lips but he turns away so that I can't see. It's all a bit strange, but what's even more strange is that I really enjoy being with him . . ."

She shook her head in bewilderment. "I can't say that I understand, but hey, whatever makes you happy, girl!"

I laughed. "What did you get up to today?"

"Nothing much – after finally making it out of bed, I've pretty much spent the day on the beach, in the sea and around the pool just relaxing and reading. It was wonderful."

"Any news from home?"

She shook her head, her eyes clouding over. "No, not a word since I sent my email yesterday."

"He needs a little time to take it all in and besides, you know how slowly men type – he probably started replying to you yesterday and is still at it now."

She laughed. "Oh crikey, that's so true. He is the slowest typist ever."

"You see, give him a little time. You've had a few days to think about things, but it's probably all new to him and he'll need time to process everything before getting back to you."

She sighed. "You're probably right."

As I made my way back to my room a while later, I couldn't help wondering where Adam was and what he was up to . . . It had only been a few days since I'd met him, but it felt like I'd known him forever. I almost missed him when he wasn't around, a feeling I'd never felt with anyone before. My feelings towards him remained a huge enigma to me as I couldn't understand my attraction to someone so broody. Suddenly an image of his lopsided grin flashed before me and I felt my heartbeat accelerate. Damn him! I didn't want him to get under my skin. He wasn't good for me.

29

ADAM

I saw Molly heading back to her room, and admired her from afar. I was like a love-struck teenager and felt ridiculous. No one had ever had that effect on me before. I actually missed her when she wasn't with me, and every time she showed up somewhere, I was so damn happy to see her. I was getting more and more frustrated at having to be crabby and not be able to laugh with her. I'd just been for a long jog way down the beach, but seeing Molly made me feel like I needed another jog to quell my frustration.

Adam, get a grip. You're falling for this girl and she will hate you when she finds out that you've been pretending to be someone you're not simply to write an article about her. I knew that whoever that little voice belonged to, it was right. She would never forgive me for not being honest with her and pretending to be someone I wasn't just for an article. I was furious with myself for still going along with this, but it was too late for me to back out now. Besides, I wanted that promotion badly. I waited for Molly to get inside before making my way back to my room. I couldn't cope with seeing her right now, but then again there was nothing else I'd rather do than be with her. *Arrgggh!* This was driving me crazy.

I was just getting out of the shower when I noticed that my mobile phone was ringing. I grabbed a towel and quickly tied it around my waist before grabbing my phone from the bedside table.

"Adam! You have to talk to them! I'm going crazy here. They still think I'm a kid!" I heard my youngest sister, Lily, wail into the phone before I could even say a word.

"Well hello to you too, squirt! Who is 'them', and by the way, you *are* still a kid."

"I AM NOT A KID! I'm fifteen years old!" she protested heatedly.

"So what seems to be the problem?" I asked as I took a pair of shorts from my suitcase and pulled them on, holding my phone between my shoulder and ear.

"I want to get a nose ring and a piercing in my eyebrow and Mum and Dad won't let me!" she exclaimed furiously.

"Well thank God for that! Why on earth would you want to do something like that at your age?" I asked, horrified by the thought.

"Oh *noooo!* You're just as old and boring as them. I thought at least you would understand!"

"I'm sorry, but I personally don't find piercings and nose rings particularly attractive," I said as I made my way across the room and settled on the sofa. "Aren't you a bit young to start having nose rings and piercings everywhere?"

"No!" she cried angrily. "And I just want *one* nose ring and *one* piercing in my eyebrow."

"Lily, you're gorgeous just as you are. You know that all the guys at your school would give anything to go out with you," I said gently, hoping that flattering her would get that ridiculous idea out of her head.

"Yes, but there's this guy . . ." she said quietly.

Damn those stupid guys. I hated the thought that she felt the need to change to please a boy.

"Lily, I know what it's like to be fifteen years old and to have a crush, but what you need to remember is that if this guy doesn't notice you or think that you're terrific exactly the way you are, then he's just not worth it. Don't change to please others. Those who are worth it will love you for who you are."

She sighed heavily into the phone. "Do you really think so?"

"I know so," I replied gently. "But more importantly, do *you* really find nose rings and eyebrow piercings beautiful, Lily? Is it truly something that you would like to do for yourself?"

She sighed heavily again but stayed quiet.

"If you honestly do, then I'll talk to Mum and Dad for you."

She remained silent, probably taking it all in. I waited a moment, giving her time to think things through.

"Lily?"

"I really love you, you know?" she finally said softly. "You always manage to make me understand why Mum and Dad say no to things. I always think they do it to just annoy me, but when you explain it, it all makes sense. Thank you."

"Anytime, sis, I'm always here for you, you know that. How are things at home?"

"What? You mean apart from Mum and Dad freaking out because their daughter suddenly wants to turn Goth at fifteen?" she said giggling. "All okay. Boring as ever. Emma called last night and is loving New Zealand and will be back on Sunday. Jo is walking around in a daze and eats, sleeps and breathes Tony! It's sickening."

I laughed, just imagining Jo in another one of her romances. She was forever falling in love and it was always "this time he's the one".

"So, tell me about Mauritius? Any gorgeous locals who've fallen under your charms?"

"No, but it's great. I love it, although it's hard having to work," I said honestly, although I didn't elaborate on exactly what it was I was working on.

After talking to Lily, I went for a long walk on the beach, enjoying the feel of the warm sand between my toes. The sea always calmed me and although I loved the sound of breaking waves, the gentle lapping of the water onto the shore was really soothing too. I lay on a deck chair on the far end of the beach to watch the sunset. At least here I was sure not to bump into Molly.

I couldn't help smiling as I thought of Molly in the taxi on the way back from the markets today. The expression of surprise and delight on her face when I'd grinned and winked at her was priceless.

As night fell, I slowly made my way back to my room. I would stay in and order room service so that I could get some work done. I settled on the sofa and spent an hour jotting down the day's events and my dialogues with Molly before switching on the TV and mindlessly channel-hopping for a while. Finding nothing to grab my interest, I switched off the TV and got up to get my book from my bedside table. I grinned as I remembered Molly on the plane. My grin was soon replaced by a scowl as I realised that I was once again grinning stupidly to myself while thinking of Molly – my subject, a girl who would end up hating me, a girl I just could not fall for. Sighing deeply, I shook my head, willing the thoughts away, and threw myself down onto my bed. I settled comfortably against my pillows, determined to think of nothing but my book for a while. It didn't take long for me to see that it was wishful thinking on my part because my thoughts kept wandering off and always in the same direction...

30

MOLLY

I didn't stay long after dinner as I was exhausted after our day in Quatre Bornes. I walked back to my room and couldn't help thinking that, all in all, it had been quite a day. Pretty wonderful, yet strangely disturbing too. I had just snuggled up comfortably in my super comfy bed when I heard my mobile shrill on my bedside table. My heart raced as I turned to grab it, knowing that it could only be my mum.

"Moll, is that you?" I heard my mother's voice whisper anxiously into the phone. My heart plummeted.

"Hi Mum, how are you?" I asked, hoping that my intuition was wrong.

"I can't breathe, Molly, I think I'm having a heart attack!" she said, her voice filled with panic as she panted into the phone. My heart constricted, then started to race. I hated this. I took a deep breath, knowing that I had to be in control here.

"Mum, just breathe deeply. You are not having a heart attack, you know that," I said soothingly, going into my doctor-client mode. "You've felt this way so many times before – you know it's just a panic attack."

"No, it's different this time. My chest is really so tight and my heart is racing like it never has before – I can't breathe Molly . . ." she said, panting heavily, her voice hoarse. "I c-an't – I can't brea-the!"

I knew that she wasn't having a heart attack as her heart was in perfect condition. We'd gone to the doctor for a full check-up last month after I'd threatened to take her under duress in an ambulance if she didn't come with me. I needed to get her to relax, but being an ocean away wouldn't make things very easy. When I was with her I just held her hand and did the breathing with her and talked her though the attack.

"I can't move, Molly, I'm so scared. I can't breathe, I can't breathe!" she cried again in anguish, still panting. My heart beat in my throat and I felt the knot tighten in my stomach. What if I couldn't get through to her? Taking a deep breath, I tried again.

"Mum, go and lie down on the couch and try to relax," I said, hoping she couldn't hear the tremor in my voice. "I'm right here with you."

"Okay, I'm lying down," she said in a shaky voice, still breathing heavily. She'd probably been pacing around her apartment. That's what she did when she was anxious. She couldn't sit still and kept sitting down and getting up again, trying to find things to do to forget her anxiousness. Luckily she was very receptive to my help – we'd been through this so many times before.

"Take a deep breath Mum, inhale – exhaaaaale. And again, breathe in deeply, hold it and exhale . . ." I talked her through the breathing routine the anxiety counsellor had taught me and heard her slowly starting to breathe normally again.

"Okay, now let's go to your safe place. Close your eyes, Mum, and think of that place where you feel completely safe and happy." I talked on in a soothing voice as we went to her safe place and tried to bring back the feelings of security and happiness she felt in that safe place. It seemed so far-fetched in a way, but it did work. I'd done it a few times with the anxiety counsellor and it was amazing the power the mind had over the body. It really ruled our feelings and emotions. She began to relax, then suddenly the panic took over again and I had to start all over again. It happened three times and then finally, half an hour later, she had calmed down.

"Are you alright now, Mum?" I asked apprehensively. I had no idea what I would do if she wasn't. I would have to call my Aunt Janine, but she wasn't very good at dealing with my mum when she had her panic attacks. She got angry at her and said things like, "Just bloody relax, will you? You're being ridiculous!" which really didn't help. I can totally understand why people who have never suffered from panic attacks or anxiety think that it's ridiculous to let yourself succumb to it, but what they don't realise is that it's uncontrollable and no matter how stupid we know it is before and after, when that fear grips you from the core, there's nothing you can do to stop it. It's terrifying and sometimes you wish you could curl up and die just so that the anxiety goes away.

When I was eighteen, I'd suffered from panic attacks for a few months, and it had been hell. It seemed that the situation with my mum had overwhelmed me. I'd refused to let it get the better of me and went to see an anxiety psychologist right away. He taught me how to cope with my anxiety when it did surface and taught me to recognise the signs of an upcoming panic attack and what to do in that case. I was so determined not to end up like my mum that I didn't give it a chance to control me. Now if it does rear its ugly head at me, I do my breathing straight away and talk myself out of it. I am one of the lucky ones because I am able to do that, but so many people can't and it ruins their lives and stops them from living life to the fullest because they live in anxiety and fear a lot of the time. In a way I'm relieved to have actually gone through it too because at least it helps me to understand, sympathise and cope better with my mum.

"I'm feeling a bit better, love. My chest is less tight and I can breathe a little easier now," she said in a small voice. "Thank you so much, Mol. I'm so sorry for putting you through this again."

"Don't worry about it, Mum. I'm always here for you when you need me. Are you sure you're going to be okay now?"

"Yes, I'm sure. I still feel anxious but I can handle it. I'll just have a hot cup of tea then get some sleep."

"Do you want me to tell Janine to come over?" I asked, hoping that she wouldn't say yes because she definitely wouldn't take kindly to being woken up in the middle of the night to go and babysit my mum.

"No, don't worry. I don't want to wake her up. She said she'd come over tomorrow morning for a visit anyway."

"Okay then, if you're sure. How about I tell you a little about Mauritius so that it takes your mind off things a bit?"

"No, love, I don't think I could concentrate. All I want to do is go to bed and sleep it off now. But thank you again. I'm so sorry – I don't know what caused it. I guess I suddenly realised that I was alone and that you were far away, and I didn't know what I would do if I got sick. And then I started feeling sick, obviously . . ."

"It's alright, I'm glad you called me. Call me back if you need to, okay? But now go have a cup of tea and try to get some sleep. You'll feel more relaxed in the morning."

I was shaking like a leaf as I put the phone down. It took a lot out of me having to talk her through the attacks. I wasn't a psychologist and it shouldn't have to be up to me to do it. I was always worried that I wouldn't be able to get through to her. There wasn't much more that I could do for her anyway. She had to learn how to control her attacks herself and she did try, but sometimes it got the better of her and she got herself into a terrible state. Once she'd called me up from a shop; she was having a massive panic attack and was tetanised and could no longer move. In the end they called an ambulance and she had been given oxygen and sedatives – it had been a nightmare.

I'd tried so hard to get her to see someone but she just wouldn't. I would keep trying, though, because I couldn't do this for much longer. It was too hard. I felt like I had the responsibility of her life in my hands, and I didn't feel strong enough to handle that alone. I wouldn't be able to cope if she ever had a really bad anxiety attack and became suicidal.

I walked outside and fell onto the deck chair on my veranda. I felt completely drained. It was so sad to see my beautiful mother reduced to the wreck that she'd become. What a wasted life. Her body was in perfect health, but her mind was sick so she couldn't enjoy life and all the wonderful things that were around her.

It was all too much for me and my eyes welled up. Most of the time I managed to keep my emotions in check after her attacks but sometimes I fell apart. It had been a while, but today, I couldn't cope. Maybe it was because I was far away, I'm not sure. My chest tightened painfully and I felt like I was having a panic attack myself. I honestly didn't know how long I would be able to keep going on like this, always having to be the one to be strong, happy and there to look after her. I wished that I had parents to look after *me*; surely that's how things were meant to be?

I curled up and let the tears fall freely. I knew I needed to let it all out so that I could put it aside and move on. If I kept it in, it would eat me whole. All of a sudden, I felt someone by my side. Just from the smell and the fluttering in my stomach, I knew it was Adam.

ADAM

"Molly, what's wrong?" I asked gently, putting my hand on her shoulder, wanting to comfort her. Unfortunately, it had the opposite effect and she began sobbing even harder. Great. I sure hoped she wasn't crying because of me. Maybe I had managed to break her spirit after all?

"N-n-nothing," she finally stuttered, between sobs.

"It sure doesn't sound like nothing to me," I said softly, sitting down on the edge of her chair. She shrank away from me and turned her head in the other direction. She visibly didn't want me to comfort her or to see her crying, but I couldn't leave her like this – I had to do something.

I looked at her for a minute, not sure what to do. What the heck, I thought, as I leaned down and pulled her into my arms. I sat down on the other deck chair with her on my lap. She resisted for a moment, but then gave in and curled up like a baby against me, her head resting on my chest. I inhaled her familiar scent and stroked her back gently as she cried.

"Do you want to talk about it?" I finally asked, when she had calmed down. A look of surprise flashed through her eyes; I wasn't sure whether it was because she hadn't realised that she was sitting on my lap or because I was being nice to her. Wanting to lighten the mood, I added jokingly, "I may be a major grouch, but I'm a great listener."

She looked up at me with a watery smile and before I could stop myself, I reached out and brushed her tears away with my thumb. She stared at me, clearly baffled by my behaviour. I was finally showing her my true colours, except she didn't know it. I couldn't play this game anymore, not when she was so upset.

"So, how about it?" I asked, when she still hadn't answered.

She shook her head and said weakly, "I don't know if I have the strength to talk about it right now. I feel drained."

I had no idea what was going on and I intended to find out, but it would have to wait.

"Okay, we'll talk later," I said as I stood up and carried her inside, laying her down gently on the bed. "There you go. Get some sleep now."

She nodded and closed her eyes. I had just turned to leave when I heard her calling my name. I stopped in the doorway, looking back towards her.

"Will you please stay with me? I don't want to be alone," she said in a barely audible whisper.

My heart skipped a beat. I couldn't believe how stupidly happy it made me that she wanted me to stay with her.

"Of course," I replied with a smile, heading back towards the bed. I settled down next to her and she scuttled over, rested her head on my chest, sighed heavily and fell asleep almost instantly.

I gazed at her and felt overwhelmed by the need to protect her. I held her tighter and heard her sigh in her sleep as she cuddled up to me. Her long hair was spread over my chest. I gently brushed a few strands of hair off her face – any excuse to touch her. She was such a quiet sleeper. I lay there watching her sleep and felt such a tug of tenderness for her that it scared me. After all, I had only known her for a few days. This time it really wasn't about jumping into a girl's pants – I just wanted to be with her, see her smile, talk to her, hold her. Well, alright, alright, I'm a guy, so of course I would be lying if I said that I hadn't thought about how amazing it would be to sleep with her . . . *Don't go there, buddy*. I mentally shook myself as I felt my body respond to my thoughts. Maybe it was time for me to get some fresh air.

I gently moved her off me and laid her head on the pillow, hoping that I wouldn't wake her. She sighed and snuggled into the pillow. She was so darn adorable. I went to fetch my book and returned to her room, not wanting her to wake up while I was gone. I had no idea what her problem was, but it looked like something pretty big. I was sad that I didn't know much about her life, but one thing was certain: I wanted to learn every tiny detail there was to know about this wonderful girl.

MOLLY

I opened my eyes slowly, feeling disorientated for a moment. Then, as it all came back to me, my chest tightened and I grabbed my phone to check if there was a missed call from my mum. She hadn't called back. I sighed in relief – no news was good news.

"Hey you . . ." I heard Adam's voice say gently from the veranda, making me jump. I had forgotten about him coming over.

"Have you been here all this time?" I asked, still a bit dazed, rubbing the sleep from my burning eyes as I sat up.

"I thought I'd stick around to make sure you were okay," he replied softly, smiling at me.

"That's so nice of you. Thank you," I answered and blushed as I remembered that I'd actually asked him to stay.

"Are you feeling any better?"

I nodded but looked away as my eyes threatened to fill up again. I was still upset and exhausted from all the emotions.

Adam sat down on the edge of my bed and looked at me. "I think you need to get it off your chest. You'll feel better afterwards," he said, laying his hand on my knee. "Trust me, I know – I have three sisters and I see how much it helps when they talk things out. Plus, they said that I have the best shoulders to cry on," he added with a grin. "So how about it?"

My face fell again and my heart plummeted down to my toes. I knew that I needed to talk about it and for some inexplicable reason, I trusted Adam completely.

"I don't know where to start," I whispered, looking down at my hands.

"Well, as the song goes, 'let's start at the very beginning, a very good place to start'," he said in a sing-song voice.

I looked up at him and couldn't help giggling, forgetting my problems for a moment. "Seriously?"

"Remember that thing about having three sisters?" he said, raising his eyebrow at me in amusement. I laughed and he smiled again. It struck me once more that he was smiling easily and acting as though he'd never been Mr McGrumpy all week. I didn't get it. Did I have to cry and be miserable for him to finally smile at me? Did my misery make him happy or something? I was about to ask him when he suggested we order hot chocolate from room service.

"That's my absolute favourite hot drink!" I exclaimed. It was exactly what I needed right now.

He grinned. "Plus it's the best drink when sharing secrets in bed at night."

I giggled. "I am *not* sharing secrets in bed with you, Adam!"

"Oh alright then, not those kind of secrets and not in bed," he said, smiling. "Outside on the veranda works too."

I went to freshen up and when I came back, I could smell the delicious aroma of our hot chocolates filling the room. Adam was settled on a deck chair on the veranda and I walked out to join him. He gazed up at me and I saw his eyes roaming over my body. He looked dazed for a moment then seemed to snap out of it and without saying a word, he handed me my hot chocolate. I felt all flustered so I decided to concentrate on the cup in my hand.

"Mmm, this smells heavenly," I said, inhaling deeply.

"Sure does." He smiled. "You can't even begin to imagine how many hot chocolates I went through during my sisters' teenage years and I haven't finished yet as Lily is only fifteen years old. Think there will definitely be a world record in there somewhere by the time I'm done."

I took a sip and grinned up at him. He was so gorgeous, lying there in jeans and a black t-shirt that stretched sexily across his muscular chest. I was still basking in the warmth of having finally discovered his smile and was under its spell. I had already noticed the way his beautiful eyes shone and crinkled on the sides when he smiled, and how they sparkled with mischief when he grinned and how expressive his eyebrows were. He made my insides go all gooey. *Oh my* . . . I groaned inwardly, as my eyes reached his mouth. There was a hot chocolate moustache on his lips and I almost had to physically stop myself from leaning over and licking it off. I blushed at the direction of my thoughts and hoped that he couldn't read my mind.

"Want to tell me about it now?" he asked quietly, pulling me out of my reverie with a start. Thinking that he had read my thoughts, my face grew hot. I looked up and realised that his features were a mask of concern and let out a shaky sigh of relief. My dirty thoughts quickly disappeared as my heart began to race again. I hated talking about my mum, but I didn't know how I could get out of it. I would simply give him as little details as possible.

"Are you sure you want to hear this? It's getting late and I'd totally understand if you preferred heading off to bed."

"There's nowhere else I'd rather be," he said softly, looking into my eyes and making my insides go weak again. Did he really just say that? Surely I must be misinterpreting the meaning behind his words? Oh well, I guess I'd better start talking. So I did. I told him about my childhood with my parents, my dad dying, my mum's illness and basically what it's been like all my life.

"About three years ago, my mum had her first panic attack. She was at the shops and suddenly started feeling sick, hyperventilating and basically thought she was having a heart attack. Obviously it wasn't a heart attack, as the doctor explained to her afterwards, but a panic attack, and since then she refuses to go out, too scared that it will happen again while she's out. The only place she goes to is the supermarket down the road, anything else is too much for her. She refuses to let me take her to the doctor because it's too far, and gets into a terrible state of panic if I try to force her."

"I tried to get her to take medication for anxiety, but she's too scared that it will make her feel worse. I ended up going to see a specialist in anxiety disorders to ask for his help in dealing with my mother when she has her attacks. He taught me how to calm her down and what to say and do. I won't give up trying to get her to go and see a psychologist or join an anxiety disorder group, or even just to take medication . . . I have to find a way," I finished, looking up at him.

"I can't imagine living with the weight of responsibility you've had on your shoulders since such an early age. I mean, how do you manage to cope?"

"I promised my twelve-year-old self that I would never let myself become like Mum and Dad. I literally decided that I would be happy and that I would look at things from a positive angle – and I must say, it works most of the time. I've always been so scared to end up like her or my dad."

"You won't. I mean look at you, you're obviously brave

and strong. So many people let themselves be overcome by every little thing that goes wrong in their lives, but despite everything you've faced, and still have to face, you just keep smiling, seeing things positively and being happy."

"Please stop! You're actually being nice to me and it's making me blush!" I said, feeling embarrassed by his unexpected praise.

"Now you know why I avoid being nice to you!" He grinned. "But seriously," he said, his face growing serious again, "it must have been really difficult for you growing up as an only child with no siblings to share your troubles with. I've been so lucky because I have a wonderful close-knit family and I've taken it for granted all my life."

He went on to tell me about his family: how wonderful his parents were and then about his sisters, describing each one with affection and tenderness. It must be amazing to have a big brother like Adam, I thought wistfully. I'd always dreamt of having a sister, someone I could share everything with, someone to help me make sense of all the things that confused me when I was a little girl and also growing up. But a big brother like Adam would also have been wonderful, someone to protect me and hold me and comfort me in all the hard times . . .

ADAM

I listened to her talk and my heart went out to her. I would never have imagined that she had gone through all that – and was still going through it. I had the answer for my article. I had everything Christine wanted. Molly was like this because she had decided to be. It wasn't always easy, but she managed to stick to her decision because the alternative for her was impossible to contemplate. In her case, it was a decision that she'd made when she was twelve years old and which had shaped the person she'd become. She had her ups and downs like everyone, but she'd learnt to focus on the good things and not give too much time to the negative stuff that upsets her. I was in awe of her. It also made me see how easily we judge people without knowing what they've gone through and who they are . . .

We talked until the small hours of the morning. It was so easy to talk to her and to be with her. When she asked me about my work, I hesitated, but ended up telling her the truth

– that I was a sports writer for *Today's News*. I didn't mention my current assignment, of course . . . and felt bad about it. She told me about her job as a photographer and her eyes shone as she described her work.

I couldn't be bothered acting grumpy and negative. To hell with it. I wanted to reveal the truth to her because after everything she had just shared with me, I felt like I owed it to her – but somehow the moment never came.

When it was time for us to get some sleep, I said my goodbyes and headed back to my room, although I would have loved to stay with her all night.

I had another restless night, thoughts of Molly disturbing my sleep. I kept seeing her curled up, crying her eyes out, and it broke my heart. I woke up feeling tired and confused by everything that had happened. I decided that I needed time to myself to think and to write the first proof of the article. I had hired a car and would be driving to Le Morne, where I planned to hire a kite-surf and have a bit of a go at kite-surfing in Mauritius before heading to one of the hotels around there to have lunch and get some writing done. I got ready to head out and hoped that I wouldn't – or would – bump into Molly. I desperately wanted to see her and check if she was alright, but then again, I just needed space to get my thoughts together before seeing her again.

MOLLY

J woke up feeling drained, but happy. Adam had been wonderful to me; he'd been kind and friendly all night. I still felt a little uneasy about the contrast between Adam last night and the Grumpy Adam I'd got to know all week, and was beginning to wonder if he hadn't simply pretended to be grumpy. But then again, why would he do that?

Maybe looking like Ian Somerhalder made him want to push people away so that they would leave him alone? Oh wow! I hadn't thought of that before. Maybe that was exactly it. He was trying to push me away by pretending to be grouchy. It might also be a way to test people to see whether they were interested in him for his looks, or if they stuck around long enough to get to know the real him. I had no idea, but whatever the story, I was hooked. I'd never felt this way about a guy before. Well not since my first love when I was seventeen – the only guy I'd ever given my heart to and who had broken it after eight months. I'd had such a hard time coping with my pain, my mum's illness and running the house after the break-up that I'd sworn never to put myself in that position again. I'd been so scared that I wouldn't be strong enough to get back to being happy again – that I would fall into the same dark hole my mum and dad had – but with sheer determination, I'd coped. It had really scared me, though. I'd never allowed anyone to get too close again. It wasn't a risk I was willing to take. So I went out with guys sometimes, had fun, but always kept it light. I would have to be careful with Adam.

Today, I was going to relax at the hotel. Adam was off to kite-surf and visit Le Morne, and I'd decided that I would work on my tan and hang out with Samantha. I'd seen her briefly at breakfast as she'd been leaving when I arrived and was quite upset because she still hadn't heard from her husband. Luckily by the time we met on the beach, she was back to her usual friendly and happy self. We spent the day sunbathing, ate a pizza by the pool at lunchtime, read, chatted, drank wine and basically chilled out big time. It was pure heaven.

At tea time, the aroma of pancakes filled the air. Needless to say, we were suddenly starving and followed the smell that led us to a table near the bar. However, everyone else seemed to have got a whiff of the smell, and there was quite a queue. We chatted in line for a bit until Samantha got tired of waiting and decided to head back to her room instead to check her emails. There was no way I was giving up on my pancakes, so I waited patiently as the queue slowly moved. I was lost in my thoughts and jumped in surprise as I felt someone tapping me gently on the shoulder. I turned to see the girl behind me smiling warmly.

"Oops, I'm sorry. I didn't mean to startle you," she said, laughing.

"No worries, I was just lost in my thoughts." I grinned back.

She smiled. "It's just that I thought I recognised your accent and was wondering if you were from Australia?"

"Sure am. But you, on the other hand, don't sound like an Aussie."

"I'm not Australian, but my family live in Perth. I lived there for a few years before coming back to Mauritius."

"So you live in Mauritius? That sounds so exotic!"

"Well, it is and it isn't actually!" she said, grinning. "The sun, sand and sea part is wonderful, but it can be a bit suffocating at times because everyone knows everyone else in our community. Most people are related one way or another or know someone you're related to – let's just say it's hard to go unnoticed."

"It must be pretty special in a way though," I said wistfully.

"Yes, it is – but having lived overseas, I sometimes wish that I could just fade into the background more often!"

"Are you at the hotel for the day then?"

"No. Matt, my boyfriend, and I are staying here tonight. We were meant to be coming with friends but they had to cancel at the last minute," she explained. Her face suddenly broke into a huge smile. "Oh, and there's Matt now."

I followed her gaze and saw a good-looking man of medium height, probably in his early thirties, with light brown hair and beautiful blue eyes heading our way. He smiled as he reached us, sliding his arm around the girl's shoulders.

"Matt, I'd like you to meet . . ." she started, then stopped short and looked at me, eyes wide. "Oh no! I'm so sorry, I don't actually know your name. We didn't introduce ourselves!"

Matt and I laughed. "I'm Molly."

"And I'm Lucy." She grinned before turning back to Matt. "Anyway, Molly's from Australia. Molly as I mentioned, this is Matt, my boyf – oh no, I keep forgetting, my *fiancé* actually," she amended, motioning from me to him and back.

"Oh wow! Congratulations!" I exclaimed, beaming at Lucy before remembering my manners and turning back to Matt. "It's lovely to meet you."

"Likewise." He smiled, his eyes crinkling on the sides.

"When are you getting married?" I asked.

"Oh no! You said the M word – watch Matt start to hyperventilate!" Lucy teased, pointing at Matt and laughing.

Matt just rolled his eyes at her good-naturedly. "You've got the ring on your finger haven't you?"

She laughed and turned back to me, "The big day is on the fourth of May."

"That's only a few months away! Are you all organised?"

"Not really. Haven't done much yet, I'm not the most organised person around, I must say. But at least my dress is getting made and the rest will work itself out I'm sure. As long as Matt's there, that's all I care about really!" she said, beaming at him.

"You couldn't stop me if you tried," he said with a wink, before leaning down to give her a peck on the lips.

"You have to know here that it took Matt four years of us going out, me to break up with him and go out with a gorgeous Englishman—" she started explaining before stopping short when Matt nudged her hard, glaring at her in mock anger. She laughed and pushed him away playfully. "Anyway, as I was saying before I was so rudely interrupted," she went on, sticking her tongue out at Matt. "Four years, me going out with a gorgeous Englishman, a crazy stalker ending up on my doorstep, before he realised that he couldn't live without me." She finished by grinning lovingly at Matt, who shrugged and smiled adoringly back at her.

"I've been known to be quite indecisive," he said to me with a smile, as Lucy burst into laughter.

"That is the understatement of the year!" She exclaimed. "Have you ever heard the saying 'I used to be indecisive but now I'm not so sure'? Well, Matt owns it!"

I burst out laughing and Matt joined in. "What can I say? I can't be perfect. Gotta have a flaw somewhere!"

We reached the table and piled our plates high with delicious-looking-and-smelling pancakes with a selection of mouth-watering fillings like Nutella, sugar and cream.

"Would you like to join us?" Lucy asked as I started to turn away.

"Sure, I'd love to."

We sat together at one of the tables and ate our pancakes, chatting away. When we parted, we agreed to meet for a drink later on. I went back to my room, showered and got dressed in a long flowing dress which was slightly less colourful than my other clothes as it was only red and white, but I loved it. As I brushed my long hair in front of the mirror and plaited it, I tried to convince myself that I wasn't doing all this with the aim of pleasing Adam. In fact, I had no idea if he would be there tonight. His room was still dark and he didn't seem to be back from his day trip. My heart sank at the thought of not seeing him tonight. *Stop it, Molly!* I scolded myself. I was going to have a good time and didn't need Adam for that.

I headed to the beach bar and ordered a tropical cocktail. The moon was out and it was a gorgeous evening. I hadn't seen Samantha since she'd left me earlier, but I knew she would show up sooner or later. I gazed towards the beach and saw the silhouettes of a man and a woman walking back towards the bar. For some reason the woman looked familiar, but I couldn't recognise her from that distance. As she approached, I realised that it was Samantha and that she was laughing with a gorgeous-looking man. When on earth had she met him? As I saw her gaze adoringly up at him, I started to worry. Was she going to do something stupid? Should I stop her and remind her that she had two kids who needed her and a husband? Or should I let her have her fun; after all, her husband never need find out. *Oh how could I even say that!* Of course she couldn't cheat on her husband. I already knew that she wasn't the sort of woman who could do that kind of thing and take it lightly. Granted, the man with her was a real stunner – tall, full of muscles, short spiky dark blond hair. I couldn't see the colour of his eyes, but I *could* see that he had an amazing smile and oozed sexiness.

I changed seats so that Samantha wouldn't be able to see me spying on them. They stayed on the beach and seemed to be deep in conversation. The man had taken Samantha's hands in his and she was smiling up at him. OMG! He was leaning down to kiss her! Oh no. No, no, *noooo*, this can't be happening. I bounced off my seat and raced towards them. They were full-on kissing now and looked like they wanted to eat each other whole. I stopped short, right by Samantha's side, and cleared my throat loudly. I'm sure that Anna heard me back in Australia. They broke away from each other with difficulty, the man's green eyes looking at me, dazed.

"Samantha, can I talk to you for just a second, please?" I said in an urgent whisper.

"What? Like *now*, now?" She replied, surprised, looking towards the man.

"Yes, now – like *right now*!"

"But I'm kind of in the middle of something," she said, looking towards the man again, clearly not wanting to let me down but at the same time not inclined to leave him even for a second.

"Yes, that's quite obvious," I replied petulantly, getting desperate. "But it's *really important*!"

"Okay fine!" she said resignedly. She told him that she would be right back and followed me a little further down the beach. I noticed the man stretching out on the wooden sun lounger – he most definitely did not look like he was going anywhere. *Damn it!* How and when had this happened?

"Do you really think you should be doing that, Samantha? Are you sure you won't have any regrets in the morning?" I said as soon as we were far enough away.

"Molly, wait . . ." Samantha said, trying to cut me off.

But I was having none of it. "Think of your husband and kids - your family, Sam! Don't do this, he's not worth it!"

"Molly, wait a minute!" she insisted, trying to get me to stop my diatribe, but I ignored her. I had to make her see reason.

"MOLLY, STOP!" she shouted loudly, finally making me stop short. "The guy I was kissing *is* my husband," she explained gently, her hand on my shoulder. "After getting my email, he begged my mum to tell him where I was and she gave in. He took the first flight he could get and got here this afternoon. He was waiting by my door when I got back."

"*That's* your husband?!" I screeched. "Did you just happen to forget to mention that he's flippin' cover-of-a-magazine gorgeous?"

She grinned and said with a half-shrug, "Well . . . I don't like to brag!"

I laughed. "Well, go on, what are you waiting for? Hurry up and get back to your Greek God and I'll just try to put a sock in my mouth to stop myself from butting into other people's lives in the future!"

She chuckled, taking my hand and squeezing it affectionately. "Thanks for caring, Mol. It means a lot to me."

We hugged and I watched her as she raced off to join her husband. His face broke into a huge smile as he saw her heading towards him and his eyes were full of love. They would be fine; I just knew it.

I headed back towards the beach bar and bumped into Matt and Lucy. We sat at a table and ordered some wine. They were so relaxed and easy-going that I ended up staying with them.

Later, on our way to dinner, I noticed Samantha and her husband in the restaurant. I waved to her as she looked our way and she beckoned me to come over. They stood up to greet me and Samantha made the introductions. Patrick smiled warmly at me. "It's so nice to meet you. Thank you for doing what you did earlier. Although it happened to be me, I really appreciate you trying to protect Sam and our marriage," he said earnestly.

"It was nothing," I said, feeling embarrassed by his praise. I stayed with them for a few minutes then left them to their dinner and offered that they meet us for a drink later if they felt like it.

I looked around and saw that Matt and Lucy had been joined by another guy about Matt's age. He was tall, with dark eyes, dark hair, olive skin and was kind of cute.

"Hi, I'm Jeremy! A friend of Matt's," he said, introducing himself as he leaned in and kissed me on both cheeks. I was taken aback by the intimacy of it, and Lucy burst out laughing. I looked at her, bemused.

"You should have seen the look on your face!" she said, still laughing, as she turned her attention to Jeremy. "In Australia, people don't greet each other like we do here. You shocked the poor girl with your kisses!"

Jeremy grinned. "I did?"

"Molly, in Mauritius we greet each other socially like the French do, by kissing each other on both cheeks," Lucy explained.

"Really? Seems a bit intimate for a greeting though,

doesn't it? Especially when you only meet the person for the first time," I said, not sure that I liked the idea.

"Nah, you get used to it. In a way it helps to break the ice because instead of just standing there and saying an awkward 'hi', you lean in and kiss each other and somehow it makes you feel less like strangers I guess."

"Do guys kiss each other too?" I asked, looking at Matt and Jeremy.

"No way!" Matt exclaimed, chuckling. "Us virile males shake hands!"

I laughed. "Okay, got it! Now that I know what to expect, I won't blush next time."

We had dinner and drank more wine. There was still no sign of Adam. I wondered where he'd got to and wished he were here, although I was having a wonderful time with Lucy, Matt and Jeremy. It was lovely to meet people from the island. They told me a bit about their lives here and it was both similar and different to my life in Perth. I loved the thought of everyone knowing everyone else. I couldn't help thinking that if we lived in Mauritius, or somewhere like here, my mum wouldn't be so alone with her problems and would have a whole network of friends and family around her, which, of course, would also be wonderful for me. Having no siblings, I loved the thought of the big families they talked about with the endless first cousins, second cousins and even third cousins they all seemed to have. I think I could definitely be happy in a place like this. I loved Perth, but it sometimes got a bit lonely.

I'd had way too much wine and was a bit tipsy by the end of dinner, but I was in the mood to have fun. The band started playing and Lucy bounced up and pulled me onto the dance floor with her. Matt and Jeremy joined us a while later, and Jeremy had me rock and rolling around the dance floor, which made me think of Adam. Where the hell was he? I would rather be in his arms than in Jeremy's, but I quickly pushed the thought away. It would only lead to heartbreak. Suddenly the tempo changed and a slow song came on. Jeremy cocked an eyebrow at me suggestively. I smiled and nodded.

We were dancing and chatting away happily when suddenly Jeremy's face changed. His eyes fixed on something – or someone – behind me. Judging from the way my heart-beat suddenly accelerated, I knew that Adam had finally showed up . . .

35

ADAM

I came up behind her and just stood there for a moment, inhaling her wonderful smell. It did all sorts of things to me, but more than anything it just overwhelmed me with tenderness. I touched her shoulder, but she seemed to have sensed that I had been standing there all along as she didn't look surprised to see me.

"Adam! You're back," she said, smiling widely. I noticed that her eyes looked a bit glazed.

"Hi, Molly," I said softly, before turning towards her partner who was still holding onto her, looking confused. "Do you mind if I take this lovely lady away from you for a minute?"

He didn't seem too pleased about it, but looked towards Molly questioningly. She nodded, moving out of his embrace. "Sorry about this, Jeremy – I'll be right back!"

Oh no you won't! I thought possessively. I had no intention of letting her go back to him. Where the hell had he sprung up from anyway? I grabbed Molly by the waist and drew her back onto the dance floor. I held her tightly and enjoyed feeling her so close to me. We danced quietly for a few minutes, my cheek resting against her hair, before she pulled away slightly, looking up at me quizzically.

"So, are you going to tell me what that was all about?"

"What do you mean?" I asked, feigning innocence. I hadn't realised that she'd noticed me sending daggers Jeremy's way.

She raised an eyebrow at me. God, she was so adorable. With a few loose tendrils coming out of her braid, her green eyes sparkling and that mouth . . . how I wanted to kiss her.

Snapping out of my lust-filled reverie, I saw that she was waiting for me to give her an explanation. "Well, I'm sorry, but you can't just let anyone grope you like that!"

"Grope me? He was not groping me! We were just dancing," she exclaimed incredulously.

"From where I was standing, it definitely looked like he was groping you!" I teased.

Noticing the amusement in my eyes, she slapped my arm playfully. "Oh just shut up and dance, will you!?"

"With pleasure, sweetness," I whispered into her ear before I could stop myself. I felt her tense up as she heard my words, but then she just relaxed into my arms. I held her tightly and caressed her back, loving the feel of her naked skin under my hand. I never wanted to let her go. *Oh jeepers, what was this girl doing to me?*

36

MOLLY

*H*ad he really called me sweetness? It seemed unlikely. I'd probably heard wrong as I was still a bit woozy from all the alcohol. But what if he had? What did it mean? Did he actually fancy me? I felt a whole roomful of butterflies fluttering in my stomach at the thought. *Get a grip, Molly!* I mentally slapped myself. Just then I felt delicious shivers spread through my body. Oh my . . . his hand was caressing the bare skin on my back and it was doing all sorts of things to my poor heartrate. *Oh, settle down!* I scolded myself again. *It's only a dance – and with ADAM for crying out loud!*

My heart sank as the song came to an end, and I felt Adam releasing his hold on me. I looked up at him, still slightly dazed, and smiled. "Thanks for the dance."

"The pleasure was all mine," he said, smiling. "And I'm sorry for interrupting your dance with Remy."

"No you're not!" I laughed. "And it's Jeremy."

"Yeah, that's what I said," he answered, deadpan, although his eyes were sparkling with mirth.

I couldn't help laughing. "Don't worry about it. Actually, why don't you come over and meet Jeremy, Matt and Lucy. They live in Mauritius, you'll like them," I said, pulling his arm and leading him towards their table. They greeted us warmly and Matt and Adam recognised each other from kite-surfing. Lucy looked at me and mouthed "So hot" behind her hand. I grinned; I couldn't deny she had a point there. Matt looked at her with a mock scowl, mouthing "I saw that", making us both laugh.

Adam was wearing a pair of Capri pants that hung loosely from his waist and a plain white t-shirt that hugged his chest snugly. His short hair was scruffy and it didn't look as if he had brushed it after his shower, and he was starting to have a five o'clock shadow again, which was mighty sexy. He had a gorgeous tan from his day kite-surfing, which made his silver-blue eyes stand out even more under his black eyebrows, and not to forget his smile . . . *Mmm* . . . delectable, I thought, sighing wistfully.

Not long after, I felt my eyelids start to droop. I didn't want to leave Adam and the others, but I was exhausted and the wine had made me sleepy. As I said goodbye to everyone, I noticed that Adam looked surprised to see me go but didn't do anything to stop me. I felt a bit disappointed that he hadn't offered to accompany me back to my room, but then again, why should he? We weren't a couple. We may have gone from being "frenemies" to friends, but we were definitely not a couple.

I was woken up by a huge bang that made me jump sky high. As my brain began functioning again, I realised that it was just a thunderstorm. I looked at my phone – four o'clock in the morning. I lay there for a few minutes, watching the flashes of light flooding my room and listening to the loud rolls of thunder that followed. I loved thunderstorms, and this one was a big one. Unable to resist, I climbed out of bed, turned the kettle on and stood behind the sliding doors, watching the flashes of lightning illuminate the sky and sea. It was nature in all its glory. I quickly made myself a cup of tea, grabbed my camera and headed out onto the veranda. My photographer fingers were too itchy to stay indoors. I stood staring out to sea, my camera ready for action as I waited for the next flash of lightning to light up the sky. As soon as it came, I started clicking away and as usual, I forgot about everything else and got lost in the moment. I bumped into the side table and heard my cup and saucer shattering to the floor. "Oops!" I muttered as I looked back at the mess.

Just then, the sky lit up again and I turned back to the view, deciding that I'd leave the cleaning up for later, but went inside to get some flip flops to avoid getting splinters in my feet. As I walked back out, Adam was standing on the edge of my veranda, rubbing the sleep out of his eyes and looking divine.

"Hey," he said sleepily with a smile, making my insides melt. "I heard something smashing and thought I'd check it out."

"Sorry for waking you up, it was just me being clumsy," I said, pointing to the mess on the other side of the veranda.

"Oh." He grinned. "What are you doing out here, at like . . . four o'clock in the morning," he asked, looking at his watch and yawning.

"Taking pictures of the thunderstorm."

"Ah, figures. Only photographers would do something like that."

"Why don't you sit down and enjoy the show, then you'll

get why I'm up at four o'clock in the morning taking photos," I replied with a grin.

"Don't mind if I do," he said, settling himself into the long deck chair just as another huge flash of lightning lit up the sky and the sea before us. "Wow!" he exclaimed in awe. "That is so awesome."

"See, told ya," I replied smugly from behind my camera.

"Looks like this is becoming a bit of a ritual – you and me together at all hours of the night," he said with a wink.

I laughed but felt a blush spread over my cheeks. I loved this friendly version of Adam, but it also made me feel uncomfortable because I was more used to the grumpy and unfriendly version. This version seemed somewhat flirty and I didn't quite know how to react towards him. Both versions were pretty damn gorgeous, though, I couldn't help thinking. The sudden urge to kiss him overwhelmed me and I quickly looked away and stared out to sea, hiding behind my camera lens. It just felt safer that way.

ADAM

I watched her standing there, chewing on her bottom lip. *Oh how I wished I could be the one chewing that lip!* I had to be careful with the direction of my thoughts because I was only wearing a pair of boxer shorts, which wouldn't be able to hide much.

She was just so beautiful. Her long curls fell down over her breasts in a messy, just-got-out-of-bed way, and her little pyjama shorts allowed me to see her sexy legs which were now olive from the sun. Her tank top was tight around her breasts – and . . . Oh jeepers! She wasn't wearing a bra! I had to stop looking at her, but my eyes were drawn back to that gorgeous face I had grown so fond of. Those large, green, almond-shaped eyes, which were hidden behind her camera lens at the moment, her cute little nose and that mouth . . .

Ten minutes later, I'd had more than enough of watching the thunderstorm and was starting to feel restless. "Okay, this was pretty amazing the first ten times, but couldn't we add a bit of excitement to this whole storm adventure now?"

She turned towards me and smiled cutely. "And what exactly would you like to do at four in the morning, Adam?"

"Did you really just ask me that, Molly?" I asked, cocking an eyebrow.

"Adam!"

"What?" I said, feigning innocence. She shook her head in exasperation and took a seat beside me. Turning to her, I reached out and brushed a loose lock of hair behind her ear. It felt like the most natural thing to do, but when my eyes fell on hers, I noticed that she was totally stunned by my oddly intimate gesture. I loved that I could affect her that way and couldn't help smiling wickedly which, to my amusement, made her blush.

I laughed. "How about we play truth or dare?"

"Truth or dare. Seriously?" she said, laughing too. "How old are you? Twelve?"

"Well it's a fun way to get to know each other. Or we could play strip poker if you prefer . . ." I teased.

She slapped me playfully on the arm and laughed. "Fine. Truth or dare it is."

"Okay, you start, seeing as you're the lady and all."

She grinned and nodded. "Truth or dare?"

"Let's start with a truth then shall we?"

"Alright . . . what's your most embarrassing secret?"

"*Oooh*, that's harsh! Okay, let me think . . ." What could I possibly tell her? Suddenly I thought of something and grinned.

"Okay, so this is *really* embarrassing and as I'm putting my ego out on the line here for you, you are not allowed a) to laugh and b) to repeat it to anyone, EVER, otherwise . . . I will have to kill you."

She giggled, propping herself up on her elbow on the lounger so that she was facing me.

"Okaaay, well, the thing is . . . I'm a romcomaholic!"

"A *what?*"

"A romcomaholic! A big fan of romantic comedies," I explained sheepishly.

Her eyes opened wide in surprise before she fell on her back laughing.

"You just broke rule number one!" I said, scowling darkly at her.

"I'm sorry," she said as she propped herself up again and faced me. "But I've never met a guy who likes romcoms!"

"Well, I do! And once again, may I remind you that—" I started before she cut me off.

"Yeah, yeah, you have three sisters. I know, I know!"

"Well I do, and they luuurve romantic comedies and being the only boy in the family, I was always out-numbered when it came to choosing something to watch, so I always ended up having to watch their movie. In the end, I decided 'if you can't beat 'em, join 'em'."

She looked at me thoughtfully for a moment then suddenly she shook her head incredulously. "You are *seriously* weird!"

I laughed good-naturedly. "Okay, smartass, what's your embarrassing secret then?"

"Mine? Umm . . . Let me just think," she said, smiling. "Oh I got one!" she finally exclaimed. "I'm a bit of an obsessive compulsive. When I buy things, they always have to be in odd numbers."

"Run that by me again," I said, flummoxed.

She looked at me, eyes dancing with amusement. "Well, if I buy bananas, I either have to buy one, three, five, seven, nine, etc. I can never buy two, four, six, eight. Same goes for anything else really."

"And you think *I'm* seriously weird?"

"Well you are, and I didn't say I wasn't, did I?!" she added mischievously, making me laugh.

"Luckily it's not even numbers because you would be in deep trouble – you'd have to buy two televisions, two microwaves, two washing machines . . ."

She giggled. "I hadn't thought of that! Just imagine the look on Zach's face if I'd showed up at the house with two of everything when I moved in!"

"What's the story with Zach?"

"Zach? He's my housemate and best friend since primary school. He's like a brother to me."

"Have you ever gone out with him?" I couldn't help asking.

She looked surprised, but shook her head and smiled. "We did try in high school, but the chemistry just wasn't there."

I couldn't believe how relieved I felt to hear that. I didn't want to imagine her living with an ex-boyfriend for some reason.

"Okay, my turn. Truth or dare?"

"Truth."

"Oh come on, be wild and choose dare," I said, wriggling my eyebrows at her as I turned and propped myself up on my elbow so that we were lying facing each other.

"No way. I don't trust you! Truth or nothing, I'm afraid."

I chuckled. "Fine, be boring then. Okay, so what can I ask you? Umm . . . how about something that scares you?"

"Ok-ay," she said, thinking about it. "Well, I'm really petrified of spiders – small, medium and large!"

I smiled and was about to comment when she added softly, "And I'm totally terrified of ending up like my mum."

She had already mentioned that to me the night before, but I realised that it was truly a deep-rooted fear when I saw the look of anguish in her eyes.

"You won't," I said, wanting to reassure her. "You told me yourself that your mum became sick because of the pressure your dad's illness had on her. She isn't genetically sick, it's her life that caught up with her and made her how she is today."

"I know, but that's not really what scares me the most," she said quietly, looking down at her hands. "I just keep thinking that if I end up like her, then there won't be anyone to look after her, but also, to look after me . . ." She ended in a whisper.

"Oh, come here, you," I said, unable to hide the tenderness I felt for her. I couldn't stay away from her a minute longer. My heart was breaking for this beautiful girl who was worried that there would be no one around to look after her if she got sick. I couldn't believe that there were people who were as alone as that in life. I was lucky enough to have a large family and an extended family, and I couldn't imagine what life would be like without them. I pulled her towards me and hugged her. She didn't resist and let me hold her for a moment. Then she pulled away and settled back onto her chair.

"Thank you," she said softly, looking up at me with one of her melting smiles.

"So, I guess it's my turn!" I said brightly, wanting to change the subject and lighten the mood. The thunderstorm had finally calmed down but now the rain was pouring down. "Alright, well here it is - I'm actually scared of jellyfish! Not scared, really, but the sight of them just makes the hairs stand on end. Pathetic, I know, but can't be helped!"

She laughed then yawned loudly. I grinned at her and looked at my watch; it was already a quarter to five and the sun would soon be rising.

"Think you'd better get some sleep now," I said softly and

she nodded, smiled and yawned again, sitting up and shuffling out of her chair.

"So I guess I'll see you tomorrow then," she said with a shy smile, seeming embarrassed all of a sudden.

"Do you want me to stay with you?" I asked before I could stop myself.

She seemed taken aback, and I thought she'd flat out refuse, but a big smile spread over her face before she narrowed her eyes and asked, "Do you snore?"

"Of course I do!"

"Definitely stay then!" she retorted as I threw my head back and laughed.

I wrapped her in my arms and was thrilled that she let me. I didn't know what she felt for me, if anything. I'd been so infuriating since we met that I couldn't imagine her having a crush on me just because I'd suddenly become nice. But I, for one, definitely had a huge, mega crush on her . . .

MOLLY

*A*dam pulled me into his arms and hugged me, still chuckling. He had changed completely in the last twenty-four hours. He was amazing, funny, smart, sensitive, kind, and well . . . perfect. But why had he changed? Did he suddenly decide to stop being grumpy after talking to me about my mum last night? Had it made him realise that life was too short to waste by being a grump? I just didn't get it. But right now I was too happy and too tired to care, and I decided to simply enjoy it. I was on holiday, after all, and deserved some fun – and lying here in the arms of my very own Adonis was definitely exactly the kind of fun I wanted. I snuggled up happily against him and felt my eyelids grow heavy.

"Let's get you to bed," he whispered as he picked me up and carried me inside, gently laying me down on the bed.

"Where are you going?" I asked sleepily as he turned and headed outside. I really didn't want him to go.

"Just locking up next door. I'll be right back," he said with a smile, before walking out.

A few minutes later I felt him settle down by my side and snuggled comfortably into his chest. He stroked my face softly, before leaning down and kissing my forehead tenderly.

"Goodnight, baby," he whispered, making me smile into his chest before closing my eyes and dozing off.

I opened my eyes and sighed in contentment. I felt so peaceful and couldn't understand what was causing the warm glow in my body. Suddenly remembering that I wasn't alone in bed, I turned towards Adam who was fast asleep beside me. He really was beautiful, I thought as I gazed at him sleeping. I wanted to reach out and draw the contours of his face with my finger but stopped myself, worried that it would wake him.

I had an urgent need for the loo and got out of bed as quietly as possible. When I returned to the bedroom, I suddenly felt awkward. Should I go back to bed and wait for him to wake up? Then what? Would we just go back to our chatter as if nothing strange had happened – and *was* happening? Or would it be super awkward? I didn't know what to do and which Adam I would find this morning, the grumpy one or the friendly one. I finally decided to have a shower, hoping he would be up by the time I finished.

I couldn't believe we only had two days left before heading home. A hundred and one questions raced through my mind as the water fell over me. Would we see each other once we got back to Perth? Even as friends eventually? I felt like I had known him forever and would love to see him again. I knew he would get along great with Zach and Anna now that he was no longer the grouchy monster I initially thought he was.

I slipped on a bikini under my shorts and my bright fluorescent pink, orange and yellow tank top and seeing that Adam was still fast asleep, I headed to breakfast alone. It was already almost ten o'clock so I didn't have much time left before the end of breakfast time. I thought I might prepare a plate for Adam as he would obviously be missing breakfast this morning, and it was pretty much because of me.

I saw Matt and Lucy at a table in a corner and Samantha and Patrick too. They all looked so happy that I decided to leave them to it. I was really looking forward to another lovely day of sun, sand and sea, and I was feeling happy and carefree. I hoped Adam would still be smiling today but I didn't know what to expect, and it made me feel uneasy. I guess I was terrified of getting hurt; I knew that I cared way too much about him already, and that I was in danger of getting my heart broken big time.

ADAM

I woke up with a warm glow and remembered the previous night with Molly. I reached out to hold her, wanting to feel her by my side, and was surprised to feel the cold, empty bed instead.

She was gone.

I sat up and looked around to see if she was in the bathroom or on the veranda, but there was definitely no sign of her. Did she regret me staying the night? Or was she embarrassed by our new-found intimacy? But then again, nothing had happened and we were still just friends – although that would soon change if I had my way.

I stretched and got out of bed, making my way back to my room where I had a quick shower before heading to breakfast. It was already quarter past ten and I was probably too late. I hoped that Molly would be there. I needed to see her to make sure that everything was alright between us.

The very light morning breeze was cool and there wasn't

a cloud in the sky. I reached the restaurant and saw that the breakfast buffet had been removed. *Damn!* I was starving. There weren't many people still around, and I couldn't see Molly anywhere. My heart plummeted. Where had she gone? I looked around again and suddenly something bright caught my eye at the far end of the terrace. My heart skipped a beat. It was Molly.

"Hmmm . . . someone sure is hungry this morning," I teased as I reached the table and saw that there were five plates piled high with a delicious array of food – bacon and eggs, toast, croissants, fruits, yogurt and cereals.

She turned and gave me a radiant smile.

"Actually, this is all for you. As I didn't know what you liked, I took a bit of everything," she said, flushing cutely.

"That's so sweet. Thank you," I said, touched, as I sat down.

"My pleasure." She smiled before motioning towards the food. "Go on, dig in."

I went from one plate to the other, savouring each bite, as she watched me in amusement for a moment.

"It'sh really delichious," I said, my mouth full of watermelon.

She cocked her head, her eyes still on me, and her brow furrowed cutely. "Do you suffer from a multiple personality disorder by any chance?"

I almost spat out my mouthful of watermelon as I let out an incredulous laugh, I just hadn't been expecting that at all.

"Run that by me again?"

"It's just that you spent the first five days scowling and complaining about everything and being a royal pain in the arse."

"Royal pain in the arse, huh?"

"And that's putting it mildly!" she exclaimed. "But now

you're suddenly this whole different person, you're happy and charming and you actually smile – and at *me*!"

"Why wouldn't I smile at you?" I said, acting dumb. I knew I would have to explain it all to her sooner or later, but I had no idea how to go about it so I needed to buy time and let her do the talking for the moment.

"Well, you seemed to have developed an instant dislike to me since you sat next to me on the plane!" she said good-naturedly. "Usually people tend to like me, but not you – you couldn't stand me from day one."

"That's not true," I said, cringing slightly.

"Well if it's not true, you had a funny way of showing it," she answered. "I don't understand your sudden change in attitude towards me. I mean, you're actually being *nice* to me? What's that all about?"

I looked at her. She looked genuinely curious to hear my answer. The problem was that I had no idea what to say.

"You're just impossible not to like!" I said, trying to coax her.

She raised an eyebrow at me, clearly not convinced.

I sighed. "Maybe I just had enough of being a grouch." Okay, so it wasn't the actual truth, but it was at least partially true.

She looked at me for a moment, seeming to be debating whether to believe me or not, and then her faced brightened. "Well, I for one am glad!"

We chatted on through breakfast, Molly stealing food off my plate now and again. We were so comfortable together that it felt like we'd been a couple for years.

"So, what are your plans for today?" I asked, putting my arm around her shoulders casually as we left the restaurant. I was thrilled that she seemed relaxed about it and didn't push me away. It was definitely a good sign.

"I'm meeting up with Lucy and Matt on the beach. Want to come?"

"Sure, but I've got to go and change so I'll meet you there later."

"Okay."

She smiled and I turned to go, then I stopped and looked back at her with a scowl.

"Is the hunky, dark-haired dancer going to be there too?"

"Probably, and you'd better be nice to him!" she said, poking my chest.

I chuckled and promised that I would behave. I couldn't wait to join Molly on the beach and be free to admire her gorgeous body in that sexy little bikini of hers . . .

MOLLY

I lay on the beach, soaking up the sun and replaying last night over and over again in my mind. I knew I had a goofy grin on my face, but I didn't care. I felt so happy. Adam had joined me on the beach for a little while earlier but had now gone off water skiing, and I wished he'd hurry back. Time dragged on when he wasn't around. *Damn!* I was seriously in lust, no matter how much I tried to deny it – or stop it. I was shaken out of my reverie as I heard someone calling my name. I rolled my head to the side and saw Matt, Jeremy and Lucy heading my way.

"Hey, guys! How's it going?" I asked, genuinely pleased to see them. I chuckled as one by one they kissed my cheeks in greeting.

"Just going for a swim, do you want to join us?" Matt asked, smiling at me, his eyes crinkling on the sides.

"Sounds great." I followed them towards the sea and laughed as Lucy ran and jumped onto Matt's back. Without missing a beat, Matt grabbed onto her then suddenly began sprinting towards the sea, throwing himself in while Lucy clung on, screeching and laughing. As soon as they came up for air, Lucy dunked him in retribution.

"They are such kids those two!" Jeremy grinned, his eyes on them.

I dived into the water, I couldn't get enough of the deliciously warm temperature of the sea in Mauritius. In Perth the sea was as blue as it is here but it was always cold, even in summer. As I looked around me and took in the huge expanse of turquoise blue sea, the mountains to my left, the coconut trees all along the beach, I sighed in contentment. I thought of Zach and imagined what amazing pictures he could have taken if he'd been here with me. There were so many colours and contrasts in Mauritius, whether it be the people, the buildings or the landscape. A photographer's dream. I actually hadn't heard from him all week and he hadn't replied to my text messages. He was probably off in some remote place in the mountains with no phone connection.

We headed back to our spot and I spread out my towel on the sand, lying on my back. It felt wonderful. I closed my eyes and listened to Matt, Lucy and Jeremy talking. My mind started wandering off as they talked on . . . I couldn't believe we were heading back in two days. It was too depressing for words. Speaking of depressing, I hadn't heard much from my mum and was relieved as no news was good news. She had sent me a quick text message to tell me that she was fine and to thank me for helping her.

Samantha had gone off to visit the island with Patrick today. I wondered where Adam was. There were quite a few boats with skiers behind them, and I didn't know which one Adam would be skiing behind. They were a bit too far out for me to be able to recognise him. I couldn't get over the fact that he went from major grump to this new amazing guy almost overnight. Okay, I had to admit that even the grumpy version of Adam had intrigued and amused me from the start. And needless to say, I had found him sexy and gorgeous too. He had actually showed signs of kindness a few times despite his scowls, and there had been something about him that I'd liked despite everything. But then again, I tended to trust everyone and it had got me into trouble before. I guess it was part of my positive outlook on life. I believed that everyone had something positive and good in them and chose to focus on that, but of course there were people who were scheming, dishonest and liars. I just hoped that I wasn't going to find out that Adam was one of the latter.

I suddenly snapped out of my reverie when I heard Matt, Lucy and Jeremy call my name. They were off water skiing and wanted to know if I wanted to join them. I declined, not being in the mood to move. I was too tired to do anything too active after our lack of sleep last night. I was quite happy to carry on dozing in the sun and wait for Adam. Jeremy said he'd leave them to it as he had to go and help his dad with something. I jumped in surprise as his face was suddenly over mine. What the? Oh that again! I thought in amusement as he leaned down to kiss me goodbye. Definitely a Mauritian custom that would take some getting used to.

41

ADAM

*T*here was that guy again! *What the hell?!* Were my eyes playing tricks on me or did he just kiss Molly? Twice! I had been dying to kiss her for days and he just sweeps in there and does it. Damn him. I had to get rid of him. Fast.

I hastened my pace towards Molly, but to my relief, saw him wave and head off. I slowed down and gazed at Molly lying on her back in her little bright pink bikini. She had got a great tan over the last few days and looked stunning. She had her sunglasses on so I couldn't tell if she was looking my way or not. As I approached her, I suddenly saw her face break into a lazy smile and I knew she'd seen me. My heart skipped a beat. I was really acting like a teenager with a crush. She sat up and I couldn't help admiring her curves and breasts.

"Hey, you!" I said, smiling at her as I sat down on the beach next to her.

She took off her sunglasses and smiled at me, her beautiful green eyes making me melt. Suddenly I remembered the dark-haired guy.

"I saw you with that guy again," I said, scowling.

"Oh no! Grouchy Adam's back! I knew it was too good to be true!"

"Be scared – be *very* scared!"

She giggled.

"But seriously, what was that kissing thing about?"

"The Mauritians kiss each other on the cheek to say hello and goodbye," she explained with a grin.

"Well I definitely think that since we are in Mauritius, we should do as the locals do!" I countered without missing a beat and leaned towards her, kissing her left cheek softly, lingering slightly, loving the feel of her skin on my lips and the smell of her so close to me. Then I went for her right cheek, doing the same thing, inching closer to her lips and prolonging the pleasure a little longer this time. I felt her breath catch in her throat and had trouble stopping myself from lunging for her lips.

She stared at me, dumbstruck.

"What? Isn't that how it's done?" I asked with wide-eyed innocence, stretching out on the sand by her side.

She shook her head and laughed.

The only problem was that now that I'd kissed her, all I could think about was that I wanted to do it again – and again and again.

42

MOLLY

*W*ow. Okay. So I guess he may be interested in being more than friends after all. The thought of that did all sorts of wonderful things to my body... His kisses had been so tender and had taken my breath away.

I suddenly felt awkward and didn't know what to say or how to act. *Snap out of it*, I scolded myself. *It's just grumpy Adam we're talking about here. And besides, he only kissed you on the cheeks, for goodness' sake!* I grinned to myself, knowing that the little voice in my head was right. It *was* just Adam, and he *had* only kissed my cheeks, and although it had felt like so much more, it was, nonetheless, just a kiss on the cheek.

"So, Mr Suddenly Smiley, what are your plans until we leave? Actually, are you also heading back tomorrow night?"

"Yep, we're on the same flight again, I'm afraid!" He winked.

"Sure will be boring compared to my flight on the way here with Mr Grumpy Dumpy by my side."

He winced slightly. "Er, yeah, definitely wasn't feeling like myself – but now the real me is back!"

"*Is* this the real you?" I asked softly, looking deep into his eyes for reassurance. "I must say, I'm pretty confused. It's like I've met two different Adams. The grouchy Adam and the friendly Adam. The two just don't add up."

He looked startled and then pained, but didn't say anything for a moment. Finally, he sighed. "I know. I don't really know how to explain it, but trust me, this is the real me. The grouchy Adam was also me to a certain extent, but I'm honestly not the grumpy person that he was."

"But why were you like that then? What happened? Why this sudden change?" I insisted. I wanted to understand. It was impossible for someone to change so radically from one day to the next. It didn't make sense. He looked anguished, running his fingers through his hair, seeming to be debating whether to tell me something or not, but finally he let out a long sigh and said, beseechingly, "Can we drop it for now, please?"

What wasn't he telling me? I was really confused. Something was up, and he wasn't being completely honest with me, but then again, I couldn't force him to open up to me. I glanced towards his brooding face and decided to let it go. Our holiday was almost over, and I didn't want to waste it by fighting with Adam. I nudged him playfully, wanting to lighten the mood. He rolled his head towards me and the weariness in his eyes was replaced by amusement when he saw my face. "What are you grinning about? You look like the cat that got the mouse."

"I was just thinking that I really don't care if you're grouchy or smiley, because as long as I get to hang around with a Ian Somerhalder lookalike, I'm happy!"

"And a much younger and hunkier version of him too!" he retorted with a wink.

"Cocky much?" I said teasingly as he chuckled, rolling his head back and closing his eyes.

I smiled and closed my eyes too, enjoying the feel of the warm sun on my skin. It was so peaceful listening to the lull of the gentle waves breaking on the shore and feeling the soft breeze blowing over us . . . this was truly paradise.

43

ADAM

*W*e finally headed back to our rooms, talking and laughing companionably. I had given up my role of grouchy Adam completely. I had more than enough of him and besides, I had everything I needed to write my article. The only problem was that I felt like a real jerk for not telling Molly the truth. I could have told her earlier when she'd asked me, but the words wouldn't come out. I didn't know how to explain it to her without sounding like the arse that I was. There was no good excuse for lying to someone and pretending to be someone you're not. How could I expect her to understand and forgive me for fooling her like that? I shook my head, pushing these thoughts away. I didn't want to think of that right now. All I wanted to do was to pull her into my arms and kiss her.

I was sitting on the edge of my bed, freshly showered and dressed, putting my watch back on, when I heard the sound of footsteps outside my door. I looked up just as Molly popped her head around the open door.

"May I come in?" she asked shyly.

I pushed myself off the bed and made my way towards her. "Do you really need to ask?" I said softly as my gaze lingered over her body. She was wearing a pair of bright orange shorts with a white and orange tank top. Her long hair was wet from the shower and hung loosely in waves over her shoulders, and her crystal-green eyes sparkled as she watched me watching her. She looked beautiful. I didn't know how it had taken me this long to see just how stunning she was. My eyes finally met hers and our eyes locked. I stroked her cheek with the back of my thumb and felt her breath catch in her throat as she leaned her face into my hand.

"I really want to kiss you . . ." I whispered, my eyes on her lips.

"Then do it," she whispered back as my eyes found hers again.

I groaned and my lips plunged to meet hers. As soon as our lips touched, I was filled with such tenderness that instead of kissing the life out of her, I found myself kissing her softly, allowing my mouth to shape itself onto hers. I delicately explored the contours of her lips, wanting to savour the moment. I gently coaxed her into opening her lips, and when she did, I moaned and deepened the kiss, lacing my fingers through her hair.

Finally. . .

44

MOLLY

*I*t suddenly registered that Adam's hands were making their way into my bra. I pulled away from him, breathing heavily.

"What's wrong?" he asked, looking a bit dazed.

"I'd like to take it slow," I whispered, looking at my feet, my cheeks burning.

He gently put a finger under my chin, wanting me to look up, but I resisted.

"Please look at me, Mol."

I finally raised my eyes to his.

"I'm okay with that," he said, running his fingers down my cheek in a gentle caress.

"Are you sure?"

"Positive," he replied with a nod, his face breaking into one of his gorgeous lopsided smiles. I felt my insides go weak and smiled back, my eyes drawn to his beautiful mouth.

"I guess we should calm things down a bit then, shouldn't

we?" he said with a wink, looking down at his shorts and the evidence that he was more than a little turned on.

I followed his gaze and grinned. "Guess you could hang a shirt on that, huh?"

He threw his head back and laughed. Oh my goodness! I *cannot believe* I just said that! I felt myself turn crimson again and broke into a fit of nervous giggles. Adam pulled me to him and hugged me tightly as we laughed.

"How about some lunch then?" he suggested, loosening his hold on me.

"Sounds like a plan." I smiled, giving him a quick kiss before getting up and pulling my top back on.

We walked hand in hand towards Les Filaos, the beach restaurant where we'd planned to meet Lucy and Matt for lunch. As they hadn't yet arrived, we headed down to the beach, settling ourselves comfortably on sun loungers.

I closed my eyes and smiled happily. I hadn't felt this happy – and been so in lust – for a long time.

I was abruptly shaken out of my reverie by the sound of Lucy's voice. "Molly! We just saw a group of dolphins swim past, it was amazing. They were so close to the shore!" she exclaimed, dropping onto the sand beside me. Adam greeted her then lay back and closed his eyes again, leaving us to chat in peace.

Lucy caught my gaze and wiggled her eyebrows, nudging her head towards Adam. I grinned and nodded as her mouth fell open in surprise. Before she could say anything, Matt and Jeremy arrived. They shook hands with Adam before sitting next to Lucy on the beach.

Adam leaned towards me and whispered, "Phew! For a minute there I was worried that they might lean down and kiss me!"

I giggled, jabbing him playfully in the ribs as he chuckled quietly to himself. We stayed on the beach for a while and as we talked, Adam either caressed my back or squeezed my hand or kissed my cheek, sending shivers all the way down to my toes. I couldn't believe how relaxed I felt with him. I was usually awkward and shy when I started going out with someone, but with Adam, I was completely me.

I caught him staring at me a few times, and each time our eyes locked, my body tingled all over. His eyes were filled with tenderness and desire and it took my breath away. No one had ever looked at me that way before.

We had a long lunch with Lucy and Matt, Jeremy having left to go back home. We laughed a lot and shared our life stories, getting to know each other in the little time that we had left. It's funny how sometimes you meet people that are completely in sync with you and it feels like you've known them forever. Whereas others you see every day, but never manage to feel any bond with them whatsoever.

We finally said our goodbyes, and Adam and I strolled down the beach hand in hand. We were leaving the next day and wanted to enjoy every last minute of this beautiful island and whatever it was that had started between us . . .

ADAM

J strolled down to the water's edge and let the waves break over my feet. It felt heavenly. "The water's wonderful," I said over my shoulder. "How about a swim?"

She scrunched up her face cutely and shook her head. "Nah, don't really feel like it right now."

As I looked at her, I felt a wicked grin spread over my face. "Oh, you don't, do you?"

Her eyes widened at the tone of my voice and she took a few steps backwards as I began walking towards her.

She laughed and kept walking backwards, her eyes never leaving me. "Adam, *don't.*"

I grinned even wider, chuckling wickedly as I kept moving forward.

"Adammm . . . *NO!*" she warned, waving her pointer finger at me. I wiggled my eyebrows and chuckled. Her eyes darted around as she looked for a way out, then suddenly, before I knew what was happening, she turned on her heel and sprinted down the beach.

"Stay away from me!" she shrieked over her shoulder, laughing.

I took off after her and caught up with her in a few large strides, but she wiggled out of my grip and raced off again in a fit of giggles. I went after her once more and as soon as I was close enough, I made a grab for her, but as I did so, my hand caught in her bikini top. I stopped short, looking down at the bikini top in my hand and up again at her naked back. Uh-oh.

"ADDAMMM!" Molly wailed in distress, her hands flying up to cover her breasts. I put my hand over my mouth to hide my amusement as she looked over her shoulder and glowered at me. "Did you do that on purpose?"

"No! Of course not!"

She turned her head, probably trying to figure out what to do. She was so gorgeous, standing there with her naked back to me . . .

I took a step forward but her head snapped back towards me, her eyes wide. "STOP! Don't you *dare* come any closer."

I stopped in my tracks, fighting down my laughter. I knew that laughing was not an option right now. "Okay, I won't. I just wanted to give you your top back."

"Oh." Her eyes flicked towards my outstretched hand and her bikini top, and she groaned in despair. "This is a nightmare – and I can't even hide my head in my hands."

My heart went out to her. She was as red as a beetroot and in distress, and it was all because of me, even if I hadn't done it on purpose. I wondered if she believed me. "I promise I didn't do it on purpose," I said, wanting to make sure that she understood that.

She sighed heavily and held my gaze. "I believe you, but

the problem now is that I have no idea how I'm going to put my top on again without showing you, or the whole beach, my breasts!"

The fact that I was struggling to keep a straight face didn't escape her notice and she shot me a killer glare. "It's *not* funny!"

I swallowed my laughter and shook my head. "No, you're right, it's not. I'm sorry."

She huffed, not impressed in the least.

"Mol, there's hardly anyone on the beach," I said, motioning around us, hoping that it would reassure her. "And lots of people go topless in Mauritius so it's—" Catching the murderous look on her face, I amended hastily, "Although, of course, just because others go topless doesn't mean that it's okay for you to, right?"

She narrowed her eyes at me and once again it took all my strength not to laugh. *Okay, Adam. Put your thinking cap on and find a way to get her out of this with minimum damage – well, with minimum* additional *damage – to her pride.*

"Hey! How about you use me as a shield?" I suggested, opening my arms wide to demonstrate. "You can hide against my chest while you put your top back on."

She stared at me in silence for a moment, and I could see her mind ticking as she contemplated my suggestion.

Finally, she let out a deep breath. "Fine. It's not like I have much choice anyway," she said, resigned. "But please promise you won't look?"

"I promise," I said solemnly, before adding with a grin. "Although it'll be *really* tempting!"

She narrowed her eyes at me, but I could see a hint of a smile playing on her lips.

"Okay, let's do it." I motioned for her to come closer. With her back to me, she took a tentative step towards me before turning around, her arms tightly crossed over her chest, her eyes fixed on mine. She looked vulnerable and beautiful, not to mention, so darn sexy . . . *Oh my!* This was going to be torture. *Focus, Adam*, I scolded myself.

"Are you sure I can't take a peek, even just a tiny little one?" I teased, wanting to lighten the mood and make the moment less embarrassing for her.

She let out a surprised spurt of laughter. "Adam!"

I laughed too, relieved to see her smile again. "Just kidding!"

I held her top out to her, but as she was about to reach out for it, she realised that if she did, she would have to let go of her breast.

"*Oh noooo!* What am I going to do now?" she wailed in despair.

There was only one other option – and she wouldn't like it . . .

"Let me put it back on for you."

Her head jerked up in surprise and she fixed her gorgeous green eyes on me. Once again, she studied me in silence for a moment, then, to my astonishment, nodded. "Okay, but *no* groping!"

I nodded gravely. "None whatsoever."

She grinned and bowed her head against my chest. I stretched the bikini top over her hands and around her back and held it there, looking the other way.

"Alright, go for it. I'm not looking," I whispered, my voice hoarse. She quickly grabbed the top with one hand and I let go. She jiggled around in front of me for a second then finally stood still. "Okay, done!"

I let out a deep breath. "*Wow!* That was so *hot!*"

"Shut up!" she cried, slapping me playfully on the arm as her face flushed again.

"But it was. And now I *really* need a swim!"

She grinned, then her face grew serious again. "Thank you," she said softly.

I smiled and pulled her into my arms in reply. I was so in love with this girl. How on earth was I ever going to tell her the truth? The thought of hurting her, or losing her, was unbearable. But I had to tell her. Soon.

46

MOLLY

Oh my God! That was the single most embarrassing moment in my life. I couldn't help giggling as I remembered the look on Adam's face when my bikini top caught in his hand – priceless! I'd so badly wanted to turn to him and squash my breasts against his chest . . . I cleared my throat, embarrassed by the direction of my thoughts. It was ridiculous; even watching him swim made my body tingle all over. I had never felt this kind of attraction to anyone before. It was unnerving and exhilarating in equal measures. *Okay, Molly, maybe a walk would be a good idea right about now.* I called out to Adam and told him that I was going to see Samantha, and we agreed to meet back at our rooms later on. I tore my eyes away from him and strolled off down the beach. Hopefully Samantha would be able to take my mind off Adam for a while and I could let my hormones calm down a little before I saw him again.

I strolled leisurely through the hotel, making my way to

the pool, and spotted her sunbathing on one of the sun loungers.

"Hi," I said, sitting down on the seat next to hers.

"Hi back!" she said, smiling. "It's great to see you. We've got lots to catch up on."

I nodded, smiling back at her as I took off my sarong and put it into my tote bag, before grabbing my sun cream and lying down by her side.

"So, where's that sexy husband of yours?" I asked as I began rubbing cream on my face.

"He's gone water skiing."

"Well, go on, tell me how it went," I asked, throwing the sun cream back into my bag and turning my gaze on her.

"Pretty good. We're getting there. Yesterday we reached a compromise on the most important issues. I think what really worked was that I told him how every situation made me *feel* instead of saying 'I don't like it when you do this or that'. He was pretty shocked by how hurt, inadequate and upset I was by some of the things that to him seemed so unimportant. Anyway, he promised to put less pressure on me and to help me out with the things he could. All in all, it was really enriching and it feels like we're on our second honeymoon," she ended, smiling goofily before patting my leg and adding with a grin, "But enough about me – your turn now!"

I grinned back, knowing full well that my news would be a huge surprise. "Well-ll, erm . . . Adam and I are kind of . . . er . . . together."

"No way!" she exclaimed. "I'm in shock!" She shook her head. "But then again, when I think about it, I often caught him gazing at you when you weren't looking, and you, my friend, had stars in your eyes every time you saw him, grumpy pots or not!" She laughed, waving her finger at me knowingly.

I guffawed, really surprised to hear that. We chatted on for a while as she asked me a hundred and one questions about Adam and every single thing that had happened between us. When she left to go and join Patrick, I walked back to my room, impatient to see Adam again. I already missed him, although it had only been an hour since I'd left him on the beach. I peeked into his room and saw him sprawled out on his bed, sound asleep. I was dying to curl up against him but didn't want to wake him up, so I returned to my room, had a long shower and settled down with my book.

When the sun began to set, I got up and headed back to Adam's room. I wouldn't let him miss our last sunset in Mauritius. He was still sound asleep so I slid in behind him and spooned him, hugging him tightly and inhaling that Adam smell I loved so much. I felt him stir and smiled. "Hey, you."

"Hey back," he replied sleepily.

I kissed him tenderly on the nape of his neck, loving the intimacy and tenderness of the moment. "I'm so sorry to wake you, but the sun's about to set and I didn't want you to miss it."

"Hmmm, I'm glad you did," he mumbled.

"Plus, I missed you," I whispered into his ear. He rolled around to face me and we lay opposite each other, gazing into each other's eyes for a moment, then he leaned over and placed a feather-light kiss on my lips. I sighed, closing my eyes as I leaned in for more. Desire coursed through every nerve ending in my body as our kiss deepened. After a few minutes, he pulled away abruptly, breathing heavily. His eyes burned into mine as my desire was reflected back at me in his eyes.

"I could stay here all day and all night, but if you want to see that sunset, we'd better head out now," he said with a wink. I gazed at him in a lustful daze. Right now, I didn't care in the least if we saw the sunset or not.

Seeing the look on my face, he chuckled. "Please stop looking at me like that," he pleaded, holding out his hand to pull me up. "Otherwise the sun will definitely set without us."

I sighed regretfully and let him pull me up. "You can't get enough of me, can you, Molly Sunshine?" he teased, pinching my butt playfully. I slapped his hand away and giggled as he captured my hand and held on to it as we made our way down to the beach.

ADAM

*H*er joyous laughter filled me with wonder. I gazed down at her in my arms and my gut clenched at the thought of having to reveal the truth to her . . . I hoped she would forgive me – the alternative was impossible to contemplate.

Her phone suddenly trilled inside her bag and she jerked up, her smile dying on her lips as she grabbed her bag and pulled it out. She looked at the screen and her face drained of colour.

"Hi Mum," she said with forced joviality as she put the phone to her ear. She listened quietly for a moment, twirling a lock of hair around and around her finger. "Mum, stop!" she finally exclaimed, rubbing her forehead with her free hand, closing her eyes and taking a deep breath. "You're going to be fine," she went on in a softer tone. "I'm heading back tomorrow night so don't get yourself into such a state for nothing."

She listened again, this time fiddling with the zipper of her bag, her face drawn. I wanted to hold her in my arms and protect her from it all, but I knew that I couldn't take away the fact that her mum was ill, that her dad had died and that she was an only child left to deal with it.

"Mum, don't even go there. I'll be back before you know it and you won't have to worry that I'm far away and that you're all alone, okay? Don't forget that Aunt Janine is just next door."

They spoke for a little longer before saying their good-byes. After hanging up, Molly threw her phone on her bag and fell back on the towel, covering her face with her hands and taking deep breaths.

I turned onto my side to face her. "Are you okay?"

"I'll be fine in a minute," she said in a barely audible whisper, rolling her head towards me. I pulled her into my arms and she curled up into my chest, letting out a huge sigh.

"I'm finding it harder and harder to deal with my mum's anxiety and being far away makes me feel so helpless," she said, moving slightly out of my embrace so that she could see my face. "I'm scared that something will happen to her and that I won't be there to help. I know that I can't take sole responsibility for her, but it's like a constant tug of war inside me – one part accepts that I need to live my life and do my thing, but the other part is forever feeling guilty if I do – like now."

I reached out and stroked her hair. "Is she alright now?"

She shrugged. "I think so. She panicked because she was worried that she may feel unwell or have another attack and that I wouldn't be there to help her."

I would have to help her convince her mother to see a psychologist when we got home. She couldn't carry on like this or she would crack under the pressure. Harry, one of my dad's best friends and a great friend of the family, was a psychologist, and I would see if he could help Molly's mum.

We stayed there for a while watching the sun sink below the horizon, talking and laughing and enjoying each other's company. Suddenly she sat up and grabbed her phone.

"Oh no! Look at the time," she exclaimed, showing me the phone. It was almost seven thirty. "We'd better get moving, Romeo, otherwise we won't have time to have a drink before dinner. Are you okay to have dinner with Samantha and her husband later?"

I pulled her up and kissed her tenderly. "Whatever makes you happy," I murmured into her lips. I was in awe of how fast she snapped out of her lows and found her smile again. She was an example to us all.

After an enjoyable dinner with Samantha and Patrick, we headed to the dance floor. It was wonderful to dance with Molly but after a few dances feeling her body pressed to mine, I couldn't wait another second to have her all to myself and told her that we should go. She seemed surprised, but didn't argue. We said our goodbyes and strolled back to our rooms, hand in hand.

"What was your favourite part of the holiday," she asked, her smiling eyes on me.

I leaned down and kissed her cheek tenderly. "You . . ."

"Ditto," she whispered, her eyes sparkling. I squeezed her hand and we walked on in companionable silence, both lost in our thoughts. However, when our rooms appeared ahead of us, I stopped in my tracks.

"What?" she asked, turning to me with a frown.

My face broke into a wicked grin. "Your bed or mine?"

Her eyes widened for a split second then her lips curled into a wide smile.

"Definitely yours," she answered. "It's closer!"

48

MOLLY

*A*dam burst out laughing. *Oh my goodness! Where had that come from?* I felt my face burn up for the umpteenth time today.

Noticing, he looked at me in surprise. "Why are you blushing?"

I groaned, hiding my face behind my hands. I wasn't usually so brazen with men, and I wasn't very comfortable with this side of me. He chuckled and tried to pull my hands away from my face, but I refused to let him.

"You don't have to be embarrassed because you want my body," he teased.

I snorted, my hands falling from my face, and slapped him playfully on the arm.

"Ouch," he groaned, rubbing his arm before grinning back at me. "*Sooo* . . . your room then?"

I stifled a giggle and peered up at him through my eyelashes, still embarrassed.

"Hey . . ." he said softly, gently caressing my cheek. I rested my cheek against his big hand and raised my eyes to his. He leaned down, lightly brushing his lips against mine. I sighed, parting my lips, inviting him to deepen the kiss. He slid his arm around my back, drawing me closer, and I looped my arms around the nape of his neck as we kissed slowly and languidly. Our kiss gradually became hungrier and his hands began exploring my body. Suddenly, the sound of approaching laughter snapped me out of my bubble, and it dawned on me that we were in the middle of the pathway, making out like teenagers. I pulled away abruptly and we stood opposite each other, breathing heavily for a moment.

"What's the matter?" he asked with a frown.

"We're on the pathway," I said by way of explanation, motioning for him to look around.

"Ah." He grinned. "Guess we'd better go inside huh?" he added huskily, nudging his head towards his room.

I nodded and took his hand, following him to the door. As soon as we were inside, I turned and threw my arms around his neck, crushing my lips to his again. I had no idea what had got into me and was embarrassed by how forward I was being, but I couldn't stop myself. All I wanted was for him to kiss me – forever. He chuckled into my lips and wrapped his arms around my waist, and without breaking the kiss, he carried me to the bed. He laid me down gently, then pulled away, searching my eyes to make sure that I was okay with the situation. I smiled tenderly before putting my hand behind his nape and pulling his mouth down to meet mine again.

"Eager little beaver aren't we?" he teased, shifting his weight onto his side so that he wouldn't crush me.

"Oh will you just shut up and kiss me already!"

He laughed, crushing his lips to mine. And kiss me he did...

49

ADAM

*W*hen I woke up, the sun was already high in the sky. Molly was still fast asleep and snoring softly by my side. I gazed at her, filled with tenderness and pure, undiluted, lust. Okay, better think of something else quick as I didn't want to wake her up just because I was horny as hell.

I picked up my phone from the bedside table as quietly as I could to see the time. It was already half past nine. We only had half an hour before the end of breakfast. I watched her sleep for a few more minutes, not quite believing that she was really here in my bed. I smiled and bent down to kiss her lips softly. Once, twice, no reaction, and then finally the third time she moaned as she opened her eyes slowly. Her face broke into a big smile when she saw me. She grabbed my hand and tugged me down gently into her arms.

"What a wonderful way to wake up," she said, hugging me to her.

I smiled, giving her a kiss on the forehead. "It's almost ten and we'll miss breakfast if we don't get moving soon."

She groaned. "I don't want to get up. I like it here. I think I want to stay here for the rest of my life."

I chuckled, leaning over and placing feather-light kisses all over her face before settling on her lips. We kissed lazily for a while until she stopped abruptly. "Breakfast, right?"

I grinned and nodded, getting up and holding my hand out to pull her up. She put her hand in mine but instead of pulling her up, I leaned down and kissed her again. She laughed, pushing me away. "Stop! Breakfast. Now."

50

MOLLY

I strolled leisurely back to my room after having gone to say goodbye to Samantha. Adam had returned to his room to pack and tidy up after breakfast, and I was meeting him there now. I stopped for a minute and turned my face up to the sun. I closed my eyes and let the warmth of the sun seep through me. It was heavenly.

When I finally got to Adam's room he was in the shower. He'd packed his suitcase - well, sort of. Basically he'd just chucked everything inside in a messy pile. I looked around the room and noticed that his laptop was on his bed with a few loose sheets of papers lying next to it. Curious to have a look at his work and what kind of a writer he was, I picked up the top sheet.

First day: Plane ride to Mauritius with Molly – me scowling and grumpy all the way, but it had no effect on her whatsoever. Seemed to amuse her more than anything. She's actually quite sassy and amusing. Will be harder than I thought. Must devise my strategy and find ways to get the information I need.

Just then, the door to the bathroom opened, and I looked up at Adam standing there looking freshly washed and shaved and cosy in a pair of jeans and a white shirt which hung loose and open.

"Hey, you," he said with a smile, his eyes finding mine. Seeing the look on my face, he frowned, looking at the sheet in my hand. His eyes suddenly widened then darted to the bed and back to me, and the smile died on his lips. "Oh no . . ." he whispered, running his hands through his wet hair. "Molly, please let me explain."

I didn't understand what I'd just read and why he had written it, but I knew it wasn't good. The pained expression in his eyes confirmed that.

"Before I explain, I want you to remember that what I feel for you is real. I've never felt like this before, and that's the truth."

I sat down heavily on the edge of the bed, feeling totally lost. I'd fallen in love with Adam, but he'd been hiding something from me all along. Finally, I raised my eyes to his. "Adam, just tell me what this is all about."

He sighed and nodded. "I came on this trip to work on an article. The theme of the article being 'Is happiness a feeling or can it be a choice?'"

My brows furrowed in confusion. "And?"

"And... you were my subject."

"Your subject? But you didn't even know me!"

He looked at me, his face pale and his eyes full of pain.

"I know. But Nicole, your colleague, spoke to Christine, a colleague of mine, about your eternal smile and optimism, and it inspired her into writing an article about people like you. She wanted to find out if you were truly happy or if you pretended to be. If happiness was a feeling or if maybe it could be a choice for some, and she decided to use you as her muse."

I frowned, still not understanding what he was getting at.

He took a deep breath and carried on. "Christine was then called away for two weeks because her mother is having an operation, and I was told that I had to fill in for her. I never wanted to do this! I'm a sports writer, not a feature journalist. It felt all wrong from the start, but I had no choice – not if I wanted to keep my job anyway," he explained, raking his hands through his hair and shaking his head despondently. "I'm so sorry, I had no idea that I would fall head over heels in love with you. The aim was for me to rile you by being broody, rude and mega annoying and see how you reacted. I had to observe if your smile stayed put despite outside influences – in this case, me. The scowling and nega-tivity isn't really me, as you now know."

I didn't know what to think and what to say. He had deceived me. I had been right to think that there'd been something amiss about his sudden change of attitude towards me.

He knelt down in front of me, but I hung my head, not wanting to look at him. He put his finger under my chin, urging me to look up, and I finally gave in and raised my eyes to his. "I'm deeply sorry, Molly. I never meant to hurt you. I wanted to tell you the truth so many times, but I was so afraid of losing you. I guess I thought that if I gave you more time to get to know me, there would be more chance that you would forgive me when you eventually found out the truth."

He got up again and walked to the sliding doors, hands in his pockets, shoulders slumped, and just stood, staring outside. I didn't move. I tried to process what had just happened. I couldn't even find the strength to be angry, to scream, to rant and rave – I felt empty, and so sad. I thought I'd finally found someone perfect for me, someone who would be there for me. I looked towards him and my heart broke into a million pieces.

Sensing my eyes on him, he turned around slowly with a big sigh, his eyes finding mine. He looked crestfallen, but I just couldn't comfort him and tell him that it was okay. Because it wasn't.

He took a few steps towards me, but I shook my head, motioning for him to stop. I couldn't bear for him to come any closer.

"Molly, you are the bravest, most amazing girl I have ever met. I admire you and I'm in awe of you," he said softly, his face drawn. "I promise that I won't write any of the personal stuff you shared with me. You can trust me," he added beseechingly.

"Trust you?" I said in a whisper, shaking my head. "How can I ever trust you again?"

"Oh Mol, no . . . please, don't do this," he begged, coming up to me and kneeling down in front of me again, hands on my knees. I could smell his aftershave, his hair, that Adam smell I had grown to love, and my heart constricted with pain. I looked down at my hands.

"I'm so sorry for not telling you sooner."

I lifted my gaze to his, tears brimming in my eyes, and swallowed hard.

"You lied to me. I asked you so many times." I shook my head as a few tears escaped and ran down my cheeks. I wiped them away quickly. "You should have told me. I would have understood."

"I'm so sorry," he said again, his voice breaking as he dropped his head onto my knees.

I looked down at his gorgeous mop of black hair, hair that

I had been running my hands through only a few hours earlier, and I couldn't stop the tears from spilling down my cheeks as sadness overwhelmed me. As the holiday flashed through my mind, the sadness was replaced my anger. How could I have been so stupid?

"I'm such an *idiot!*" I exclaimed angrily, shaking my head and pushing him away abruptly, making him fall back and land on his butt. If I hadn't been so angry it would have been funny, but I was in no mood to laugh. I stood up and stormed out of his room. Adam stayed on the floor and watched me leave. He didn't try to hold me back. I was both disappointed and relieved.

For the first time since I was seventeen years old, I had allowed myself to get attached to a guy, and this is what I got for it. I should have trusted my instincts. I was such a fool.

If only he had trusted me enough to tell me the truth, I would have understood. After all, work was work, and he hadn't known me when he'd taken on the assignment. I'd given him so many opportunities to come clean, but he'd lied to me over and over again. Okay, so maybe he hadn't lied, per se, but he'd omitted to tell me the truth time and again – and it was just as bad.

51

ADAM

J sat on the floor, staring outside for a while, feeling numb. Damn it, I was such a fool! Why hadn't I just told her the truth? She'd given me enough opportunities to come clean and I'd just been too much of a coward to fess up, and now I had lost her . . .

She would never forgive me. No, actually, she probably would because she was that kind of person, but she would never trust me again. I already knew from the little time I'd spent with her that she didn't give her heart out very often or very easily because her life was hard enough as it was.

I just wished I could go to her and try to convince her to forgive me, but I knew that she needed time to get her thoughts together, and I figured I owed her at least that. Maybe with time we would be able to be friends again. *Friends?* Are you kidding me? How in the world could I be "just friends" with her after knowing what it was like to hold her in my arms and kiss her. *Well, tough for you, Adam. You made your bed, now lie in it, buddy*, my annoying conscience pointed out. I sighed heavily. I guess I didn't deserve any better than that. Besides, who was I fooling? Torture or not, if friendship was the only way I could have her in my life, then of course I would take it.

I kept my distance at the airport, but my eyes followed her as she strolled through the duty free and then browsed in the bookshop. Her usually bright face was drawn and her shoulders were slumped, and I hated myself for being the cause of it. She was so beautiful and still multicoloured despite her sadness, I thought with a smile, as I took in her bright jeans, multicoloured blouse which hugged her body beautifully, and a red hibiscus flower clip holding her long curls up in a ponytail.

When our flight was called, I made my way to Gate 5 for boarding. I was lost in my thoughts as I headed to the plane. I simply wanted to go home, get into bed and sleep – anything to forget this nightmare. I didn't see Molly walk into the plane and didn't know where she was sitting. At first, I'd wanted to try to make sure I was sitting next to her, but then thought the better of it. I settled into my seat and was glad to see that there was no one next to me.

Once we were airborne, I flipped though the movies and saw that *Two Weeks Notice* was still on. Feeling that it would somehow make me feel closer to Molly, I pressed play. I enjoyed seeing it again. Sandra Bullock is a great actress, and the chemistry between them was pretty special. When it ended, I climbed out of my seat, needing to use the bathroom and stretch my legs a bit. I tried to convince myself that it wasn't because I wanted to see Molly – but who was I fooling? As I walked to the toilet, my gaze fell on her. She was sitting alone in a window seat. She must have felt my presence because she looked up from her screen and our eyes locked. My heart tightened when I saw the anguish in her eyes as she held my gaze. Gradually, her eyes brightened, and she finally smiled shyly at me, making my heart race wildly. I smiled back and was about to slide in next to her, when she turned her head away and focused on her screen again, making it clear as day that she had finished with me. My heart sank. Oh well, at least she had smiled.

On my way back, I saw that she'd just been served dinner. I was held up by the food trolley so I waited in the aisle, happy to be able to look at her without her knowing. As I neared her seat she glanced up and quickly looked away again when she saw me.

I waited for the trolley to move and watched her as she took the foil off the main dish and removed the knife and fork out of the plastic wrapping. The trolley finally moved out of the way and, unable to stop myself, I slipped into the seat next to her. She looked up at me in surprise, her fork midway to her mouth.

"Hmmm, that fish looks *soooo. . . . fishy,*" I teased.

She laughed softly, and my heart soared at the sound of it.

"God, I love that sound." I sighed tenderly. Her face clouded over, but she turned away without a word. Desperate to draw her into a conversation, I suddenly thought of something that would make her smile.

"Hey! I've got a rom-com movie quote for you!" I exclaimed. "Who complains to whom that he is the most frustrating man in the world?"

She stared at me as if I had grown two heads, then all of a sudden seemed to catch on, and cocked her brow at me. "Me to you?"

"We-ll . . ." I said, stroking my chin with my thumb, pretending to be considering her answer seriously. "Yeah, I guess that could definitely be applicable too, but no, it's in a movie I just watched. Okay, a bit more info: then he tells her something along the lines that she can't possibly say something like that because it's impossible for her to have met all the men in the world."

She looked away, and I could tell that she was having trouble finding it. Suddenly, she spun back towards me and her face lit up.

"You watched *Two Weeks Notice!*"

"I did," I said with a grin.

She beamed at me then turned back to her food. I was hoping that she would talk to me, but after eating silently for a few minutes, she glanced towards me and frowned. "Aren't you going to go back to your seat now?"

"Er . . . yeah. Okay, I guess I am," I stuttered, amused. "And here I was thinking that we were having a great chat," I added wryly as I slid out of the seat. She peered up at me, biting down on her lower lip, clearly stifling a smile. I saluted theatrically before making my way back to my seat, my heart lighter. Maybe, just maybe, there was hope . . .

MOLLY

*M*y heart was doing cartwheels and somersaults as I watched him walk away. I felt weak all over just from being close to him again for a few minutes. I wish I could pretend that he hadn't lied to me, but I couldn't. I'd already forgiven him. But forgiving didn't mean forgetting, and I didn't know if I could trust him again.

I settled down to try get some sleep. I was tired and emotional and hadn't had much sleep over the last few nights. I fell into a fitful sleep and was woken up by the air hostess telling me it was time for breakfast.

Before I knew it, we'd landed in Perth. It was so surreal to see the Perth International Airport -Mauritius already felt like a dream, one that hadn't ended too well, but a dream nonetheless.

I passed through immigration and went through "nothing to declare". I didn't know if Anna would be there to pick me up as I hadn't contacted her to ask, too caught up in

Adam. Speaking of Adam, I could see him further ahead in line, waiting to go through. I so badly wanted to run up to him and have him hold me in his arms, I gave myself a mental shake and reminded myself that he had lied to me for days – but somehow I couldn't quite work up much energy to feel angry. I was just sad, if anything, because it felt like I had lost one of my best friends. I'd shared so many things with him that I'd never told anyone except Anna and Zach. I somehow knew in my gut that I could trust him to keep everything I'd told him to himself. But if so, didn't that mean that in my gut I thought he was trustworthy? I groaned inwardly. I was so confused and had no idea what to think anymore.

He suddenly looked back and our eyes locked. He gave me one of his lopsided smiles, but his eyes looked sad. I just wanted to hug him and tell him that everything would be okay, but I couldn't. So I just smiled back and turned away.

I finally walked through the exit and was greeted by the welcoming shrieks of my two best friends. Before I could react, they had both jumped into my arms and were hugging me as if I had been away for years, not just a week. I laughed, hugging them back affectionately. Zach finally pushed Anna out of the circle. "My turn *alone* now, because we both know that I missed her more than you did," he said, sticking his tongue out at her like a child. Anna snorted, slapping his arm playfully but nevertheless giving him his moment alone with me.

He hugged me, but before I could respond, he pulled away again, frowning,. "Er . . . Mol," he said, looking behind me. "Why is that tall, dark-haired, muscly and somewhat familiar-looking guy over there looking at me like he wants to kill me?"

I chuckled, knowing it was Adam. I turned to make sure and was met by his familiar scowl. *He was jealous of Zach!*

I turned to Zach with a grin. "Oh, don't worry about him, that's Adam," I said with a dismissive wave of the hand.

"*That's* Adam?" Anna screeched, pointing behind my shoulder. "You didn't tell me he looked like Ian Somerhalder!"

I shrugged and picked up my bag, getting ready to head off.

Zach folded his arms and pulled a stern face. "We are not going anywhere until you have introduced us to this Adam person, who I've actually never heard of before now, but who Anna here seems to know all about!"

Before I could say anything, Anna leaned over towards me and whispered loudly, "For your information, he's walking this way and looks like he's heading straight for you."

My heart began hammering as he approached us. I felt dizzy and realised that I had forgotten to breathe. I quickly took a deep breath and tried to shake myself together before he reached us. *Get a grip, Molly! How old are you, for goodness' sake?* I mentally scolded myself.

He stopped in front of me, his eyes searching mine. "I didn't want to leave without saying goodbye." I felt a lump in my throat and couldn't get a word out. He reached out, taking my hand and holding it in his. "Can I call you?" he asked, eyes pleading.

I shook my head and finally regained the power of speech. "I don't think so . . . not right now."

He looked crestfallen, but nodded. "If you ever change your mind, just ask Nicole for my number, okay?"

I looked away, not trusting myself to speak without crying. He squeezed my hand gently, then leaned towards me and kissed me tenderly on the cheek. I had to do everything in my power to stop myself from throwing my arms around his neck and kissing him to kingdom come.

He began pulling away, then stopped midway and whispered in my ear, "Why is it that every time I turn my back, you're being hugged or kissed by some guy?"

I couldn't help myself; I burst out laughing. Turning to Zach and Anna, who had been standing behind me watching the whole exchange in silence, I smiled and said, "Adam, I'd like you to meet my two best friends, Zach and Anna. Zach and Anna, this is Adam." I motioned to each one in turn. We spoke for a few minutes, talking about Mauritius and our trip, but seeing Adam talking and laughing so easily with my two best friends made the knot in my stomach tighten. I couldn't help thinking "what if" and knew that I couldn't let myself go there. Oh jeepers, I needed to get away from him – and fast. I cleared my throat and said as jauntily as I could, "Sorry, guys, but we should get going."

As we said our goodbyes, I felt my heart shatter. I so badly wanted to grab his hand and tell him to stay, but I couldn't. Zach and Anna were watching us intently, their eyes darting from me to Adam and back again, and I knew I would be subjected to a major inquisition as soon as we were alone. I felt Adam's gaze on me as we walked away and was desperate to look back just one last time. *Don't do it, Molly*, my little inner voice said heatedly, but I couldn't resist and glanced over my shoulder. He was still standing in the same spot, eyes on me, and he looked so sad. "I'm so sorry", he mouthed, smiling forlornly before he turned and walked away.

I felt completely bereft as I watched him leave and finally tore myself away and went to join my friends, who were waiting a little further ahead.

"Whoa! There is so much emotional tension between you two, it's electrifying!" Zach said, shaking his head in wonder. "I have definitely been kept in the dark about this Adam person!"

I smiled, glancing back to watch Adam again. As I did so,

the outside door opened and three stunning brunettes ran in, hair flying through the air, looking around for someone. Adam spotted them instantly and waved. His three sisters. Oh *wow*! What a beautiful family they made. He put his suitcase down and opened his arms wide as the three girls ran and jumped into his arms. My heart melted at the sight, and all I wanted to do was to run up to him and join them.

I heard Zach clearing his throat rather loudly and turned back.

"Just let us know when you've finished ogling Adam, okay? But do you think you could give us a rough idea as to how long that might take because I need to make sure that I have enough money on me for parking."

I laughed, walking towards him and shoving him playfully. "Ha-ha, very funny!"

"You've got it bad, girl," Anna said, linking her arm through mine. "I've never seen you like this before."

"As soon as we get into the car, you're going to tell me everything," Zach said firmly. "As your housemate and best friend, I think that's the least I deserve!"

I laughed and agreed. After putting my suitcase into the boot and settling down in the front seat – Anna insisted – we took off. I began telling them the whole story. It felt good to let it out and share my thoughts and feelings. I knew they would be honest with me, and I could trust their judgement. They couldn't stop laughing as I told them about the many grumpy Adam situations; the plane ride, the suitcase-stealing episode, the cancelled glass-bottom-boat ride, the snorkelling, Henry, the markets, the quad riding . . .

When I got to the end, their faces were drawn and Zach was frowning.

"So? What do you think?" I asked, looking from one to the other, wanting their opinion but feeling anxious to hear what they had to say.

"I agree that he should have told you sooner, but I can understand why he didn't," Anna said, squeezing my shoulder affectionately.

Zach nodded. "I have to agree with Anna on that one. The guy is clearly crazy about you, Mol, and didn't want to lose you. It doesn't make him a liar or a bad person. It just makes him human really."

I groaned. Hearing Zach put it that way made me feel bad about my reaction towards Adam. But then again, even if deep down I knew they were right, I didn't know if my fragile heart wanted to take the risk. Maybe it was better to end it before it really began . . .

I nodded. "You're right. I know you are," I said quietly, looking at them. "But maybe this was a sign – a way for me to get out before I got in too deep."

"Mol, you have to let yourself fall in love, it's a part of life. One of the most important parts of it," Anna said softly.

"I know, and I did fall for him. But then when all this happened, it gave me the opportunity to take a step back and see things more clearly."

"And?" they said in unison.

"And . . . I'm just terrified of the depth of my feelings for him. If I go back to him and it doesn't work out, I'm too scared that I won't be able to handle it."

"Molly Malahan! You are *not* your mother!" Zach said sternly. "You're strong – by God, you've proved it over and over again. Give yourself a bit of credit and let someone love you and look after you for a change."

I shook my head sadly and looked out the window. "I can't . . ." I whispered, my voice breaking.

After a few minutes of feeling sorry for myself, I realised that I was sitting in the car with my two best friends who I hadn't seen in a week, and that I was not going to sit here staring into space and feeling miserable. It was time to focus on something positive.

I plastered a smile back on my face and turned to Zach. "Okay, your turn now! Where were you and why didn't you text me at all?"

Obviously deciding to let the subject of Adam go for now, he grinned and answered, "I was up in the mountains in Peru in a remote area that had no electricity and definitely no mobile phone reception, but I promise I thought of you every day."

I laughed and he leaned and gave me a friendly peck on the cheek.

"As for me," Anna said, "I didn't get to travel anywhere interesting like you two lucky people, but everything went well workwise – although it's not the same without you."

"Aww, I missed you both too," I said, touched. "I would have loved it so much if you'd been there. And, OMG Zach, the photos you could have taken! Mauritius is an island of contrasts and colours – the people, the landscapes, the weather, the buildings, everything! I took so many photos myself, I'll show you later."

We fell into our usual easy banter as we headed back home. I couldn't believe I was back. The contrast between Mauritius and Perth hit me hard. I'd never noticed just how neat and orderly it was here. There was a sense of order that was totally lacking in Mauritius. I'd always loved this, but right now I really missed the hustle and bustle of Mauritius and wished I was still there.

As we drove past the Deep Water Point Café, I suddenly realised that we weren't heading towards our house.

"Erm, where are we going?"

They looked at each other sheepishly. "We're going to your mum's," Anna admitted.

I groaned. I was exhausted, both physically and emotionally, and I just wanted to go home. I didn't have the energy to deal with my mum right now.

"We're sorry," Anna said. "But she made us promise to take you right there on our way back. She seemed so desperate to see you that we couldn't refuse."

"Fine," I pouted, although I would have done the same thing if I had been in their shoes, and I knew that she would be dying to see me. My stomach tightened as we arrived. I just hoped that she was having a good day, because I just couldn't cope with one of her bad days right now.

She'd probably been watching out for us through the window because before we even had time to get out of the car, she was running towards us with a big smile. My heart soared at the sight of her smile.

"Molly! I'm so happy to see you, love," she exclaimed, throwing her arms around me and holding me tight. "I thought you'd never come back."

"Mum, I've only been gone a week."

She smiled again. "I know, but I missed you," she said before giving Zach and Anna a hug too.

"Please come in and have a cup of tea or coffee or something hot – I went to the supermarket and bought a bit of everything yesterday."

My heart broke at the sound of her enthusiasm. I wished that this could be my mum all the time. We went inside and I told her about my trip as she busied herself making coffee for everyone. She had bought biscuits, croissants and cakes. This was the mum I remembered from my childhood. She'd been so full of life, always inviting people over and making way too much food. Everyone had loved her because she'd been warm, generous and loving. As I looked at her, a wave of sadness washed over me. She was still beautiful with her long sandy-coloured hair, her olive skin and her large almond-shaped green eyes (both of which I had inherited from her). She asked us all endless questions. Zach and me about our trips and Anna about work, and we chatted for quite a while. I began to feel exhausted and waited to catch Zach's eye, nudging my head towards the door, signalling that it was time to go. He caught on and got up, telling my mum that he was sorry but that we had to leave as he had a meeting he needed to get to soon. I was so grateful to him for knowing that my mum would be sad and hurt if it had come from me. I hugged her tight, savouring the feel of her arms around me. How I wished they could provide me with the security and safety haven I so desperately craved, but I knew they never would. She would never be like other mothers, and I was the one who had to look after her. It wasn't easy, but she was the only mum I had, and I loved her with all my heart.

Ten minutes later, we pulled up into our driveway. I was so relieved to finally be home. Zach pushed the door open and held his arm out, gesturing for me to go in.

"Home sweet home," he said, walking in behind Anna and me, rolling my suitcase in. I smiled and inhaled the familiar "home" smell. I had no idea what it smelled of exactly, but it just represented "home". I felt like I'd been away for a year, instead of a week. Something had changed inside of me. I think I'd found out what it was like to fall in love - although it was over before it had even begun.

I really needed a shower. Anna told me to go ahead and that she'd put the kettle on and wait to have a cuppa with us before heading to work. As the warm water poured over me, I couldn't help but think of Adam. I missed him so much already and wondered what he was doing right now . . .

ADAM

My sisters talked all the way home, hardly allowing me to get a word in edgeways. Emma told me excitedly about her trip and how she had only got back the previous morning. Jo told me about her new man and how this time he was "really, truly the one", while Lily and Emma rolled their eyes, making me grin. Lily told me that she was relieved that I'd convinced her not to get any piercings because she had met a really great guy at a party the following night and he'd invited her to the movies later in the week. I grinned and ruffled her hair. "Told you – you're perfect just the way you are!"

I phased out as they started arguing about goodness knows what. All I could think about was Molly. I couldn't believe it when I'd seen Zach hugging and kissing her. I'd felt so jealous. It was shocking as I'd never been the jealous or possessive type, but with her it was different. Both Anna and Zach had seemed genuinely nice, and I could see how they were Molly's best friends. I couldn't wipe away the memory of the look of anguish and longing on her face when she'd looked over her shoulder before leaving. I could only hope that she would come back to me. I guess I needed to give her some time. I had to get that stupid article written and then maybe we could move forward.

It was great to be home and see my parents again. Spot, our dog, was over the moon to see me and jumped up and down non-stop like a spring until he crashed down, totally exhausted, at my feet.

We had a usual Wilson family dinner; they were always rowdy, my sisters all trying to talk at the same time and outdo each other in every story. My parents tried in vain to ask me about Mauritius, but in the end they gave up. I didn't mind though, as after hearing Molly's story, I was just grateful for having them. It was sad to think that some people were really alone in life. I had always been surrounded by my crazy but wonderful and loving family, and I don't remember ever feeling alone. Molly, on the other hand, had gone through so much and had had to face it all alone. I really needed to talk to my dad about Harry. I was sure that he would be able to help us out one way or another. At least I had to try to do something to help Molly's mum.

After dinner, my dad settled comfortably in his favourite chair and turned on the television. The girls went into the kitchen to help my mum clean up. Realising that it was the perfect time to talk to him, I sat down next to him and told him about Molly and her mother. He listened intently, asking a few questions now and then, and agreed to contact Harry to ask for his help.

"I can tell this means a lot to you, Son, so I promise I'll do everything I can to help," he said gently, patting my arm affectionately.

"Thanks so much, Dad. It is very important to me."

"So, when are we going to meet this special lady?" he asked with a smile, as I felt my heart plummet.

"One day I hope, Dad. But it's a bit complicated . . ."

He looked at me and frowned, waiting for me to explain, but I couldn't – not yet.

"I'll tell you about it soon, but right now I just want to try to help her mother. Please don't mention her in front of the girls. You know how they are, and I'm just not ready to talk about her yet."

He promised that he wouldn't, and I knew I could trust him. We chatted a while longer, about my trip, his work and my article, and we were then joined by my mum. I was finally able to tell them a bit about Mauritius before my sisters followed, and then it was back to listening to their banter, bickering and commentaries until we settled down to watch a movie.

The next day my alarm went off at what seemed to be the middle of the night, but when I pulled the curtain to the side, I was surprised to see that the sun was definitely up. *Couldn't be!* My eyes still half closed, I threw my hand out and grabbed my alarm clock from my bedside table, trying to read through the haze: seven thirty. *No way!* The batteries had probably died while I was away. Then suddenly it dawned on me that I was still on Mauritian time and that made it half past three in the morning for me. No wonder I could barely keep my eyes open.

I made it to the office pretty much on time. I was greeted warmly by everyone as I walked into the office. It felt like I had been away for a year, not a week, and it felt strange to see that nothing had changed because I, for one, felt like my whole world had been rocked to its foundations during my week away.

I walked into my office, threw my jacket over the side of

the chair, switched on my computer and fell on my chair. I couldn't believe I was already back.

"Adam! Get in here," Luke called out from his office door.

Oh well, time to get back to work. I sighed and made my way to his office, where he bombarded me with a hundred and one questions about my trip and where I was at with my article. To my relief, he seemed satisfied with my answers. I finally headed back to my office and fell heavily down onto my chair once again. Talking about my trip and the article had brought everything back to the surface and once again, Molly was all I could think of.

I'd woken up thinking that I would see her by my side, and then reality had hit me hard. I knew I wouldn't be able to stop myself from getting into contact with her. Maybe I could write to her? That would be innocent enough, surely? That way, if she didn't want to communicate, all she'd have to do is not reply, although I hoped to God she would. I decided to ring up her office and ask to speak to Christine's friend, Nicole, to ask her for Molly's email address. Luckily she was at the office and didn't ask any questions. I typed Molly's address into my address bar and felt my heart race in apprehension and anticipation. I didn't know how she would react to my email because she had specifically asked me to leave her alone.

I began writing:

Hey little Miss Sunshine! How's the jetlag? Was awful waking up in the middle of the night to come to work, but the worst part definitely was waking up and knowing that I wouldn't be seeing you today . . .

I stopped and re-read what I'd written. My finger hovered over the send button. I didn't know if I should do this to her. She had asked me to leave her alone and after what I'd done to her, she deserved some time to process everything and think things through. No matter how hard it was for me, I needed to give her the space and time she needed. I sighed deeply and pressed delete.

MOLLY

I'd been back for ten days already but I was still feeling miserable, which is completely unlike me. I couldn't get Adam out of my mind and desperately wanted to see him. I'd thought long and hard about what had happened and spoken at length to Zach and Anna about it, and I knew they were right; Adam had messed up by fear of losing me and not because he was cruel or dishonest. Deep down I knew that he was someone good and kind and that I could learn to trust him again. I was so scared of getting hurt, though. He'd respected my wishes and not contacted me since we'd returned and I was grateful, but miserable too. Maybe he'd already forgotten about me and was relieved that things had turned out the way they had after all. My heart plummeted at the thought.

I went to see my mum every day after work as she was on edge and tense. I sensed that she needed to be reassured that she wasn't alone anymore. Me not being here for a week had been hard on her and she'd obviously had to fight hard against her anxieties while I'd been away.

Zach had flown off to Bali a few days after I got back and the house had felt way too empty while he was away. I was so happy that he was back now. I'd never felt lonely when he was away before, but somehow, this time, I had. I guess I wasn't feeling my usual happy self since I returned, and I hated that. It made me feel anxious. On the other hand, having all that time to myself in the evenings had given me the time to print my holiday shots, and I had hundreds of amazing photos of Mauritius, not to forget a few great photos of Adam, including the one of Adam and me at Casela. I loved that photo. I'd had it framed and it was now sitting on my bedside table. *Good one, Molly,* my annoying inner voice said sarcastically. *Great way to get over someone – put a photo of him next to your bed!*

"Oh shut up!" I snapped out loud. Of course my little voice was right, but I didn't want to hear it right now.

I drove to work and decided to do my "list of things to be grateful for" to try to drive my nostalgia away. First of all, I had a great work day ahead of me with two photo shoots that I was really looking forward to: the baptism of a little girl and a photo shoot of a pregnant woman. I smiled, feeling better already. No more thoughts of Adam. *Only positive thoughts, Molly! You have so much to be grateful for,* I reminded myself.

I walked into the office with a smile and poked my head into Anna's office to say hi. She was on the phone but smiled and waved, mouthing that she would see me later.

I sat down at my desk and switched on my computer, waiting for it to boot so that I could check my emails. I always did this first thing in the morning as I often had requests for photo shoots and most were rather urgent and needed to be dealt with straight away. I scanned the long list of new messages and as I was doing so, a new message arrived in my inbox. I did a double take as I saw that it was from Adam Wilson. *No way! It couldn't be.* My heart raced wildly as I clicked on it.

To: Molly Malahan
From: Adam Wilson
I watched the *Wedding Date* with my sisters last night, and when the guy tells the girl that he would miss her even if he'd never met her, it made me think of you . . . because now that I've met you, I honestly don't know how I lived twenty-six years without you in my life.
I know I said I would leave you alone, but surely ten days is long enough?
Adam xxx
P.S. I'll be holding my breath awaiting your reply . . . so please don't wait too long because then I'll become all blue and pass out or maybe even die or something.

I snorted with laughter as I read the P.S. and brushed away a tear that was making its way down my cheek. I read his sentence "because now that I've met you, I honestly don't know how I lived twenty-six years without you in my life" again. Wow. Oh wow. He wasn't playing fair. How was I supposed to resist him when he said stuff like that?

I re-read his message over and over again, grinning every time I got to the P.S. I'd missed him so much. I didn't know what to reply. If I reacted to his beautiful words, it would mean that I was letting him back into my life again and although there was nothing I wanted more, at the same time I was so scared.

I decided to buy myself some time and concentrate on the P.S. so that I could just keep it light for the moment.

To: Adam Wilson
From: Molly Malahan
You're such a dork 😊

I had just started scrolling through one of my new emails when I saw another message arriving, once again from Adam. Seems that he'd really been waiting in front of his inbox for my answer. My heart skipped a beat as I quickly opened it.

To: Molly Malahan
From: Adam Wilson
Hmmm . . . Okayyy . . . I'd kind of hoped for something somewhat more heartfelt or maybe even poetic in return, but hey, I guess "you're a dork" works too!

I laughed out loud – I should have known he wouldn't let me get away with saying so little.

To: Adam Wilson
From: Molly Malahan
Fair enough, Mr Wilson! I was buying a little time . . .
Not only did I need to process the fact that you were writing to me again, but all those wonderful things you said completely caught me off guard and I didn't know what to say.

To: Molly Malahan
From: Adam Wilson
"I really missed you too" would have worked great, you know!

I spurted with laughter again. He was incorrigible. Before I could answer, another mail came in.

240

To: Molly Malahan
From: Adam Wilson
So did you? Miss me, I mean.

I grinned, and wrote back.

To: Adam Wilson
From: Molly Malahan
Maybe, maybe not 😊

To: Molly Malahan
From: Adam Wilson
Maybe maybe or maybe definitely?

To: Adam Wilson
From: Molly Malahan
What do you think?
I have to go now – lots of work to do and you're distracting me.

My heart was racing. I couldn't fall for him again. Okay, fine, so I'd never actually un-fallen for him, but that's not the point. I couldn't let him get me to give in to him. I had to keep my distance like before.

To: Molly Malahan
From: Adam Wilson
I think that I really hope you did 😊
I must say that I like the thought that I'm distracting you – that means that you aren't completely indifferent towards me. . .

I sighed heavily. The idiot! As if he didn't know that I wasn't in the least bit indifferent to him. I pressed reply.

To: Adam Wilson
From: Molly Malahan
You know I'm not . . . Now go away!

To: Molly Malahan
From: Adam Wilson
Okay ☺
See ya!

I laughed, imagining his pouting face. He was totally irre-sistible, and I was in deep trouble if he carried on writing to me like this. But then again, I couldn't wait for him to write to me again. I groaned. *What are you doing?* I had no idea, but all I knew was that all I could think about was Adam and that I'd been staring at a photo shoot request on my screen for the past half hour. It was no use, I couldn't concentrate. I finally gave up and went to get myself a cup of coffee. It was as if we were back in Mauritius and things were all good between us. I had missed him so much.

As I had a meeting with a client soon, I decided that I would gaze into my coffee and dream of Adam until then. Work would have to wait until my mind was functioning normally again.

After lunch, I opened my inbox and saw another email from him waiting for me. My heart lurched.

To: Molly Malahan
From: Adam Wilson
Want to go out for a drink tonight?

Oh my goodness. He didn't waste any time, did he? My heart raced and I quickly typed my reply before I could let myself be tempted.

To: Adam Wilson
From: Molly Malahan
No!

To: Molly Malahan
From: Adam Wilson
Ouch! Couldn't you at least try to sugar-coat your "no" a little?

I burst out laughing.

To: Adam Wilson
From: Molly Malahan
No. But thanks.
Better?

To: Molly Malahan
From: Adam Wilson
I guess . . .
But I would definitely have preferred a yes 😊

To: Adam Wilson
From: Molly Malahan
I'm sorry . . .
Maybe next time?

To: Molly Malahan
From: Adam Wilson
I won't insist, but just know that I won't give up that easily.

Oh my goodness, he was going to make this staying away from him thing so hard to stick to. Or did I even want to? I was about to reply when he sent another email.

To: MOLLY MALAHAN
FROM: ADAM WILSON
By the way, do you forgive me for Mauritius and the article?

To: ADAM WILSON
FROM: MOLLY MALAHAN
Yes.

To: MOLLY MALAHAN
FROM: ADAM WILSON
You do???

To: ADAM WILSON
FROM: MOLLY MALAHAN
Yes. I forgave you almost immediately. I don't bear grudges very well. Besides, I understand why you did it.

To: MOLLY MALAHAN
FROM: ADAM WILSON
Now I'm confused . . .
Why won't you see me then?

To: ADAM WILSON
FROM: MOLLY MALAHAN
It's complicated.

To: MOLLY MALAHAN
FROM: ADAM WILSON
Oh Mol, it's only as complicated as you make it.

To: ADAM WILSON
FROM: MOLLY MALAHAN
I know – but I can't help the way I am and the way I feel.

To: MOLLY MALAHAN
FROM: ADAM WILSON
I know (Note: I am sighing heavily and looking very anguished).

To: ADAM WILSON
FROM: MOLLY MALAHAN
You're an idiot (Note: I am laughing out loud)

To: MOLLY MALAHAN
FROM: ADAM WILSON
So my anguish makes you laugh, huh? Maybe you're not as nice as I thought you were ... (Note: I'm scowling at you big time!)

I giggled, imagining his scowling face as I received yet another email.

To: MOLLY MALAHAN
FROM: ADAM WILSON
How's your mum, by the way?

To: ADAM WILSON
FROM: MOLLY MALAHAN
She's been a bit on edge since I got back. I think me being away took a lot out of her. I just wish she'd let me take her to the doctor.

To: MOLLY MALAHAN
FROM: ADAM WILSON
If she won't go to the doctor, we'll just have to make the doctor come to her, won't we?

How would we do that? Was it even possible? I wondered and replied.

To: Adam Wilson
From: Molly Malahan
Wish it were that easy.

To: Molly Malahan
From: Adam Wilson
I'm working on it . . .
Bye Mol – see you soon 😊

What did he mean by that? How could he do anything about it? I didn't have time to dwell on it further as I heard a knock on my door announcing the arrival of my afternoon photo shoot.

I dropped off to see my mum on my way home from work. She was back to her usual negative self. She was worried she had something wrong with her because she'd had a headache since this morning. I asked her if she'd taken some Panadol or Nurofen and of course, she hadn't. It was so frustrating because she refused to do anything to try to make things better. It's like she enjoyed being a martyr. I went to get her some and made sure she swallowed them in front of me before leaving.

I was happy to see Zach's smiling face greet me when I got home. He had been cooking and our apartment smelled of garlic and herbs. My stomach rumbled at the smell.

"I cooked spaghetti bolognaise – easy for me, and delicious for you!" he said with a grin, as he handed me a glass of white wine. In a way we were like an old married couple when he was around, and he took good care of me. Unfortunately, he was never back for long. We sat and ate, and I told him about Adam's emails.

"I like this guy." He laughed. "He's funny, and I love the fact that he seems to get you. So, you told him about your mum?" he added, clearly surprised.

I nodded and told him what had happened.

He twirled his wine glass in his hand as he listened intently. When I stopped talking, he stayed silent for a moment before putting his glass down and looking at me. "You do realise this guy's special, don't you?"

"I know . . . but it scares the crap out of me. When I was in Mauritius, it was like we were in a bubble. Real life seemed miles away so I let myself get swept up in Adam. But now that I'm back here with Mum, I don't know if I want to take the risk of letting myself fall in love with him in case it back-fires and I get hurt."

"Don't run away from him," he said softly, reaching over to squeeze my hand.

I shook my head desolately. "I have to, don't you see? I won't be able to cope if he lets me down. I'm finding it harder and harder to cope with my mum as her panic attacks are becoming more frequent. It's so hard. I know I'm a happy person because that's how I've chosen to be, but sometimes, when I'm alone in bed at night and I think of my mum and the huge responsibility that I have on my shoulders, I start hyperventilating and almost have my own panic attack."

"Oh Mol, why didn't you tell me it was getting this bad?" he said, his eyes full of sympathy. "You can come and wake me up when that happens, you know? I'm always here for you."

"Thank you. I know you are, but you aren't often around." I smiled.

He leaned over the table and gave me a hug. I loved him like the brother I'd never had. Zach and I spent the evening looking at his amazing photographs of Peru, as we hadn't had time to do so before he'd left for Bali. He was so talented, and his shots blew me away. I showed him the photos I had taken of Mauritius, and he loved the colours and contrasts of the place. He laughed at my photo of grumpy Adam and me, and asked me about Lucy and Matt and Samantha. We ended up drinking way too much wine for a week night and getting to bed after midnight.

When my alarm went off the next morning, I slammed my hand over it to shut it up.

"*Nooooo,*" I groaned, hiding my head under my pillow. I just didn't have the energy to get up. I finally managed to get myself dressed and to work, but my eyes were still heavy with sleep. Our office was in Applecross, so only a few minutes' drive from our house in Brentwood. After saying hi to Anna, I went to my office and turned on my computer, hoping to see a message from Adam.

It had been so great emailing him yesterday. My heart sank when I saw that he hadn't written. I sighed and got to work. I had quite a few quotes to prepare for various upcoming events and was glad to be busy. Half an hour later I already felt exhausted and went to the kitchen to grab a cup of coffee, hoping to see Anna so we could have a chat. But the kitchen was empty and everyone seemed hard at work. I walked back to my office and sat down, sipping my coffee, savouring the taste. Why hadn't he written today?

ADAM

I'd waited ten days before giving in. I'd written to her at least three times a day, sometimes telling her how much I missed her and cared for her and other times just telling her about something funny that had happened during the day, but I'd ended up pressing delete every time because I knew that that was what she wanted and expected me to do. Poor John had had to bear with me and listen to me rant about missing her and what an idiot I'd been.

Then yesterday I hadn't been able to stop myself. I'd been too desperate to hear from her. I couldn't believe it when she'd replied straight away and seemed happy to hear from me. I felt like a love-struck teenager again. I'd finally decided to go for it and see how it went. I desperately hoped that she would agree to see me soon.

I had to finalise my article today, and I wanted her to see it before it was sent to print because I didn't want there to be anything in it that she was unhappy with. I'd made sure not to put her name in it and not to mention her mum directly, although I included the fact that her father had passed away and that her mother wasn't well because it only made her cheerfulness all the more amazing – and I wanted the world to know how wonderful she was.

My dad rang me before lunch and told me that he had managed to talk to Harry, who was willing to help as a favour to him. Harry told my dad that I should call him to organise a meeting with Molly and her mum. He thought that it may be a good idea to initially present it as being for both Molly and her mother, with Molly saying that she needed to learn how to cope better with her mum's attacks so that she could be there for her. I thanked him and told him that I would get back to him as soon as possible. I just hoped that Molly's mum would let him help her so that Molly could finally be relieved of that huge burden.

A few hours later, I'd finally finished my article and was quite happy with the result. I walked to Luke's office and knocked on his door.

"Come in!" he called out.

I walked in, waving my article in the air. "It's done," I said, handing it to him. He took it from my outstretched hand and motioned for me to have a seat, his eyes already scanning it. I twirled my pen in my hand as I waited nervously for him to finish reading it. I wasn't sure that the angle of my article was exactly what they'd had in mind when they'd given me the assignment, so I was apprehensive of his reaction. Finally, after what seemed like hours but was probably only a minute or two, he looked up and I was reassured to see him smiling widely at me.

"Well, well, well . . . looks like I was right. This is great work, Adam. Not exactly what I'd been expecting, but excellent nevertheless," he said, shaking the sheet of paper in his hand.

I let out a breath I hadn't realised I'd been holding in and smiled. "Thanks. Glad you like it."

"We'll need the final version for print tomorrow afternoon so make sure you have finished it by then," he said with a nod. I nodded back and turned to leave. "Oh, and Adam," he called out as I reached the doorway. "I'll let you know as soon as I have more information about that promotion."

"Thank you, Luke, that would be great," I answered, trying to hide my excitement. So he hadn't forgotten. The promotion was still on the cards. I couldn't believe that I may have the chance of covering international sports events one day.

I walked back to my office and fell on my chair, sighing contentedly. Things were finally looking up. I had finished the article, and now I just had to find a way to get Molly back.

MOLLY

OMG! An email from Adam. Finally! It felt like I had been waiting for years instead of just a few hours. Bursting with happiness, I clicked on the mail.

To: MOLLY MALAHAN
FROM: ADAM WILSON
I dreamt of you all night . . . what a cruel wakeup call it was when I realised you weren't by my side this morning.
Can I take you out?

Oh. Okay. Wow. He wasn't wasting any time, was he? I was both ecstatic and in a total panic. Did I really want to do this? Was I ready to see Adam again?

I picked up my phone and dialled Anna's extension.

"He wants to see me!" I exclaimed as soon as she picked up the phone.

"Well hello to you too," she said, clearly amused. "I'm guessing we're talking about Adam here?"

I sighed in annoyance. "Yes, of course. So what should I do?"

"You should definitely see him."

"Anna!" I wailed.

"You asked me and I told you. If you don't want to hear my answer, then don't ask me."

"What if it all goes horribly wrong?" I asked, biting my lower lip, thinking of all the ways it could go wrong and I could get hurt.

"It won't. But if it does, Zach and I will comfort you and help you through it."

"ARRGH! Not helping!"

"Molly you need to see him again – you've been miserable since you got back. You have to take a chance and see where this goes," she said gently.

I finally knew what I was going to do. She was right. I was miserable without him, and I really wanted to see him again. I would give this thing a chance, but I was going to make sure we took it real slow. I wanted to be sure that there was really something between us and that we hadn't just been caught up in a holiday romance.

I hit reply.

To: Adam Wilson
From: Molly Malahan
Okay. But we can't just pick up where we left off. We have to start over.

I pressed send and waited for his reply, which came almost instantly.

To: Molly Malahan
From: Adam Wilson
Sure! So where exactly would you like to start?

Where did I want to start? If I was really honest, I wanted to start off where we had left off just before I found the notes on his article. In his arms, kissing him . . . I sighed and typed.

To: Adam Wilson
From: Molly Malahan
At the beginning.

I wondered how he would react to that. I didn't have to wait long to find out.

To: Molly Malahan
From: Adam Wilson
What? So you want me to do the whole Mr McGrumpy thing again?!

I burst out laughing.

To: Adam Wilson
From: Molly Malahan
Ha-ha, very funny! No, I just meant starting at the beginning as if it were a new relationship. Getting to know each other, going on dates etc.

My heart raced at the thought of being alone with him again.

To: Molly Malahan
From: Adam Wilson

Sounds perfect. How about I take you out to dinner at Il Ciao's tonight? Is that okay for a first date?

My eyes widened as my heart began to race.

To: Adam Wilson
From: Molly Malahan
Tonight? As in today, tonight?

I felt a knot of anxiety in my stomach. I hadn't expected it to be so soon. I thought I would have a few days to psych myself up for it.

To: Molly Malahan
From: Adam Wilson
Breathe Molly. BREATHE and relax – it's just me. Besides, there's something I really need to talk to you about...

Curiosity got the better of my anxiety as I wondered what he was talking about.

To: Adam Wilson
From: Molly Malahan
Now I'm really intrigued. If you were a girl I'd think that you were going to tell me that you're pregnant or something, but as that's not an option . . .

I wondered what he could possibly have to tell me and quickly clicked on open as his answer pinged into my inbox.

To: Molly Malahan
From: Adam Wilson
No, that's definitely not an option 😊 It's nothing bad, don't

worry. It's about helping your mum. I may have found a way and I want to run it by you.

He'd found a way to help my mum? What did he mean by that? I hastily typed a reply.

To: Adam Wilson
From: Molly Malahan
You have?

I couldn't imagine what he'd done but I was desperate to find out.

To: Molly Malahan
From: Adam Wilson
Yes, we'll talk about it later, okay? I'll pick you up at seven thirty. Just send me your address.

Oh well, it obviously wasn't something he wanted to say by email and I understood. Wait! What? Pick me up? No way. He couldn't come to my house; it would just be too awkward. No. I had to meet him there.

To: Adam Wilson
From: Molly Malahan
No. I'll meet you there. Seven forty-five at Il Ciao's?

My heart was racing again just imagining myself arriving at Il Ciao and looking for him in the restaurant, walking up to him, saying hi . . .

To: Molly Malahan
From: Adam Wilson
Seven forty-five at Il Ciao it is. Ciao Ciao 😊

My heart thumped as it sunk in. I was going to see him tonight! The coward in me wanted to find an excuse not to turn up so that I could hide from Adam for a little longer, but the other part of me was dying to see him and lose myself in those silver-blue eyes of his.

I had butterflies in my stomach as I dialled Anna's extension again.

"I'm going out to dinner with him *tonight!*" I screeched.

"You do know that you're supposed to greet the person you call before screaming down the phone at them, don't you?"

"I talked to you ten minutes ago! Surely, I don't have to say hi again, do I?"

"Well come to think of it, you didn't say hi when you called ten minutes ago either!"

"Anna! Please focus. This is really important!"

She laughed. "It's really great, Molly. I'm so glad for you."

We talked for a few more minutes before I hung up. I felt both elated and very nervous at the thought of seeing him again.

I tried on ten different outfits before settling on a pair of dark purple jeans with a white, violet and pink striped fitted top, a long necklace made of purple, pink and white beads and a pair of long purple feather earrings the same colour as my jeans. I put my hair up into a ponytail, then tried a loose bun followed by a braid, before ending up just leaving it down.

"Okay, here goes . . ." I murmured with a sigh, heading out towards my car. My legs felt like jelly, my palms were sweaty and my heart was beating abnormally fast. *Breathe, Molly, just breathe*! I told myself. I couldn't help wondering whether it would be awkward between us or if we would just fall back into our usual friendly banter. Five minutes later, I had already reached the restaurant and slowly made my way towards the entrance. I glanced at my watch and saw that it was seven fifty, making me just a little late. I pushed open the door and looked around nervously to see if Adam had arrived, but I couldn't see him anywhere. I was just about to head back outside to wait for him when I jumped in surprise as I felt delicious frissons spreading through my body as his breath caressed my neck . . .

ADAM

"*H*ey sweetness," I whispered in her ear, my heart racing just from being so close to her and smelling that wonderful Molly scent again.

Clearly startled, she jumped then swirled around, her eyes wide. As her gaze locked with mine, her face broke into an ear-splitting grin. Before I could stop myself, I enveloped her in a big hug. It was just so good to see her again. To my surprise and delight she hugged me back and I could swear she was smelling me again, not that I hadn't done exactly the same thing as I held her.

I grinned into her hair. "You're smelling me again, aren't you?"

She pulled away and laughed. "Still as cocky as ever, aren't you?"

I chuckled, grabbing her hand and guiding her into the restaurant. "Let's find a table, I'm starving."

I saw a table in a quiet corner and we sat down opposite

each other. I ordered a beer for me and a glass of Merlot for her and we began chatting easily. I needn't have worried because we just picked up from where we'd left off without any awkwardness, and she didn't seem to hold a grudge against me for the article episode. Speaking of the article . . . I opened the flap of my black leather jacket and pulled out the brown envelope I'd brought for her.

"I've got something for you," I said, holding the envelope out to her. "But you can't read it now. Read it when you get home and tell me what you think, okay?"

She looked at the envelope and back at me, her brows furrowed.

"It's my article."

"Oh." She was clearly surprised as I handed it to her. "Thanks."

"Read it first, then see if you still want to thank me," I said with mock severity.

Her head jerked up and she gaped at me, making me bark with laughter. "I'm only joking, Molly!"

She reached over and slapped me playfully on the arm, grinning. "You jerk!"

"But seriously, if there's anything in the article that makes you uncomfortable or that you want me to remove, tell me at latest midday tomorrow, and I'll do it before it goes to print, alright? Anything at all."

She nodded, looking touched, then twisted to the side to put the envelope into her bag. When she turned back, she looked me square in the eye. "Can you tell me about my mum now, please?"

So I did. She thought it was a wonderful idea and said there was no way she would refuse Harry's help. She promised she would make sure her mum at least tried to work with him.

"She will have to let Harry in, and once he's there, I'm

sure he will be able to get her to talk one way or another, and let's hope she'll listen to him. She just has to . . ." she said, looking down and rolling her glass in her hand as a tear rolled down her cheek.

"Oh Mol, please don't cry," I pleaded as I leaned over the table and gently wiped it away with my thumb.

"They're happy tears," she said, smiling through her tears. "Just imagining that maybe, just maybe, my mum might get better makes me so happy."

We chatted on, trying to settle on a day to start. I suggested that I bring Harry to her house and then she could take over from there and introduce him to her mum.

She sighed heavily, taking a sip of her wine. "I just hope this works."

"It will," I answered with conviction. It had to.

After that, our food arrived, and we ate in comfortable silence for a while. She then asked me about my sisters and what I'd been up to since we got back. Before I knew it, it was eleven o'clock and time to go. My heart plummeted at the thought of leaving her already. I knew I couldn't ask her over to my parents' place as it would freak her out. She'd asked to start at the beginning, so this couldn't go anywhere else tonight. I walked her to her car and we stood awkwardly facing each other. Finally, I leaned in and kissed her tenderly on the cheek. "It was so good to see you."

She nodded shyly and smiled. "You too."

"So, can we do this again sometime?" I asked, as she was getting into her car. "I want us to start over too so I can prove to you that I'm a good guy and that you can trust me. We'll take it slow – I promise."

She looked up with a smile and nodded. "I'd love to."

"Fantastic! So how does eight o'clock tomorrow morning sound? We could have breakfast!"

MOLLY

I burst out laughing as he looked at me with laughing severity. "What? Don't laugh, I'm serious."

I put the key in the ignition and grinned. "*That's* taking things slow?"

He shrugged sheepishly. "So, what do you say?"

I grimaced and shook my head. "Nope, sorry, but I don't really do mornings."

"What does that even mean? How can anyone not *do* mornings?" he exclaimed, throwing his hands in the air. "Sorry, lady, but just for your abysmal use of the English language, I think you now *owe* me breakfast tomorrow morning!"

I rolled my eyes. "Oh, *alright* then."

"Yes!" he cried out, pumping his fist in the air, making me laugh again.

"But where on earth can we go around here at eight o'clock in the morning? I have to be at work at eight thirty."

He was lost in thought for a moment before finally looking at me with a satisfied smirk. "I know! Let's meet at a quarter to eight at McDonald's on Leach Highway and then we can go straight to work from there."

I swallowed down my laughter and looked at him with exaggerated wide-eyed astonishment. "How did you know?"

He looked puzzled. "Know what?"

"That I've always *dreamt* of having breakfast at McDonald's!"

"Yeah, yeah, make fun of me all you want but it just so happens that their McCafé is actually pretty good," he said with a grin. "Besides, weren't you the one who thought airplane food was amazing?" he added, cocking an eyebrow at me.

"Fine, so I'm easy to please." I shrugged good-naturedly.

"Perfect. So I guess I'll see you at seven forty-five tomorrow morning, Molly Sunshine!"

I smiled and reversed out of the parking space, waving over my shoulder as I took off. I stole a glance in my rear-view mirror and saw that he hadn't moved. He stood where I had left him, hands in his jacket pockets, and watched me leave. Oh my, he looked so sexy in snug faded jeans and a white shirt which hung loose under his black leather jacket. I had forgotten how beautiful his eyes were and what that lopsided smile of his did to my insides, not to forget the way his eyes crinkled up at the sides when he laughed . . . I couldn't not give this a second chance, no matter what happened in the end. But we had to take things slowly. I needed to be sure that I could truly trust him before we even thought of getting intimate again.

59

ADAM

*I*t was already eight fifteen and there was no sign of Molly. I tried her mobile but kept getting her voicemail. At eight thirty I admitted defeat and knew that she wasn't coming. Not one to dramatise, I deduced that she'd probably overslept. Oh well, this is definitely new, I thought, grinning. I'd never been stood up before.

As soon as I got to work, I powered up my computer, hoping that she would have sent me an email to explain or apologise, but nothing. I tried her phone again but got her voicemail once more. This time I left her a message asking her to call me. I tried her office but was told that she hadn't come into work yet. Looks like she'd definitely overslept. Oh well, we'd just have to make up for it tonight, I decided. I didn't have time to ponder over it for long as Luke called me into our weekly planning meeting.

An hour later, I made my way back to my office and checked my mail and phone again. It seemed strange that she hadn't excused herself by now, so I dialled her number again.

To my surprise, I heard Molly's sleepy voice answer.

"Oh! Hey, you," I said smiling into the phone. "Are you still in bed?" I added incredulously.

"Adam?" she said, sounding confused, before suddenly exclaiming, "Oh my God! What time is it?"

I glanced at my watch. "Ten o'clock. Molly, is everything okay?" I added, sensing that something wasn't quite right.

"Oh, Adam, I'm so sorry. I missed our breakfast," she said tiredly. "I've only just woken up. I didn't hear my alarm this morning. I had a rough night . . ."

"Hey, it's okay, just tell me what happened."

She sighed into the phone, but said nothing.

"Mol?" I insisted gently.

Then I heard her sniffing quietly. She was crying! Damn it! What had happened to her again? I had to go to her. I bounced off my chair, grabbed my car keys and jacket and walked out of the office.

"I'm coming over."

"Adam, wait! Don't worry about it, I'll be fine," she said, her voice breaking.

"I'll see you in fifteen minutes!" I said and hung up.

I knew Molly's address as I'd managed to get it from Nicole. She never seemed very interested in the details and gave out any information I asked quite freely. It came in very handy.

Fifteen minutes later, Suzy, my friendly GPS, announced that we'd arrived. I pressed the doorbell and Molly opened the door looking half asleep, but very sexy, in a pair of shorty pyjamas with a tight-fitting tank top, her hair pulled up into a messy bun.

"Hi," she said softly, looking at me with a small smile, her eyes still red and puffy from crying.

"Hey, you," I replied, giving her a peck on the cheek before pulling her into a hug. She didn't push me away as I'd expected her to, but instead just relaxed into my arms. After a moment, I pulled away slightly and looked at her drawn features. "Do you want to talk about it?"

She nodded. "But let's go in first."

I followed her in, closing the door behind me. She walked to the couch without saying a word and threw herself on it, sighing heavily.

"Thank you for coming," she said with a tired smile as I sat down next to her.

I took her hand and gave it a little squeeze. "I'm glad to be here."

She smiled gratefully then leaned her head back against the sofa and closed her eyes.

"Talk to me, Mol."

She rolled her head in my direction, lost in her thoughts for a moment, and then took a deep breath and began talking. She explained that her mum had called her at a quarter to twelve the previous night in a terrible state, and Molly had driven straight over to her house.

"It was awful," Molly said, her voice shaking. "She kept telling me that she was dying, that she couldn't breathe and it honestly sounded like she couldn't. It was really bad. I was so scared. Then she began saying that she wanted to end it all so that she wouldn't feel like this anymore, and I couldn't get her to calm down. Nothing I tried worked. I had no idea what to do . . ."

Tears poured down her face and she began sobbing. I pulled her into my arms and comforted her as best I could as she cried. After a few minutes, she removed herself from my embrace and leaned back against the sofa once again, her eyes looking into the distance.

"Finally, at about two o'clock in the morning, she was a

bit better but didn't want me to leave, so I stayed with her. She grudgingly agreed to take some sleeping pills and ended up drifting off to sleep at about four o'clock this morning."

"This has got to stop. I'm going to call Harry right now and see if he can come over this afternoon," I said, leaping off the sofa.

Molly looked at me, eyes full of apprehension. "I-I don't know if it's ideal today because she's always a bit fragile after a bad attack."

"It doesn't matter, and it might be better this way as at least he'll be able to see how she is on less good days," I said firmly, deciding that enough was enough. It was time to react.

Although somewhat reluctant, Molly finally agreed to let me call him and we arranged to meet at Molly's house at five thirty. When I was reassured that Molly was alright, I headed back to work. I realised that I'd completely forgotten to ask her if she'd read my article . . .

MOLLY

J called Anna and asked her if I could work from
home. I was totally drained, both emotionally and
physically. I told her briefly what had happened, and she said
she'd come over later in the evening to have a chat. I lay on
my bed and took Adam's envelope out of my bag. I still
hadn't read it. For some reason, I didn't have the courage to. I
knew without a doubt that it would be wonderfully well
written and that there would be nothing in it that would hurt
me. I knew Adam enough by now to be sure of that. But then
again, I was still worried about what he had written in there .
. . I just didn't want to stir up the disappointment I'd felt
when I'd found out that he'd "used" me, so to speak, to write
an article. I may have forgiven him, but I just didn't feel like
rehashing the subterfuge of Mauritius. I guess I felt stupid
for not having realised that he'd been playing me along at the
beginning. So, for now, I preferred not to read it – one day I
would, but not right now.

After last night, I wasn't sure it was a very good idea for me to get involved with Adam after all. It was too risky. He had too much power over me already, and I just couldn't let myself grow even more attached to him. I needed to stay strong for my mum because I was all she had, and I couldn't risk anything disturbing the balance I had so carefully worked on finding in my life. I was happy. I had friends, a job I loved and a home I loved. I had a lot to be grateful for, and I needed to keep focusing on that. I knew that Adam could rock my world completely if I let him. In fact, he already had. But I couldn't get in deeper than I already was. Not yet. Not until my mum was better. I didn't know how I would explain this to Adam. I might not say anything – after all, I'd already told him that I wanted to take it slow, so maybe we could do that. After dinner last night I'd pretty much decided to forget about the "taking it slow" part because it had felt so right to be with him – but now I didn't think it was such a great idea after all. Maybe we could just be friends for now?

At five thirty, Adam and Harry, or rather Dr Edwards, arrived. He was younger than I'd expected, probably in his late forties, tall with blond hair cut short in a crew cut and large friendly hazel eyes. I invited them in and we discussed my mother over coffee. Dr Edwards asked me questions about her and her illness, listening intently to my answers. He had a gentle and friendly manner that made me feel at ease, and I liked and trusted him immediately. After about half an hour, he suggested we go over to see her. I wasn't sure how she would react as I hadn't talked to her about it, but he seemed to think it was better this way. It felt wonderful to have someone else decide for me for once, so I agreed. Adam left us, telling me to call him later to let me know how it'd gone. I nodded, waving him off before getting into the car with Dr Edwards.

To say that my mum was surprised to see me standing at

her door with a man, one who was about her age, was an understatement. She looked from me to Dr Edwards and back a few times, mouth agape and clearly at a loss for words.

"Hi, Mum," I said with a smile. "I'd like you to meet Dr Edwards, my psychologist."

"Your what? Your psychologist? Honey, I had no idea that you were seeing one again," she said, sounding anxious, her eyes darting from me to him once more.

"Can we come in?" I asked, trying to sound as normal as I could. I was worried about how she would react to Dr Edwards. I really needed this to work out. She suddenly remembered her manners and greeted Dr Edwards, ushering us both into the lounge.

"Molly, I'm not really sure I understand what you and Dr Edwards are doing here," she said, frowning and glancing at Dr Edwards from the corner of her eyes.

"Dr Edwards has been helping me to learn how to cope with your panic attacks so that I know what to do when they occur. But last night really scared me, Mum . . . I can't do this anymore. I can't be solely responsible for you. I'm only twenty-five years old and I have no idea what I'm doing. I'm petrified half the time that I'm doing it wrong or that you won't listen to me and that you'll end up doing something to yourself. It's getting to be too much for me to handle alone . . ." I explained softly, my voice breaking.

"I'm so sorry, love," she said, with tears in her eyes. "I wish you didn't have to go through all that, but I'm sick, you know that."

"I do, and I don't blame you for any of it. It's just that you need to help me help you. By that, I mean that you have got to at least *try* to get better. Dr Edwards kindly offered to carry out our session here at your house, and I thought it was a great idea since you're scared of going out. What do you think?"

"But what will I have to do?"

"Nothing much, just listen and talk when needed. Dr Edwards will teach me relaxation methods that I can pass on to you, and you'll be able to hear them and maybe try them out too. I want you with me so that we can work through it together. Will you at least give it a go for me, Mum?"

She looked hesitant and anxious, not seeming to understand what would be expected of her. I held my breath because if she refused, there was nothing I would be able to do to change her mind. I knew that much. Finally, she took a deep breath and sighed loudly, before nodding. "Okay, I'll do it. It's the least I can do for you after everything I've put you through."

Dr Edwards and I exchanged relieved glances and he suggested we get to work. I was the guinea pig this time, and so he worked with me on methods of relaxation, encouraging my mum to help me out and do it with me. She wasn't too keen but went along anyway. After half an hour, Dr Edwards ended the session, and I could tell that my mum was both intrigued and scared by his presence. I accompanied him back to his car and thanked him. He told me that he would come back in three days and asked me if I would agree to go with my mother to an anxiety disorder support group he held at his practice once a week. He thought it would be a great way for Mum to realise that she wasn't alone and that life did go on. He said that it would also help me to know that I am not alone either. I told him that I would do anything to help my mum and that of course I would go with her. The plan was that eventually she would be able to do all this by herself.

I felt a heavy load lift off my shoulder. I couldn't believe that someone was finally here to help us. Adam was a miracle worker, and I quickly sent him a message to thank him. I was so grateful to him. I had no idea if my mum would react positively and agree to work with Dr Edwards, but at least it gave me hope that maybe, just maybe, she would get a bit better.

61

ADAM

*M*olly had been pretty taken up with Harry and her mum over the past month. Things were moving along nicely and Grace, her mum, was reacting really positively to Harry's treatment. The support groups had also helped her to make new friends and feel less alone with her troubles. It would take time, but he seemed confident that Grace would be able to start leading a semi-normal life again and learn to cope with her anxiety attacks herself when they did occur. She now had to understand that life could go on, even if she was prone to having panic attacks. She had also finally agreed to take some medication to help calm her anxieties and that too would improve her state no end.

As for Molly and me, things hadn't really progressed much since our dinner at Il Ciao's. The incident with Grace that night had scared Molly, and she had shut down on me since. I knew that it was because she was afraid of getting hurt and then not being strong enough to help her mum if needed, but I was getting really frustrated. I kept reminding myself that Grace was getting better and soon Molly would be able to live her life freely, but until then I had to make do with emails, phone calls and dinner or a drink once or twice a week – as friends, of course, except for the odd cuddle or hug or kiss on the cheek from me. I was too crazy about her to give her an ultimatum at the moment, but I honestly wasn't sure how long I could carry on like this without going mad. I craved to hold her, feel her soft skin against mine, and kiss her delectable body from head to toe… One day, I convinced myself, one day it would happen. Despite every-thing, I loved being with her and she made me happy. So if friendship was all I could get, I would take it – for now.

As the weather was amazing, I called Molly to see if she wanted to go down to Cottesloe Beach with me for a sundowner and some fish and chips. She said she'd come, but with Zach and Anna. It didn't surprise me as this happened a lot. She didn't seem to want to be alone with me and always found a way to bring Zach or Anna with her. I didn't mind, though, as I liked them both a lot and we had a good laugh together. Once, when neither of them had been free, she'd convinced me to bring John along, using the excuse that he was my best friend and so it was really important that she got to know him.

When we arrived at Cottlesloe, there were people every-where – some swimming and surfing, others just lazing on the beach chatting, or others, like us, who had come to watch the sunset. We found a spot on the grass not far from the beach and laid out the rugs. The girls settled down, opening the cooler bags and getting themselves a drink as Zach and I headed off to the fish and chip shop across the road. We placed our order, grabbed a beer and sat at a table outside, waiting for our order to be ready. We were discussing Arse-nal's victory against Manchester United when I looked up and thought that I was seeing a mirage. Were my sisters really walking towards us? What were they doing here? I blinked a few times and looked again. Yep, still there – and they'd seen me. They began waving wildly and I grinned at them affectionately and waved as Zach leaned forward to see who I was waving to.

"*WOW*," he whispered in awe. I grinned; I kept forgetting how beautiful they were with their long legs, gorgeous silky brown hair that fell down their backs and their silver-blue eyes – a family trait. Although they looked quite alike, Emma was taller than the other two, Jo's hair a little lighter and wavier than the others and it was easy to see that Lily was much younger, but at a glance, they sure made a gorgeous trio. I got up to greet them.

"Hey, Adam!" they chimed.

"Hey, girls!" I said, hugging each of them in turn. I was about to ask them what they were doing here when I noticed that the three of them had lost all interest in me and were now standing gawking at Zach behind me.

"Wow! He's *hot*!" Jo blurted out loudly, nudging Emma, who was by her side.

"Look at those biceps . . ." Emma sighed wistfully, her eyes not leaving Zach's body.

"And his eyes! They look just like Liam Hemsworth's," Lily exclaimed, looping her arms with Emma and Jo's as she continued studying Zach.

"Do you think he's got a girlfriend?" Emma asked, looking from one sister to the other then back at Zach. My mouth twitched as I took in Zach's dumbstruck expression. I wanted to see how far they would go, and how long it would take for Zach to react, so I remained quiet and tried to keep a straight face.

"Looking like that, he's got to have one!" Jo replied with a pout.

Zach cleared his throat loudly and fake-coughed, seeming to have finally snapped out of his shocked trance. "I'm sitting right here girls, and can actually hear you," he said, waving a hand towards himself.

I chuckled, hiding my mouth behind my hand. He didn't know my sisters!

"Oh that's okay, we've got nothing to hide," Emma said, grinning mischievously at him before turning to me. "Adam, you haven't introduced us."

I rolled my eyes at them. "As if you actually gave me the opportunity! Lily, Emma and Jo, this is Zach. Zach these are my crazy *sisters* – Lily, Emma and Jo."

Zach's eyes popped out as his head swung towards me and he raised his eyebrows questioningly. I nodded with a grin. His face broke into a huge smile but before he could say anything, Lily turned to him, hands on hips.

"So, which one of us are you going to ask out?" She clearly had no intention of dropping the subject.

"Jo doesn't count because she's already got a boyfriend," Emma cut in, pointing to Jo.

"Well, it's not like it's serious or anything," Jo replied with a shrug.

"JO!" Emma and Lily cried in unison, looking at her in shock, making me chuckle again.

"What? I've got to keep my options open, I'm still young," Jo cried out in her defence.

Emma and Lily shook their heads incredulously and turned back to Zach, who was now having a hard time stifling his laughter.

"Lily, may I remind you that you are fifteen years old?" I cut in, trying to sound stern but failing dismally.

"No, you may not. And besides, I like older guys," she said, sticking her chin up defiantly.

I caught Zach's gaze and we threw our heads back and

laughed. The three girls looked from Zach to me and back, eyes narrowed, clearly not impressed.

It was Emma's turn to put her hands on her hips. "So?" she asked, raising her eyebrows at Zach. "Who's it gonna be? Surely you find one of us hotter!"

Just then our number was called, and Zach jumped up with relief.

"Saved by the food." I grinned as Zach nodded and raced inside.

I turned to my sisters and scowled. "Okay, that's enough now! You are embarrassing. Hasn't anyone ever told you that it's not becoming to throw yourself at guys like that? Have you no shame?"

They looked at me and rolled their eyes.

"You're so boring!" Emma grumbled.

"And who even says 'it's not becoming' anymore?" Lily exclaimed, pulling a face.

"Okay, let's go, girls," Jo said good-naturedly as she placed an affectionate peck on my cheek. "We're not wanted here."

I laughed and pulled the three of them into a group hug before sending them on their way just as Zach walked back out.

"By-ye Zaaach," the three trilled over their shoulders, waving. He laughed, waving back, before turning back to me, shaking his head.

I chuckled. "I know, mate – crazy, right?"

Zach laughed and nodded. "Sure are. Bloody beautiful, though."

I nodded and grinned, taking some of the food from him before we made our way back to the girls. Zach told them about his encounter with my sisters and both girls were in stitches. Molly seemed disappointed not to have met them, but Zach assured her that she'd had a lucky escape.

We chatted away as we ate, watching the sunset, drinking

wine and beer. I couldn't help stealing glances at Molly – she was just so gorgeous, and her smile beguiled me. Our eyes locked a few times and she smiled warmly, but she never made a move towards me or tried to get closer to me. I had no idea what was going on in that beautiful head of hers.

"Okay, toilet break," Molly exclaimed, breaking me out of my reverie as she bounced up, holding out her hand to pull Anna up. Girls just didn't seem to be able to go to the toilet by themselves. It was always a two at a time thing. I took a sip of my beer and tried to stop myself from staring at them – well, okay, at Molly – as they walked off, but my eyes were drawn to her like magnets.

Zach, who had obviously been watching me watching her, chuckled.

"Oh wow! You've got it bad, buddy!"

"That obvious, huh?" I sighed.

"So when are you going to do something about it?"

"What do you suggest I do exactly? Kidnap her, tear all her clothes off and kiss her senseless?"

"Well . . . yeah. I guess that could work." He shrugged, amused.

"I have no idea what to do! She knows I'm crazy about her, but she wants to take things slow, which basically means - stay friends for now."

"It's obvious that she's also crazy about you, though," he said, glancing at me as he reached out and took a chip.

"She sure has a strange way of showing it," I muttered despondently.

"She's terrified of getting hurt, that's all," Zach said with a half-shrug as he munched on a chip.

"Well, aren't we all?" I snapped in frustration, before downing the last of my beer.

"I know. But she thinks she's more fragile than us because of her parents. But honestly, she's one of the strongest people

I know," he said, taking a swallow of his beer. "I guess she's built a wall around her heart to protect herself, and she won't let it down."

"I know! All I want is to be there for her, protect her and love her, but she won't let me!"

"Well, why don't you tease her a little and pretend to be interested in someone else," Zach suggested, grinning wickedly.

I gazed at him in astonishment. "Aren't you supposed to be her best friend?"

"Desperate times call for desperate measures," he answered with a cheeky shrug. "Besides, it's for her own good. I don't want her to mess this up and regret it when it's too late."

"I'll think about it, but I don't know if I could do that to her."

"Just think of it as helping her come to her senses," Zach said with a wink as the girls headed back towards us.

I'd just laughed at something Molly said when I noticed that we were being watched. There were three little girls standing a little further away, staring at me and whispering to each other. Following my gaze, Molly saw the girls and nudged me, grinning widely. "Fan club?"

I pulled a face, making her laugh as the girls approached us. The oldest looked not a day over twelve years old, and the youngest looked as young as five. I couldn't help smiling warmly at them as they came up to me.

"Excuse me," the eldest said shyly. "Can we have your autograph, Ian?"

"Say *please*!" the middle one hissed loudly, making me chuckle.

"Hey there, girls," I said, smiling widely. They were

adorable. "I'm really sorry, but I'm not actually Ian Somer-halder, you know."

"Yes you are!" the three girls chimed.

I laughed and shook my head. "I'm sorry, but I'm really not."

"I don't believe you," I heard a little voice say as I gazed down into the eyes of the youngest little girl, who was observing me suspiciously.

"I promise. Scout's honour," I said gravely, doing the scout's salute.

"I'm not a scout so I don't know what that means," she said, unimpressed.

"Oh, okay. Well, you'll just have to take my word for it then," I said, winking at her.

She narrowed her little eyes at me, pouting. Molly, Zach and Anna had been following the exchange and burst out laughing. Molly, obviously taking pity on me, turned towards the girl and said kindly, "It's true, you know. He looks a lot like Ian but it's not him. If you look closely, you'll see he's actually much uglier."

I nudged her hard, laughing good-naturedly. The little girl looked from Molly to me and back again, then put her hands on her hips and stared me down defiantly, "Can I see your ID?"

"My what?" I replied incredulously.

"Your ID. I want to see it," she repeated, looking pretty scary. I chuckled, getting my wallet out of my back pocket and pulling out my ID.

"There you go," I said solemnly, biting down my laughter as I handed her my card.

She grabbed it from me as the other two surrounded her to have a look. Their faces fell as they read my name. I told them how sorry I was and asked them their names: Ella,

Alexa and Sasha and they were twelve, nine and five years old.

Sasha, the five-year-old, wasn't happy. "Now I won't have anything exciting to tell my class in *Show and Tell* on Monday!"

"Hey, you could still say that you met an Ian Somerhalder lookalike. That would be pretty cool too, you know," Molly said, trying to make her feel better.

Sasha perked up and asked Ella, the eldest, for her mobile phone, which she then handed to Molly, instructing her to take a photo of her with me. Molly grinned and winked at me as I put my arm around Sasha's little shoulders and did my best Ian Somerhalder lopsided smile. She was thrilled, and needless to say, Ella and Alexa then also wanted a photo, so I posed with them too. Finally satisfied, they said their goodbyes. I gave them each a big hug and they strolled off, giggling excitedly.

"That was *so-o-o* cute! You were great with them," Molly said with a big smile as they left.

"Cute? Are you crazy! They were really scary," I said, eyes wide in mock horror.

She giggled, her eyes sparkling with mirth. I grinned back and as our eyes met, we had "a moment", as they say in romantic comedies. I don't know what she felt, but for my part it felt like a bolt of lightning spread through my body. It took all the strength I had not to pull her into my arms and kiss her. Things had to change between us or I would go crazy. One thing was certain: I couldn't go on being "just friends" for much longer . . .

62

MOLLY

*I*t had already been almost a week since our sundowner at Cottlesloe and the episode with the three little girls and, of course, "the moment" Adam and I had shared. You know what I mean – when you look into someone's eyes and everything and everyone around you disappears and you feel like you're the only two people on earth, your heart rate accelerates to thirty times the normal rate, your legs feel like jelly, your palms go all sweaty . . . yeah, well that type of "moment", and all I'd wanted to do was jump into his arms and kiss him. But it had only been "a moment" and in a few seconds it had passed and I'd luckily managed to calm myself down and act normal again. Adam and I had pretty much pretended that "the moment" had never happened, but I knew that things were changing between us, or had to change, and I still didn't know if I could allow them to.

But today I had more pressing matters to worry about.

For a few weeks now, Adam had been begging me to come meet his family, and so far I'd managed to find excuses to avoid going. I guess I was worried that it would mean too much to Adam – and even to me – if I met them. However, having run out of excuses, I'd finally given in and tonight was the night. I was so nervous, not because I was worried I wouldn't like them or vice versa, but more because of the situation between me and Adam. I was worried they would ask questions that I wouldn't be able to answer.

I'd just finished getting ready when Adam arrived. I opened the door and my heart skipped a beat at the sight of him, as it always did. He looked freshly washed and shaved and so sexy in a cosy pair of faded denim jeans and a red t-shirt.

"Hey, you," he said, smiling, as he leaned down and kissed me tenderly on the cheek before walking in. I could smell his aftershave, his hair, his skin . . . My breath caught in my throat, but luckily he didn't notice. "You ready?" he asked over his shoulder.

I nodded. "As ready as I'll ever be."

"Oh, come on, it won't be that bad!" he said, turning back towards me with a grin. I pulled a face and made my way towards the side table to grab my bag and keys.

"I'm really nervous," I admitted as I slipped the strap of my bag over my shoulder, pulling at a few strands of hair that had caught beneath it.

"Relax, they'll love you. Just be yourself."

I sighed, knowing they would hate me if they knew how I had been treating Adam.

Seeing that I was ready to go, Adam headed back towards the front door and motioned for me to follow.

"We're not even going out, so what are you stressed about?" he said teasingly as we walked down the path towards the car. "As far as they're concerned, I'm just bringing a friend over for dinner. I didn't even specify that it was a girl."

My mouth fell open, and I stopped dead in my tracks. "You didn't tell them it was me?"

He looked over his shoulder and seeing my expression, stopped too. He turned to face me, shaking his head sheepishly. "To be honest, I couldn't be bothered with the questions it would raise, so I just asked my mum if I could bring a friend to dinner tonight. My dad's the only one I spoke to about you because I had to get his help in contacting Harry, and I have no idea whether he said anything to my mother or not. All I know is that they love me having friends over and were delighted that I was bringing someone for dinner. Mum probably thinks it's John."

Somehow it bothered me that he hadn't told them it was me. *Molly Malahan, you don't deserve to be treated any better,* my annoying little inner voice reminded me, and I knew it was right. I understood how difficult it would be for Adam to answer questions about us, but I wondered if doing it this way wouldn't lead to even more questions.

"Hmmm . . . not sure if it's better or worse, but I guess we'll find out soon enough," I said, taking off again towards the car.

"Trust me. It's better this way. At least they'll have less time to think of questions to bombard you with!"

"Not helping!" I cried out, glaring at him over my shoulder.

"I'm only joking! Well . . . maybe not too much – but you'll be fine," he said with a laugh. "They are really easygoing – except for my sisters, who are rather crazy."

63

ADAM

She giggled in that cute way of hers and as was often the case these days, I wanted to grab her and smother her with kisses. She was beautiful in a pair of pink skinny jeans with a white blouse and a long necklace with pink, purple, white and light pink beads on it. She had long silver dangly earrings and was wearing a touch of black eyeliner which accentuated her gorgeous green eyes. Her long curls fell over her shoulders and down her back in shiny waves. I sucked in my breath at the thought of kissing every single part of her gorgeous body . . . I shook my head, trying to rid myself of thoughts of Molly's body, and pulled my keys out of my back pocket, unlocking the car.

She opened the passenger door, looking over at me. "What's our story then?"

"What do you mean?"

"Well, why am I having dinner with your family all of a sudden?"

"Oh, don't worry about that, I've got it sorted," I replied, sliding into the car. She got in too and looked towards me expectantly. I bit down on my bottom lip, trying to keep a serious face as I put my seatbelt on.

"Well," I finally said, looking at her with a straight face. "I'm going to tell them that we've been having wild sex since Mauritius and that we are now friends with benefits."

She snorted with laughter, giving me a playful punch on my arm. "Don't you dare!"

"Well a man can dream, can't he?" I answered, with a wink. She rolled her eyes and grinned but didn't say anything.

She dropped the subject and asked me about my day instead and we chatted on until I turned into my parents' driveway ten minutes later.

"We're here," I announced with a smile, turning towards her. She was staring at the house like a rabbit caught in a car's headlights. I squeezed her hand, leaning over to give her a soft kiss on the cheek. "You'll be fine. They'll love you."

Jo and Emma's cars were parked outside, so they were here too. It was going to be the whole family then. I hoped that my sisters would be on their best behaviour and wouldn't scare Molly off with their questions and comments. Wouldn't surprise me if they tried to marry us off during dinner! I went to open the car door for Molly and took her hand to help her out, then kept hold of it as I led her to the front door. Suddenly she pulled her hand out of mine and stopped short.

"What's wrong?" I asked, annoyed that she wouldn't even let me hold her hand.

"We can't arrive holding hands! I'm just a friend, remember!"

"*Ohhh*, that's right. Good point, Ms Malahan." I grinned.

"Funny how I keep forgetting that little detail…" I murmured.

She playfully slapped me again, but her eyes were sparkling with amusement as we walked up the steps to the front door.

"Muu-um, we're here!" I called out as we made our way in.

"We're in the lounge, come on in," she called back.

I led the way down the hall towards the lounge. We could hear Jo and Emma arguing about something to do with nails, it seemed. The lounge was a big, cosy room with large, super-comfy sofas full of colourful cushions. The walls were covered in family photos, the shelves piled high with books and more photo frames and the piece de resistance was the large, rustic fireplace in the centre of the room. It was our favourite room, and we'd spent a lot of time hanging out in here when we all still lived at home.

"Hey, Adam!" My sisters chimed as I entered the room, barely looking up from their nails.

"Hi, love," my mum said, smiling up at me. I bent down to give her a kiss on the cheek, and that's when everyone noticed Molly standing behind me.

"Everyone, this is Molly. Molly, this is my mum, Claire, and these are my sisters – Jo, Emma and Lily."

"Hi, everyone," Molly said smiling shyly. "It's really nice to meet you. Adam's told me so much about you."

"Well he hasn't said a word to us about you!" Emma cried, looking none too pleased.

"Emma!" my dad said sternly as he entered the room and came to greet us.

"It's lovely to meet you, Molly. I'm Robert," he said, smiling, but as Molly opened her mouth to reply, she was interrupted by Emma.

"Well, it's true, I've never heard anything about her!" she exclaimed, clearly annoyed.

"Emma, you're making poor Molly really uncomfortable. Can't you at least let her sit down before you start bombarding her like it's the Iraq war or something?" I said in exasperation, looking apologetically towards Molly who was clearly hoping the earth would swallow her up. I squeezed her hand quickly to reassure her and led her to the free sofa. She sat down and I sat on the arm of the sofa to act as her shield. I could see that she would need it.

"Sorry Molly," Emma said, shamefaced. "I can't quite seem to stop myself from saying absolutely everything that pops into my head. I don't seem to have been born with a filter!"

"Or a stop button," Jo added teasingly, before adding in a conspiratorial whisper to Molly, "She even talks in her sleep."

"I do not! That happened *once*!" Emma exclaimed in outrage, then seeing Jo raise an eyebrow at her, she added sheepishly, "Okay, maybe twice!"

My dad asked Molly what she would like to drink and this gave her a few seconds of peace from my nosy sisters, but I knew they wouldn't keep quiet for long – I could see the look of determination in their eyes.

"So, Molly? Where did you meet Adam?" Lily blurted out a few seconds later, making Molly grin.

"Lily, I thought I said that we should wait for Molly to have a drink before you girls started on her."

"You didn't say a drink, you said that we had to wait for her to sit down. And look, she's sitting down, isn't she?" Lily said, pointing towards Molly on the sofa.

Molly laughed softly. She now knew that they were all crazy anyway and that there was no point in being stressed out.

"We met in Mauritius," Molly finally answered, smiling.

"In Mauritius?" the three girls cried out incredulously.

I grinned down at Molly and decided to take over. "Yes, we met in Mauritius. We were sitting next to each other on the flight there and we hit it off straight away."

Molly let out a burst of laughter and I looked down at her and winked. My sisters looked from Molly to me and back, frowning. I decided to go on before they interrupted me. "Anyway, then we realised that we were actually staying in the same hotel and ended up hanging out together quite a bit."

"So, are you in love then?" Lily asked seriously.

"Lily!" my mum reprimanded her before turning to Molly. "Molly, please excuse my girls. I just don't know how I did such a terrible job raising them."

Molly laughed good-naturedly. "I don't mind, honestly. I might just let Adam answer this one though . . ."

MOLLY

I waited, intrigued to see what Adam would say.

"No, we're friends," he finally answered, smiling at me.

"But *why?*" Lily asked, clearly puzzled.

"Lily!" Robert said sternly, coming back with my wine. "That's enough! Leave Molly alone."

I thanked him and grinned up at Adam.

"But Lily has a point there!" Jo said, looking at her parents then back at us. "Why are you just friends, and if so, why did you bring her to meet us?"

"Can't I bring a friend home without them, or me, having to face the third degree from you?"

"Women and men can't be friends," Emma said with quiet determination, looking down at her nails.

Molly chortled and cocked her eyebrow at me.

"Well, we can, okay? Now shut up and let's talk about

something else," Adam said, sounding annoyed for the first time.

They pouted but stayed quiet – for all of two minutes – while Adam and I talked to his parents about Mauritius and my work. The girls then joined in with questions about our trip and my family life. They were all funny and warm and made me feel right at home. Dinner was delicious and fun. I wondered what it would have been like to grow up in a house like this, full of laughter and love. Adam was wonderful, and I loved seeing him talk to his sisters and parents. There was so much affection and love between them. It showed me yet another side to Adam, and I liked him even more. As we were leaving the dining room, I went up to Adam's dad and thanked him for sending Dr Edwards to us. He told me that it had all been Adam's doing, but that it was nevertheless a pleasure. He asked me how my mother was and as he listened to me, I noticed that Adam had his eyes. He was a very handsome man and must have been quite a heartbreaker in his youth. After dinner, we went back into the lounge, where everyone lazed comfortably in the sofas.

"Okay, Molly, now you've had time to drink, eat, sit and get to know us . . . so *now* can I ask you why you're not dating my brother?" Lily blurted out, clearly not able to keep it in for a second longer.

I hadn't been expecting her outburst and spurted with embarrassed laughter. "Well, actually, I'm desperately in love with Adam, but he only likes me as a friend," I finally replied, pouting cheekily and making sure not to look at Adam.

"Molly Malahan! What a blatant lie, you should be ashamed of yourself!" Adam exclaimed, wide-eyed, with a laugh.

"What's a blatant lie?" Lily asked, looking from me to Adam and back.

"That she's in love with me," Adam said quietly, looking

directly into my eyes, making my heart race. I swallowed hard and looked away quickly, not wanting him to notice the blush that was spreading from my neck up to my face.

"Well, she should be. You're kind, smart and the best brother ever and all the girls find you gorgeous," she said seriously, as Adam grinned at her affectionately.

"To be honest, I'm not much into the whole Ian Somerhalder look – all those muscles and that basic gorgeousness . . . just not my thing really," I said, deadpan, wrinkling my nose in distaste and shaking my head.

Adam snorted with laughter as his sisters stared at me wide-eyed and mouth agape, while his parents looked on with amused smiles.

"Are you for *real*?" Lily finally exclaimed, still looking shell-shocked.

"She's joking, Lily. She finds both Ian and me drop-dead gorgeous, but it's just that she's more into girls if you must know."

"ADAM!" I said in amused horror.

"Poor Molly, she'll never come over for dinner again," Claire said, shaking her head, although it was obvious that she was having a hard time stifling her laughter.

"Don't worry, Mrs Wilson, I'm used to Adam's sense of humour, and besides, I'll get him back for that one!"

"All this is well and good," Emma said, looking at Adam and me. "But we still don't know what Molly is doing here, why we haven't heard about her before now and if you two are going out or not?"

I looked at Adam and raised my eyebrow. To my surprise, he looked at his watch, stood up, stretched and put out his hand to pull me up. "We have to get going actually, so your questions will have to wait until next time. That'll give us the opportunity to come up with juicy answers for you!" he said, winking at them.

I giggled as his sisters glowered at him. He hugged his mum and dad while I thanked them all for the wonderful evening. "I hope you'll come again soon," Mrs Wilson said, hugging me as if she had known me all my life.

"I would love to," I replied, touched. I didn't want to leave and would have loved to stay with this wonderful, funny and warm family and sit and laugh with them some more, but Adam seemed quite in a hurry to leave.

"Well, that went pretty well," Adam said, chuckling, as we walked to the car.

"They are pretty amazing – crazy, but wonderful," I replied with a smile. "Why didn't we stay a bit longer? I was enjoying that."

"You were? I thought you would want to leave as soon as possible!" he said, looking at me with surprise.

"No," I said shaking my head. "I loved being with your family."

"Then I'll bring you again real soon because I loved having you here," he said with a smile as he took my hand, giving it a squeeze.

We drove off and didn't talk for a while, both lost in our thoughts. I loved that about being with Adam. The silences between us never felt uncomfortable; they were totally relaxing.

"Um . . . Mol?" Adam said, breaking me out of my reverie.

"Yeah?" I replied, glancing at him. He was staring straight ahead, looking rather serious. I frowned, wondering what was up.

He glanced briefly in my direction, seeming to be debating whether or not to go on. Finally, he asked softly, "Did you end up reading my article? You've never said anything about it, and I've been too scared to ask."

I shook my head but was too embarrassed to look him in the eye. I felt terribly guilty for not having read it yet, and suddenly all the reasons which had once sounded so reasonable now seemed ridiculous when I thought of explaining them to Adam.

"Not yet," I finally answered in a barely audible whisper.

His head swung towards me as his forehead creased into a deep frown. "But *why*?"

"Because . . . I guess I didn't really want to think about the whole Mauritius episode again. I've got enough on my plate as it is and don't really want to re-hash the whole *you pretending to be someone you're not and lying to me* thing."

"Oh Mol, we're over that now, and the article – it's all good, you know?"

"I know . . . I'm trying . . . but there's a part of me that's just so scared of getting hurt and losing the plot completely."

He sighed deeply, and added softly, "I can't force you to trust me and to open your heart to me, but I love you, and I don't know if I can do this for much longer . . . it's too hard."

I spun my head towards him, but he wasn't looking at me. His eyes were on the road and his face looked drawn and sad. My heart began to race in a panic. I couldn't lose him. I couldn't imagine my life without him in it – his smile, his hugs, his phone calls, his sense of humour, his kindness . . .

"Adam?" I whispered as my heart raced on.

"Mmm?" he murmured, still lost in his thoughts.

"Do you mean that?"

He turned to me, and I could see the sadness in his eyes. My heart plummeted.

"I think I do, Mol," he answered, sighing heavily before fixing his eyes on the road again.

I didn't know what to say. My heart was in turmoil. A part of me wanted to jump into his arms and drive away into the sunset with him. But the other part was still holding me back, telling me not to go there because I had to protect my heart and my sanity.

We drove in silence for a while, both doleful and then suddenly Adam turned the radio on full blast and said loudly over the music, "Okay! I'm taking a page out of the Molly Sunshine book and duly declare that there shall be no more moping for today. We are going to the Left Bank to parrr-tyyy!"

"We are?" I repeated dumbly.

"Yep! There's a great band playing there tonight so we'll have a few drinks and do some dancing. John and a few other friends of mine will also be there."

"Sure," I mumbled, a bit dumbstruck by his sudden change of mood. As he sang along to the music, I glanced at him from the corner of my eye and couldn't help smiling, feeling the heaviness lift from my heart a little.

"Could I tell Zach and Anna to join us too? I know they weren't doing anything tonight," I eventually shouted over the music.

He turned down the volume and replied, with a smile, "Sure. That'd be great – the more the merrier!"

Anna texted me to tell me that they were keen to come and would meet us there in twenty minutes. They had been on their way out for a drink anyway so were ready to leave right away. I was relieved that they would be coming because although Adam was smiling again, something had definitely shifted between us, and it made me feel uneasy.

The Left Bank, a pub near the river in Fremantle, was packed when we arrived, but Adam spotted John straight away.

"How's it going, Molly Sunshine?" he said, pulling me into a friendly hug as I greeted him back.

"So how was dinner at the Wilsons'?" he asked with a grin, brushing his sandy coloured hair away from his eyes. "Did they run the Spanish inquisition on you?"

"Yep, pretty much," I nodded, laughing.

We chatted on a bit as Adam went to get us drinks. John was funny and easy-going and I could see why Adam and he were friends. Adam came back with a glass of white wine for me and a beer for him.

"How about some tequila shots?" John asked Adam.

Adam turned to me and cocked his eyebrow.

"You don't have to ask for my permission, you know? Go have fun," I said, smiling and gesturing him to follow John to the bar.

"Why don't you have one with us?" Adam suggested.

I hesitated, but seeing as I really needed to relax and forget about our conversation in the car, I decided to go for it and have some fun. "Sure! Why not. But just one – otherwise you'll have to carry me out of here."

We got served our shot glasses and Adam waggled his eyebrows at me. "You ready?"

"As ready as I'll ever be!" I grimaced, making him grin into his glass.

One, two, three . . . and down they went. I spluttered and coughed as Adam and John made fun of me.

"Not much of a shots type of gal," I said, pulling a face. "Think I'll stick to wine, if you don't mind." They laughed good-naturedly and ordered themselves a few more rounds. I sensed that Adam was out to get drunk and realised that I had never seen him like this before. I felt uneasy as I could tell that he was troubled and had been since our conversation in the car, and it was completely understandable.

To my relief, Anna and Zach soon arrived and I went over to greet them.

"I'm so glad you're here, I get the feeling that Adam is out to get drunk, and I'm not sure I feel very reassured."

"What did you do to him, Molly?" Zach asked sternly.

"What do you mean *what did I do to him*? I didn't do anything!"

"Well, that's exactly the problem!" he said in exasperation. "He won't wait for you forever, you know."

"Please don't . . . just drop it for now," I begged him. I noticed his jaw clenching, but he nodded.

We headed to the bar, where Adam and John were now talking to a few other guys. When he saw us coming, Adam stood up to greet Anna and Zach and then introduced us to everyone – Nick, Mark, Michael and James, or was it Alex and Dave, I didn't quite catch all the names. He pulled Zach in with them after getting Anna a drink and ordered another round of shots. Anna and I went to sit outside on the terrace, where the band was setting up, getting ready to play.

I told Anna about our evening and our conversation on the way here. She agreed with Zach and thought that I had to decide once and for all if I was going to go out with Adam or not, and if not, then I had to let him go, because Adam was in love with me and it wasn't fair to string him along any longer. I knew she was right, and my heart was torn in two. I knew I loved Adam and I couldn't imagine not having him in my life, but then again, the thought of depending on someone that way made me break out in a sweat.

As the band began to play, people came out and started dancing, and Anna and I happily joined them. The boys were still holding up the bar and we could hear frequent raucous barks of laughter coming from there. Adam had come out with Zach a few times to check on us, and each time his eyes seemed more glazed, but he was still charming and kind and wanted to make sure that we were all good.

When the band started singing "Anything, Anything" by Bananarama, they all suddenly burst outside, talking loudly and obviously rather drunk, and started jumping up and down and shouting along to the lyrics. After a few more loud and fast-paced songs, the tempo changed and the band began to play "My End and My Beginning" by Derek Stiles. I was about to leave the dancefloor when I felt Adam grab my hand from behind. As I turned, he tugged me into his arms, whispering in my ear, "Would you like to dance with me?"

I smiled and nodded. He pulled me closer and I rested my head on his broad chest. I felt so safe there, and as we moved slowly in time to the music, he caressed my back. Every single nerve ending in my body reacted to his touch. All of a sudden, I felt his chest rise as he sighed deeply. I looked up. He was looking at me, his eyes burning with desire. I was taken aback by the intensity of his gaze, but couldn't draw my eyes away from his. "God, Molly, you don't know how beautiful you are," he whispered, sucking in a shaky breath. He leaned his forehead against mine and suddenly his lips were on mine, soft and gentle, with so much tenderness that it was my undoing. I groaned and kissed him back and he deepened the kiss, gently parting my lips so that our tongues could meet. It was everything I remembered it to be – and so much more. I loved everything about this man and couldn't get close enough to him. Suddenly, I realised what I was doing and pulled away abruptly.

"Adam! I can't . . . we shouldn't . . ." I cried, despondently, as he looked at me, eyes still clouded with desire.

"*Why?*" he whispered hoarsely, his eyes searching mine.

"Because we're meant to be taking things slow, remember?"

"Oh, Mol, we're taking it so slow that we've stopped moving altogether." He sighed, shaking his head. "I can't do this anymore."

He leaned his forehead against mine again and we stayed like this for a moment in silence, my heart drumming against his chest. He finally looked at me and whispered despairingly, "I love you, Molly, but it's obvious that you don't feel the same way about me, because if you did, there's no way you would be able to keep going on like this either."

"Adam, you know why I can't . . ."

"No, I don't!" he snapped angrily. "You're scared of getting hurt. Well who isn't? Don't you think it scares me too? It scares the living daylights out of me because I've never felt this way before and I don't want to get hurt. But I still think it's worth taking the risk. What's life without taking risks? If you don't risk anything, you don't get anything!"

"I know . . . but I just can't. I-I . . ." I stuttered, before he cut me off.

"You can't hide behind your mum's problems for the rest of your life. She's much better already and she'll end up managing fine without you. It's pretty obvious that you don't love me, because if you did, you'd throw caution to the wind."

"I really care about you, Adam, you know I do," I said, as tears rolled down my cheeks.

"But not enough," he whispered sadly, brushing my tears away with his fingers, before kissing my forehead softly and turning to leave. I felt totally bereft and stood there frozen, staring at his retreating back as tears flowed down my cheeks. I couldn't move. I couldn't think. I couldn't breathe.

"Here, drink this," Zach said, appearing out of nowhere. I stared dumbly at him, still completely in shock.

"Drink. Now!" Zach said sternly, pushing the shot glass into my hand and snapping me out of my trance. I took the glass and poured it down my throat. I actually enjoyed the burning sensation it left as it made its way down.

"Did you really just let Adam go, Mol?" Zach asked softly.

I nodded sadly. "Well, I think so. He said something about being at a standstill and that he couldn't do this anymore."

"I don't understand you," he said, raking his fingers through his hair with a sigh. "But you said no lectures tonight, so I'll get you drunk instead. I'll be right back."

I looked around, wondering where Anna had disappeared

to, but I didn't have too much time to dwell on it as Zach came back with two more shots for me. The alcohol soon began to numb my confused heart and I was able to push all thoughts of Adam and me aside for the time being.

"Where's Anna?"

"She seems to be getting quite intimate with Adam's friend, John," Zach said, grinning and looking behind me.

"Really? Where?" I asked, turning around trying to spot them as Zach pointed in their direction. "Don't be so obvious about it!" I hissed, pushing down his finger with a giggle.

He laughed quietly, downed the last of his beer and cocked his eyebrow at me. "Wanna dance?"

"Yes please!" I said beaming happily, the alcohol having definitely reached my head. I absolutely loved dancing. They were playing "Dangerous" by David Guetta and we jumped up and down like we'd had too much sugar or something. Zach stayed by my side, talking and dancing with me, making sure that I was alright and didn't leave me alone for a minute. He really was the best friend a girl could have.

As a group of people moved outside to come onto the dancefloor, I was left with a full view of the inside bar and, to my horror, I saw Adam standing near the bar with his arm around a gorgeous blonde bombshell.

"Zach, look!" I shouted, pointing towards them.

"Now who's being obvious?" he muttered, rolling his eyes and pulling my hand down. "Well you don't expect him to wait for you forever, do you? He's a man and has needs."

"You're gross! It's only been like . . . one hour!"

"You know I don't just mean tonight. He's been waiting for months," he said gently.

I kept quiet because I knew it was true. Adam had been really good about it, and tonight was the first time he'd told me how hard it was for him. I hadn't wanted to see it and had been too centred on myself, on what I felt and what I needed because of everything that was going on with my mum, I acknowledged to myself in shame. I carried on dancing but my eyes didn't leave the Baywatch lookalike and Adam, who was now whispering sweet nothings into the girl's ear, making her laugh.

"Look at her batting her eyelashes at him and pushing her big fake boobs into his face!" I screeched, pinching Zach hard without even realising.

"Ow!" He winced, rubbing his arm. "Calm down, Molly!"

I felt like I would burst with jealousy and ignored Zach, who was trying to drag me away from their line of vision. As the girl leaned over and kissed Adam's cheek, I couldn't take it anymore.

"That's it!" I cried angrily, pushing my glass into Zach's hand and storming off towards them.

"Molly, wait!" Zach called out, but I was having none of it. I was getting Adam out of that girl's claws.

65

ADAM

I had finally managed to walk away from Molly. I couldn't do this "taking it slow" or "just friends" thing anymore. It was driving me crazy. I needed to put some distance between us for a while. Maybe eventually we would be able to be friends, but for now, I had to let her go completely. No matter how hard it was.

I'd been chatted up by Lia, a stunning blonde, who unfortunately felt the need to tell me that I looked just like Ian Somerhalder two seconds after saying hello, her eyes sparkling like she'd just won the lottery. She'd lost my interest there and then. But as I had to stop myself from mooning over Molly, and as I was actually quite drunk, I decided "what the heck?" and started chatting her up. She would be a sure bet tonight at least. If my heart couldn't be fulfilled, then I might as well enjoy myself any way I could.

I had just whispered another stupid joke into her ear when I noticed, in the corner of my eye, someone marching determinedly towards us. I turned just in time to catch Molly, who had launched herself into my arms, entwining her legs around my waist and looping her arms around my neck.

"Whoa! What the—" I exclaimed in surprise, holding her to me, a bit dazed.

"Adam! Her boobs – they're totally fake! Blown up like balloons, that's all!" she said in a loud whisper as she pointed to Lia, not even trying to be discreet about it. I bit down a laugh and tried to put her down, but she hung on tightly. "Mine, on the other hand, are one hundred percent real!" she added before leaning back and pinching them all over theatrically to prove her point. I couldn't stop my burst of laughter this time as she looked up at me, smiling proudly.

Then, all of a sudden, her brow furrowed cutely and her eyes suddenly darted to Lia's chest and then back down at her own. She sighed heavily. "Fine, I guess I have to admit that mine are much smaller than hers." She pouted, before suddenly jerking her head up again, her eyes sparkling with delight. "But at least you won't run the risk of popping them when you touch them! That has to count for something, right?"

I spurted with laughter again. She was clearly drunk, I could tell from the way her thoughts were all over the place, going from pouting to excitement and back. Unfortunately, she was absolutely adorable even when drunk, I thought, groaning inwardly. Why couldn't she be one of those terribly annoying and loud drunks, one that you wanted to run away from as fast as possible? As I looked down at her, I realised that she was still in my arms. I tried to prise her arms gently from around my neck, but she was having none of it. She tightened her hold on me and looked at me determinedly with a look that said "don't even try". I really needed to get away from her. *Now.*

"Molly, can I put you down now, please? You're getting a bit heavy for me," I lied, trying to extricate myself from her again.

She scoffed. "Yeah right, Mr Hercules. As if!"

I grinned. "Okay, but could you maybe just get down so we can talk?"

"I don't want you looking down her top anymore," she said sternly, before adding just as seriously, "You can look down mine if you want."

"Okay, I promise I won't look down her top," I agreed solemnly, trying to keep a straight face. She was looking very serious, and I didn't think that she would appreciate me laughing right now. But didn't she understand that hers was the only top I was interested in looking down anyway? I thought I'd made that more than clear.

"Look, she's already gone anyway," I said, motioning to Lia's now-empty seat. I hadn't even noticed her leaving, which pretty much said it all. "Gee, thanks a lot by the way," I added, faking a scowl. "I was actually enjoying chatting to her . . . and her boobs!"

Molly scowled at me, narrowing her eyes angrily. She was so cute and looked so annoyed, and I couldn't help laughing. She slapped me playfully and loosened her grip from around my neck, slipping off me and standing silently by my side, suddenly looking lost.

"Mol, what are you doing?" I asked softly, not sure she even knew herself.

"Will you dance with me?" she said in lieu of a reply.

I decided to let it go for now. The thought of holding her in my arms was just too tempting to resist, despite my earlier resolve. "Yes, I'll dansh with you," I teased.

"I *did not* say dansh!" she huffed, taking my hand and pulling me towards the dance floor.

"No, of course you didn't," I replied gravely, grinning into her back.

I held her against me and we moved slowly in time to the music. It was wonderful to have her in my arms. Suddenly, I came back to earth with a thud. *Adam Wilson, what are you doing?* I had finally managed to walk away from her and what did I do the minute she appeared in front of me again? I agreed to dance with her! Damn fool I am. I pulled away from her and whispered, "I don't think this is such a good idea . . ."

She put her finger to my lips. "Shush, listen to the song, it's beautiful."

I sighed. "Molly, I can't."

She gazed deeply into my eyes for a long time, as various emotions flickered through her beautiful eyes. Finally, she leaned up and put her lips softly to mine. I forced myself not to react, but she insisted and kept kissing me, teasing me and willing me to part my lips and kiss her back. I finally groaned and gave in. Her lips were so soft . . . The alcohol in my blood stopped me from acting rationally, and all I knew was that I wanted Molly more than anything, and I couldn't stop myself from giving in to the pleasure of feeling her body pressed to mine and having her lips on mine. Suddenly conscious that we were kissing like love-struck teenagers on the dance floor, I pulled away gently.

"Let's get out of here, sweetness," I murmured into her ear.

"Don't stop kissing me, Adam. I really want to kiss you some more," she whispered, holding onto me tightly.

"Oh baby, so do I," I said, full of desire. "But not here in front of everyone."

I took her hand and pulled her back inside, looking for Zach and Anna. I found Zach and told him I was taking Molly home to their place. As we walked out of the pub, I pulled my phone out of my pocket to call a taxi, before nudging her teasingly. "Hey! I was actually counting on you to drive me home, you know."

"You were? Well sure, no problem. Give me the keys," she said, dead serious, holding out her hand as if she hadn't just drunk I-don't-know-how-many shots and wasn't way over the limit.

"Are you crazy? You're totally drunk!" I said, laughing at her.

"I am not! I'm perfectly fine," she said petulantly.

"Sure you are. But I'd rather not take the risk," I said grinning, scrolling through my list of contacts, trying to find the number for the taxi.

"Look! Look! I'm walking totally straight," she said, balancing with difficultly as she walked along the edge of the pavement. Once she'd done that, she put her thumb to her nose and lifted her knee, attempting to touch it with her little finger. I looked at her and did my best to keep a straight face.

"See! I'm *so* not drunk!" she said proudly – before falling head-first onto the grass. A burst of laughter escaped my lips as my hand flew to my mouth in both amusement and shock.

"Oh my God, are you alright?" I exclaimed, running up to her. She looked up at me and as our eyes met, we both exploded with laughter.

We calmed down just in time to see the taxi pull up beside us and climbed into the back seat together, still grinning like idiots. For the first five minutes, she sat quietly by my side, gazing out the window, and then suddenly she crawled onto my lap and cuddled into me without saying a word. It felt wonderful to have her in my arms and it reminded me of when I'd held her for the first time in Mauritius on her veranda. It was the day I realised that I had feelings for her.

Twenty minutes later, we pulled up outside her house.

"Could you give me a minute please, mate?" I asked the taxi driver.

"No worries," he replied pleasantly as I turned and followed Molly to the door. She unlocked it and pushed it open before turning back to me.

"Stay with me," she whispered, taking my hand.

I stared at her in surprise, not knowing what to do. I was so tempted to stay, but I didn't want her to regret anything in the morning.

"Please."

Deciding to be reasonable, I shook my head.

"Stay . . ." she whispered again, tugging my hand, coaxing me to come inside.

Oh no. I knew that I was going to give in, I couldn't resist her. "Okay. I'll go pay the taxi driver."

As I walked back to the taxi, I knew that I should jump right back in and go home, but I couldn't do it. Molly was waiting for me in the doorway and gave me one of her melting smiles. It was ridiculous the effect this girl had on me.

"I still meant what I said at the pub earlier," I said softly as I reached her, gently stroking her cheek with my thumb.

"But I didn't. I want you, Adam," she whispered, her eyes full of yearning. She wanted me; I couldn't believe she had finally accepted that. There was a part of me that couldn't help worrying that it was because of the alcohol, but as she pulled me down to her and kissed me, I pushed the thought aside and concentrated on the here and now. I was finally kissing Molly again . . .

66

MOLLY

"*A*re you sure you know what you're doing?" Adam asked, looking worried.

"Yes, I know exactly what I'm doing," I said, rubbing my fingers gently over the creases on his forehead, wanting him to relax.

Adam was sitting on the edge of the bed and had pulled me so that I was standing between his legs. I laid my hands on either side of his shoulders and looked down at him in awe. I couldn't believe that this beautiful man was in love with me. I leaned down, planting feather-light kisses on his forehead, cheeks and down his neck, before making my way back up to his lips. As my mouth met his, he groaned low in his throat and kissed me until my knees grew weak. He pulled me down onto the bed with him and began caressing my body all over.

His eyes were burning with desire as he whispered, "Can I take your top off?"

I nodded and heard his breath catch in his throat as he reached out for me. He slowly pulled my top up and over my head before throwing it on the floor. I stood before him in my bra, glad that I had chosen to wear one of my special lacy bras – maybe subconsciously hoping that this would happen – and my body burned with desire for him. I tugged at his t-shirt and he leaned forward, helping me to remove it. I began kissing his gorgeous body all over and loved it that his breath caught in his throat and that he had goose bumps all over because of me.

"Oh Molly . . ." he whispered as our lips found each other again.

The first thing I noticed when I woke up was that I was naked from the waist up and alone in bed. The second thing was that I had a major headache. I moaned, stuffing my head back under my pillow. Flashes of me and my less-than-sober state at the Left Bank last night made me flush with embarrassment, but I couldn't help finding some of it quite funny. I wondered if Adam had been up for long and decided to go see where he was. I looked around the room, trying to find my top, and finally spotted it on the floor on the other side of the bed. I stretched over to grab it before sitting up and pulling it on. I was about to get up when my mobile phone vibrated on my bedside table. I reached over and picked it up, wondering who could be calling on a Sunday morning. My heart lurched as I saw that it was Dr Edwards and I froze. *Something had happened to my mum.* By the time I snapped out of my daze, it had stopped ringing. I quickly pressed redial, biting on a nail as it rang.

"Hello, Molly. Thanks for calling me back," he said as soon as he picked up.

"Hi, Dr Edwards. What's wrong?"

"Don't worry, it's nothing bad, but I still thought you should know. Your mother had one of her panic attacks yesterday evening when she was at the supermarket. She began hyperventilating and couldn't breathe, so the manager called the ambulance who took her to the hospital. She eventually gave them my phone number and asked them to call me. I went over to see her and she was already much better by the time I got there."

"But she didn't call me!"

"I know. And that's a really good sign. It shows that she's finally no longer dependent on you, Molly. She also rang up Alison from our support group to talk about it, and it was a relief for her to know that she had us and didn't have to disturb you. She didn't want me to tell you, but I do think it's important that you know how things are going."

"Is she okay now?" I asked my voice shaking.

"She's fine, Molly, honestly."

I thanked him and hung up, my emotions in a jumble. I wasn't sure what upset me the most – the fact that she'd had a bad attack and gone to hospital, or the fact that she hadn't called me. I knew I should feel relieved that she could now ring up Dr Edwards and friends from her support group as it took a big load off my back, but for some reason it made me feel sad too. It was ridiculous. I stayed on the bed, sitting with my legs crossed for a moment, thinking about it. Suddenly I felt Adam's presence and looked up to see him standing in the open doorway looking at me with that gorgeous lopsided smile of his and a cup of coffee in his hand.

Just seeing him made my heart lift and my face broke into a smile. My heart skipped a beat as my eyes roamed over him. He looked so sexy standing there bare-chested, in last night's jeans, his hair ruffled and his cheeks housing a five o-clock shadow. Everything would be okay, and I now had

Adam to hold me in his arms and comfort me when they weren't. I sighed in relief.

"Adam . . ." I whispered, shaking my head to push away the image of my mum in hospital from my mind, wanting to just enjoy being with Adam. But as I looked into his eyes, the smile disappeared from his face and his eyes became dark with... what? Anger? But why?

ADAM

I walked back to the bedroom, coffee cup in hand, my heart bursting with happiness. Stopping in front of the open doorway, I stood there for a moment, admiring her. She was sitting cross-legged on the bed, lost in her thoughts. Obviously feeling my presence, she looked up and smiled. As my eyes locked with hers, my heart plummeted and my smile died on my lips. *Oh no. No, no, no, please no*, I pleaded as warning bells drilled.

"Adam..."

And I understood – she regretted what had happened between us last night. I felt the blood drain from my face and stood there frozen for a minute before closing the distance between us and handing her the coffee.

"Adam?" she said tentatively, looking confused.

"Don't worry, I get it," I replied tersely, turning around and grabbing my shirt and shoes from the floor, before leaving the room and heading towards the front door.

I heard her running out of her room, calling my name, but I walked out, slamming the door behind me. I needed to get as far away from her as possible, not even glancing over my shoulder as she opened the front door and called me again. I had no intention of sticking around to hear her tell me that she was really sorry but that she had made a mistake and didn't feel that way about me. No way. I'd had enough. I tugged my shirt on as I stormed down the road, holding my shoes in my hand.

"You *I-D-I-O-T*! You STUPID *IDIOT*!" I hissed under my breath, furious with myself. As if she would have changed her mind in an hour last night and suddenly decided to blow caution to the wind and be with me just because I was flirting with another girl. I knew it! I just knew that it had been the alcohol talking. Why hadn't I followed my instinct?

"DAMN IT!" I shouted out loud to the empty street, kicking a rock on the pathway and enjoying the pain it inflicted on my bare feet. When I was far enough to be sure that she couldn't catch up with me, I took my phone and called a taxi.

I sat on the grass on the side of the road, waiting to be picked up. I replayed last night over and over in my mind and couldn't believe what an idiot I'd been. One minute she tells me she can't be with me and that we need to keep taking things slow, and an hour later she's suddenly diving into my arms, telling me to look down her top, and then we're dancing and making out. Did I want it so much that I turned into an idiot? Why did I fool myself into believing that she finally wanted me too? I raked my hand through my hair, wanting to punch myself for the idiot I'd been. Just then the taxi pulled up and I got in, relieved to finally be heading home. I would pick my car up from the Left Bank later. Right now I just needed to hide under my covers and sleep off this anger, disappointment and heartache.

MOLLY

*W*hat had just happened? I stood leaning against the doorway as I watched Adam storming off into the distance. Why had he done a 360 on me in the space of a few seconds? I had no idea. I sighed, closing the door behind me. I headed back to my room and threw myself onto the bed. I grabbed my phone, pressing "Adam". It went straight to voicemail. *Damn it!* I threw the phone on the bed and fell back against my pillows, closing my eyes and taking a few deep breaths.

My mind was racing, and Adam's reaction kept playing over and over again in my mind as I tried to figure out what had gone wrong. This led me back to Dr Edward's phone call. I still couldn't believe my mum hadn't called me, but I knew that Dr Edwards was right, it was a really good thing. It made me feel lighter because she finally had other people to lean on. I was no longer alone and I was so grateful to Dr Edwards, and Adam, for their part in helping her. She was now taking anti-anxiety pills, had started going to a yoga class which was apparently excellent for anxiety, and went to the support group led by Dr Edwards every week. The best part was that she had met two other ladies in the group and they had already gone out for coffee together a few times. She was still too scared to go into town, but at least she was okay to leave the house and go to the supermarket to do her shopping or go out for coffee with her friends. The most wonderful thing was that she was really motivated to start living again.

My thoughts switched back to Adam once more. What had happened? I dialled his number again – voicemail. Damn it, I definitely needed more coffee and Panadol to think this through. I flipped the kettle on and leaned against the counter, staring outside. Had he changed his mind and regretted what had happened? Surely not, he'd wanted this for so long it just didn't make sense. I poured myself a coffee and sat down heavily at the kitchen table.

I jumped in surprise as Zach walked into the kitchen a few minutes later dressed in Homer Simpson boxer shorts, looking half asleep.

"Hey," he said sleepily, rubbing his eyes tiredly and groaning. "I've got such a headache."

"Tell me about it," I said, grimacing. "How many shots did I drink last night? You do know that you're solely responsible for my hangover, don't you?"

He grinned tiredly. "Well at least it gave you the courage to tell Adam what you felt."

My face fell and Zach looked at me, baffled. "What's wrong, Mol? Didn't you guys come home together last night?"

I nodded, taking a sip of coffee before answering. "We did. But he stormed off a few minutes ago."

"Why?"

"I have no idea. One minute he was standing in the doorway with one of his heartbreaking smiles, bringing me a cup of coffee and the next minute his face drained of colour and he said *'Don't worry, I get it'* before storming out the room and the house without a backwards glance."

"What did you say to him?" Zach asked, putting his hand in front of his mouth to hide a yawn.

"Nothing! I didn't even have time to say a word."

"Call him," he said, reaching out and nicking my cup from me, taking a large gulp before handing it back to me.

"I tried, but it goes straight to voicemail."

Zach got up and made himself a cup of coffee before heading to his room without another word. I looked on, wondering why all the men in my life were acting so weird this morning.

Zach strolled back into the kitchen, his phone to his ear. "Voicemail," he confirmed with a nod as he sat down again, sipping his coffee.

"See, I told you."

"Mol, he's crazy about you, has been for months – there's no way that that's changed suddenly. There must be a reasonable explanation."

Just then, Anna walked into the kitchen.

"Oh, and by the way, Anna crashed here last night," Zach said, his mouth hovering over the rim of his coffee cup.

My mouth fell to the floor. "What-t-t? *You and Anna?*" I exclaimed incredulously, pointing my finger from Zach to Anna.

"*No way!* Beurrrk!" Anna cried out, pulling a face, before turning to Zach with a grin. "No offence."

He chuckled. "None taken."

"We were both too drunk to drive so we figured we'd just get a taxi to your place as it was closer than going back to mine," Anna explained, jumping up and sitting on the kitchen counter.

"Coffee?" Zach offered and Anna nodded gratefully.

"So Anna, what was all that about with John last night?" I asked, waggling my eyebrows.

"What was what about?" she said as Zach handed her a cup of coffee. She smiled gratefully, taking a sip and sighing with pleasure.

"You and John seemed quite cosy," I said, pretending that I hadn't noticed her evading my question. I glanced over at Zach and caught him looking at me, eyes wide, shaking his head vigorously. Oops, too late. Guess it was a sore subject.

"Cosy? What are you on about? He's an idiot! Have you ever talked to him?" she cried heatedly.

"Of course I have – and I like him. He's funny."

"Funny? He's not funny! He just thinks he is!" she snapped, sipping her coffee, her brows furrowed.

"Well, I happen to find him funny," I said with a shrug, grinning at Zach, who was hiding his smile behind his cup.

"Well you have a terrible sense of humour then!"

I burst out laughing. "Well you sure seem to have lost yours!"

"Molly!" she exclaimed incredulously, as Zach snorted with laughter and got glared at by Anna too. John had obviously seriously annoyed her last night, and I had no idea how.

"I'm joking, Anna, but I don't understand why you're so angry with him. He's honestly a good guy."

She downed the last of her coffee before jumping down from the cabinet and going to put her cup in the sink. "He's a jerk – that's all you need to know," she said over her shoulder.

"But you have to admit that he's a pretty hot jerk," I mumbled into my cup, trying not to smile.

She swivelled around and glowered at me but I looked back at her in wide-eyed innocence. "What? Well he is," I insisted with a half-shrug, turning to Zach for confirmation. "Isn't he?"

Zach laughed and didn't bother answering. He was finding the whole situation hilarious but clearly had no intention of getting involved.

"It seems that not only do you have a terrible sense of humour, but your taste in men is also appalling – Adam excluded of course. Can my best friend Molly just come back out now? I don't like this new version of you at all!" she wailed theatrically.

I kept laughing as she scowled at me again for a moment, then suddenly her lips started twitching and her face broke into a huge grin.

"Feel better now?" I asked, amused.

"Much!" She laughed.

"So wanna tell us about it?" Zach said, realising that it was safe for him to join the conversation again. "You ranted and raved all the way in the taxi last night but you never told me what had happened."

"Okay . . ." She sighed, rolling her eyes. "We hung out, talking and having a good laugh together. Then we danced and ended up making out for a while, and it was pretty wonderful. Then, before leaving, he told me that he's not really into the relationship thing, so not to feel hurt if he doesn't call!"

"You're joking!" Zach and I cried in unison.

She shook her head.

"What a bastard!" I said. "Okay, so you win. He's a jerk."

She looked up and grinned. "Thank you."

"I'm so sorry, Anna," I said, reaching out to take her hand.

"Me too," Zach said, putting his hand over ours.

"Okay enough about that, I really don't want to talk about

it anymore," she pleaded, and we nodded in agreement. "Where's Adam?" she suddenly asked, obviously only just noticing that he wasn't around.

I told her what had happened and she was as confused as me and Zach.

"Obviously something upset him, even if you don't know what it is. You need to talk to him, he's worth it, Mol," she said, her turn to put her hand on mine.

I looked at her, then at Zach. "What are you waiting for – go!" he said, nudging his head towards the door.

"You're right, you're right. I'm going!" I said, bouncing up and racing towards the front door, grabbing my keys from the side table on my way out. Halfway to my car, I stopped dead in my tracks. "Oops, need to get dressed first." I giggled as I looked down at my flimsy little pyjama shorts and top.

Zach and Anna saw me race past the kitchen on the way to my room and burst out laughing.

ADAM

I was glad to have the house to myself. I had no idea where everyone was, but I was relieved not to have to act happy or answer any questions. That was defi-nitely the downside of no longer having a place of my own. I couldn't be alone if I wanted to be. I really hoped we'd find a house soon. I had a long shower and knowing that I would go crazy cooped up inside, I decided to go surfing to vent out my anger. I wasn't angry at Molly; I was furious with myself. I'd been an idiot. She'd been honest all along. I'd just chosen to believe that she would come round one day because I loved her so much and couldn't believe that she didn't feel the same way.

I rang John on the off-chance that he would answer, seeing as it was quite early after a night out, but he did. He sounded a bit worse for wear but agreed to come with me. He said he'd pick me up in twenty minutes and that we'd go get my car on the way home.

I told John what had happened as we drove to Scarborough, and he comforted me as best he could. He felt that I should have stayed and talked it through in case I'd got it wrong. But I'd seen the expression in her eyes and knew that I was right.

Wanting to change the subject, I asked John about Anna. He laughed, "Hmmm . . . Anna, wow, she's quite a girl. Sure does the angry thing well, though," he said, grimacing.

"Why would she be angry with you?" I asked with a frown, glancing at him. "John, please tell me you didn't mess with Molly's best friend?"

He groaned, pulling his mouth to the side, looking very guilty.

"John!"

"I didn't intend to. It was all a bit of fun. But then I realised that I hadn't had that much fun with a girl for . . . well, never really, and things heated up a bit. I actually really like her."

"Why do I know there's a 'but' coming? What did you do?"

"Well, we talked for ages, danced, made out and had the best time. Then when I left, I kind of told her that I didn't do the relationship thing and not to be hurt if I didn't call her."

"John! Couldn't you have chosen someone else to mess with?"

"I know, I know." He sighed. "But I just freaked out because I liked her so much. I can't stop thinking about her and it's driving me crazy. Why do you think I was so keen to come surfing this morning when I could be sleeping off my hangover comfortably in bed?"

I took my phone out of my pocket and turned it on. "Call her."

"What? No!"

"You know you want to and I'm sure she wants you to. So do it!"

He shook his head. I scrolled down the list of names and clicked on Anna, holding it up next to his ear as it began to ring.

"Adam, don—" he began and stopped short as he heard Anna's voice.

"Adam?" she said, sounding confused.

"Er-um . . . no, it's me, John," he stuttered, making me chuckle. I'd never seen John unsure of himself. "You know John from the Left Bank last night," he said lamely.

I laughed as I heard her shout, "Of course I know who you are!"

I motioned for him to say something because he was just sitting there, jaw slack and eyes wide.

"Well . . . erm . . . listen, I wanted to tell you how sorry I am for acting like such a jerk last night. The thing is – I panicked. All I wanted to do was take you home with me and it freaked me out, so I pushed you away instead."

He listened for a second before nodding. "I know I was a jerk and you have every right to be furious, but I really want to see you again."

He waited a moment, and then said, "Hmm . . . I think this is the part where you either tell me that you'd also love to see me again or to take a hike, but either way, *please* say something."

She finally said something and his face broke into a huge grin as he let out a sigh of relief. "Oh, thank goodness. How does tonight sound?"

"Yes, tonight as in later today? Or if you prefer we can do lunch in an hour?"

I chuckled and he grinned at me with a shrug, mouthing, "She's awesome."

"Okay, dinner it is. I'll pick you up at seven. Send me your address and lovely Yacintha will guide me to you."

He listened and burst out laughing. "She's my GPS, Anna."

They said their goodbyes and John handed me my phone back.

"And that, my friend, is how it's done," he said with a wink.

I grinned and quickly switched off my phone again, not wanting Molly to call me to say how sorry she was. I couldn't bear to hear her voice right now.

John and I hit the water and it was therapeutic to be in the sea, just my board, the waves and me. I had forgotten how exhilarating it was to ride a wave, and at least it helped me not to think of Molly for a few hours . . .

MOLLY

I drove to Adam's place, my heart racing and my palms sweating. I hadn't even brushed my hair, in too much of a rush to get to him. My heart plummeted as I saw that there were no cars in the driveway and that the house seemed empty and silent. I couldn't believe it. Where could he have gone? And where was his family? I didn't know what to do. Should I wait or just leave? I could go to John's parents' place, but I had no idea where that was and no clue as to where else Adam would go. I might as well just go home for now.

I decided to drop off to see my mum instead, thinking it would take my mind off Adam. She greeted me with a warm smile and we settled down and had a cup of coffee. I told her about Dr Edwards' phone call and asked her why she hadn't called me.

She smiled and reached for my hand. "Because I didn't need to Mol."

"But Mum, you know you can call me any time, don't you?"

"I know, love, and thank you. I feel so relieved and happy that I don't have to burden you with my troubles anymore because I have a support group who are there to do just that. I want you to live your life and not worry about me all the time. I don't want to hold you back anymore."

"You never held me back, Mum, don't say that."

"I did, love. You were always worried about me and I relied on you way too much. It wasn't healthy and I'm deeply sorry."

"Don't be, Mum. You would have done it for me too." I smiled, giving her a hug.

She then told me a bit more about her support group, Dr Edwards, her new friends – Laura and Alison – and how much more in control she was feeling. Her eyes lit up when she spoke, and I could tell that she was much better.

She finished her coffee and put her cup down on the table, and then looked at me intently for a moment, her eyes searching mine. "Molly, what's wrong, love?"

I was startled as I hadn't heard her ask me that for a very, very long time. I was the one who usually asked that question.

"Er . . . nothing, why?"

"You're smiling, but your eyes look sad," she said, taking my hand again and squeezing it affectionately. "Tell me what's wrong. Please."

I felt the tears welling up in my eyes. It had been so long since my mum had acted like a mum that it made me want to bawl my eyes out. I shook my head, not sure that I should be telling her my problems. I couldn't help worrying that it might make her anxious that I wasn't my usual happy self and trigger an attack.

She seemed to read my mind and squeezed my hand again. "You can tell me. I want you to talk to me."

So I did.

"Do you love him?" she asked, when I'd finished.

I nodded.

"Then go get him. Maybe he just needs you to show him that you love him too. He's been doing all the running since you got back and maybe it's your turn now."

I looked at her, my eyes full of hope. "Do you think so?"

She nodded. "He seems like one of the good ones, Molly. Don't let him go."

I drove straight back to Adam's house and this time there were a few cars in the driveway. My heart fell when I saw that Adam's car still wasn't there, but then again, maybe he hadn't gone to pick it up from the Left Bank yet. I walked to the door and rang the doorbell, my heart drumming in my chest. I heard footsteps and saw Emma's smiling face as she opened the door. Her smile faded and turned into a glare when she saw that it was me. I had no idea why she was looking at me like that – unless Adam had said something...

"Hi," I said, feeling a bit intimidated.

Not bothering to reply, she turned and called down the hallway, "Girls! Molly's here!"

Jo and Lily came racing towards us in two seconds flat, making me grin despite their less-than-friendly demeanours.

"What are you doing here?" Jo asked, hands on hips as Emma and Lily stood on either side of her, looking equally scary.

"I'm looking for Adam."

"He's not here," they chimed.

"And we're glad because we need some answers from you now that Adam isn't here to play at being your bodyguard," Emma added, still glowering at me.

I couldn't help grinning at their stern and determined

faces, suddenly finding their whole attitude hilarious. "Sure. Fire away!"

"Adam's been miserable lately and we couldn't figure out why – until you showed up with him last night. We saw the way he was looking at you . . . but what are you doing to him? Why is he unhappy? Don't you like him?" Jo asked, looking both angry and confused.

"Well—" I began, but was cut off by Lily.

"We won't let you hurt him, you know?" she said sternly.

It was really adorable the way they were protecting Adam.

"I don't want to—" I started, before being cut off by Jo this time.

"Why don't you love him?" Jo said indignantly. "What's not to love about him? He's a great guy."

"And he looks like Ian Somerhalder for goodness' sake – girls love that!" Emma added.

"Don't let him hear you use that as a reason or he'll kill you," Jo said to Emma, who rolled her eyes and mumbled, "Yeah, well he does . . ."

"So, we want answers and you're not giving us any!" Jo said, putting her hands on her hips as Emma and Lily nodded gravely.

"Well, if you would just let me get two words in, I would!" I said, laughing.

"Oh. Right." Emma smiled sheepishly. "Well, go on, we're listening now, aren't we, girls?" she said, as the two others nodded solemnly.

"Okay, so I am madly and completely in love with your brother. And not because he looks like Ian," I said, grinning at Emma. "But because he's wonderful, funny, kind, generous, caring and the most amazing person I have ever met."

"So why aren't you going out with him?" Lily asked, clearly confused.

"I was scared. My mum isn't well and I was worried that if I went out with Adam and he broke my heart, that I wouldn't be able to cope with both my heartbreak and my mum's problems. She doesn't have anyone else to look after her and I need to be there for her."

The three of them looked at me, eyes wide and faces drawn.

"I'm so sorry." Jo was the first to speak. "We didn't know."

"It's okay, I didn't expect you to know, and I think it's pretty wonderful that you're here to kick my butt because I'm hurting your brother!" I said, grinning.

"But—" Emma started, but I needed to get this over with.

"Wait, please let me finish . . ." I said gently, and she nodded. "Last night, after having dinner here, we went to the Left Bank and I had a bit too much to drink. To cut a long story short, we finally ended up getting together, but for some reason, he took off this morning. I have no idea why, but he must have thought that I regretted last night. It's the only explanation."

"Well why don't you call him and talk things through?" Lily exclaimed, rolling her eyes.

"I've tried non-stop but he's switched off his phone and I have no idea where he is!" I exclaimed in despair.

They looked at each other, and as if reading each other's minds, they all took their phones out at the same time and speed dialled his number – but all fell on his voicemail.

"I'll try John," Jo said, pressing dial. "Damn, he's not picking up either," she said, looking up with a sigh.

"Okay, so do you have any idea where he could be?" Emma asked, putting her phone away.

I shook my head.

"So, what are you going to do about it?" Jo asked sternly.

"I can't go home, it'll drive me crazy just waiting for him there. And if I wait here, the three of you will probably drive me crazy," I teased, making them giggle. "I might just go down to the Left Bank to see if he's picked up his car yet. If it's still there, I'll wait for him. Anything's better than staying at home and waiting. If he comes back before I see him, please tell him he's got it all wrong and to call me."

The three girls nodded, smiling.

"Do you want us to come with you?" Jo asked, as the two others nodded excitedly.

"No thanks, girls," I said, unable to hide my laughter. "But thanks for offering. I love it that you care so much about him."

They came to group hug me and I was overwhelmed by their affection. I knew that they would love me like a sister if I treated their brother right, and I had every intention of doing so – as soon as I found him . . .

ADAM

*A*fter surfing for a few hours, we went to get a hot dog and a drink and sat on the beach, soaking up the sun and chatting. John told me about a house that was on show the next day and thought it would be perfect for us. I agreed to go with him to have a look. It really would be great to be independent again. I was definitely too old to be living at home with my parents – no matter how much I loved them.

John was all excited about seeing Anna again, and it was nice to see him caught up in a girl for once. He'd had a three-year relationship which had finished when he was twenty, the girl leaving him for someone else, and he'd had a hard time getting over her. Since then he'd had a few casual relationships but mostly just hooked up with girls for a night here and there, and had never been really interested in anyone until now. It would have been nice if things had worked out between me and Molly as we could have double-dated and done things together, I thought with a sigh. Now every time I saw Anna it would only serve to remind me that I'd lost Molly . . . I couldn't do the just friends thing anymore, that much was sure. I would have to move on and get on with my life – without Molly in it. I couldn't believe how miserable that made me feel.

72

MOLLY

I parked my car along the road, opposite the Left Bank, and could see Adam's car from where I was. I'd been waiting for about an hour and hoped that he would end up showing up. I was so bored. I'd already been for a walk along the river, listened to music, read a magazine, done a crossword puzzle. I was getting hungry and picked up my bag to grab the muesli bar I'd brought along. Of course, I couldn't find it anywhere as my bag was a mess. It was full of old receipts and bills, and I decided that now was as good a time as any to clean it up. I emptied its contents on the front seat and began sifting through the mess. I had a few envelopes which were bills I needed to pay, lots of old super-market receipts that I could throw away and then I fell on the brown envelope Adam had given me that night at Il Ciao's. His article. I'd kept it in my bag so that I could read it as soon as I was ready . . . Poor Adam, he'd wanted me to read it and I never did. I had a lot of apologising to do. I pulled out the A4 sheets of paper and began to read.

Is happiness a feeling or a choice?

When I was asked to write an article about whether happiness is a feeling or a choice, to say that I wasn't particularly enthusiastic would be an understatement. My area of expertise was sports, and this type of psychological feature was just not my thing. Besides, it seemed pretty obvious to me that either you felt happy or you didn't.

The subject of my article – who we'll call Little Miss Sunshine – was apparently one of life's happy bunnies, always with a smile on her face, finding the positive side to every situation. I was to use her as my muse to obtain the answer to the question. Basically, I would need to spend time with her and do everything I could to ruin her days by being cantankerous, grouchy and unfriendly to see how she reacted. In so doing, I would supposedly be able to determine whether she was a fundamentally happy person, if she had chosen to be happy or eventually if her happiness was just a facade.

All this was well and good, but there was still one very important point that hadn't been dealt with: how do you suddenly find yourself involved in a stranger's life – well, at least, often enough – to be able to test her and taunt her? A solution was finally found – two tickets and seven days' free accommodation in a hotel in Mauritius! (Okay, so I have to admit that that part was a treat. Mauritius, can you imagine?) So there it was – I was going to find myself seated next to Little Miss Sunshine on the plane, then in Mauritius my room would happen to be right next door to hers . . . From there on, I would have to follow her around and find myself doing whatever it was she was doing and basically become the bane of her existence.

Being a pretty happy-go-lucky guy myself, I wasn't sure how I was going to pull off being a grouch for a week, but surely it couldn't be that hard, right?

Then in walked Little Miss Sunshine . . . and out flew all my confidence. She completely beguiled me from the word go. Her feistiness and amazing sense of humour caught me off guard every time, and I was at a complete loss on how to do the job I had been sent to do. I tried so hard to scowl, to moan and groan and just be as unpleasant as possible, but the more I scowled and the more despicable I became, the funnier she found me. Nothing I did upset her for very long and her amazing smile was always back in place before I even had time to blink. And annoy her I did: I stole her suitcase, cancelled a glass-bottom-boat trip and put her down for marlin fishing instead, got a Steve Urkel lookalike (remember the guy on Family Matters?) to chat her up, pretending that she had told me she was really into him, I ruined her quad bike ride by being a terrible back-seat driver, and although I did get her angry a few times, she'd let me have it but would then be smiling again a few minutes later. She was just incredible.

As I got to know her during the week, I discovered that her life had been anything but easy, and that she was happy because she had chosen to be. She explained that, for personal reasons, she had promised herself at the age of twelve that she would be a happy and positive person – and so she is. Easier said than done, you say? Well, yes and no. She admits that at times it's hard and she does cry and feel sad like everyone else, but she simply refuses to let herself wallow in it. "I just make myself think about, and focus on, all the good things in my life and I soon find a reason to smile again," she explains – with a smile.

What an amazing life lesson I learnt from this brave and wonderful woman. It's so easy to let ourselves be overwhelmed by our problems and the little things that go wrong in our lives every day, but to see the way she handles life and her problems was truly inspiring. So, to answer the article's initial question – whether happiness is a choice or a feeling for Little Miss Sunshine . . . well, initially it was a choice, a decision. However, over time, it's become second nature to her to think positive and to see the glass half full instead of half empty, which thus makes her "feel" happy a lot of the time.

As to my own opinion on whether happiness is a choice or a feeling – well, I still believe that happiness is a feeling, but now I see that it's a feeling you have power over. Of course, no one can feel happy all the time, and everyone feels sad or upset sometimes – even the Little Miss Sunshines of this world – but I realise now that it's the way we choose to deal with these moments that makes all the difference. I believe that there's so much happiness that can be found by simply choosing to look at the good side of a situation instead of focusing on all the not-so-perfect sides of it.

So, to all of you out there, what I'd like to say before signing off is that although life isn't always easy, you can choose to be happy. Just remember that there's always something to smile about, even if it may not feel like it . . . Sometimes you may have to dig a little deeper to find it, and it may just be the smallest thing, but it's there – and when you find it, hold on to it and . . . smile.

— ADAM WILSON

Tears were rolling down my cheeks as I finished reading. It was beautiful and so full of admiration and love for me, and I hadn't even bothered reading it until now. I was such a fool. Poor Adam. I really needed to see him. Where on earth was he? I tried his phone again – still on voicemail. I contacted Zach to see if Adam had called or come over, but he hadn't.

I put the article aside and carried on tidying up. I had about five pens in my bag and tried them out, finding that three out of the five no longer worked. Suddenly I thought back to something Lucy had told me that Matt had done to try to win her back, and I realised that it was the perfect way to help pass the time. I grabbed a few receipts and Adam's article, turned them over and began writing.

73

ADAM

*J*ohn dropped me off at the top of the hill and I strolled down towards my car, hands in pockets, shoulders stooped, probably looking like the miserable fool that I was. As I approached my car, I noticed that there were dozens of bits and pieces of paper sticking out from under my front and back window wipers. What the...? *My car's been paper-napped.* I walked faster, annoyed that people had nothing better to do than mess with my car.

As I reached the front, I yanked out the pieces of paper that had been stuck behind my wipers, not bothering to look at what they were. But when I pulled out the last one, an A4 sheet, something caught my eye and I stopped to look at it more closely. It was a page of my article. Surely it couldn't be? How on earth had it got here? I found the other A4 sheet – yep, my article again. Turning the first sheet over, I saw something scribbled at the top. *No way!* How was that even possible?

My heart raced and I frowned down at all the bits of paper in my hand. There were old receipts and used post it notes and when I turned them over I saw that Molly had written comments on all of them. What was going on? I sat down on the hood of my car and pulled out the first receipt.

She had circled a deodorant. "Never, ever buy this – it really stinks!'" I snorted with laughter. What on earth was going on?

Another receipt and another item circled. The receipt was older and a bit faded so I had to look closely. I chuckled when I saw that it was from a bookstore for the book *Coming Home* by Harlen Coben. All she had written next to it was "Remember the flight to Mauritius ☺ ???" How could I forget? She had tried so hard to get me to talk to her. I cringed as I remembered how unfriendly I'd been towards her.

Then came an old supermarket receipt on which she had circled *Lindt white chocolate* and written "If you want me to forgive you for walking out on me this morning, no questions asked – this is what you have to buy me."

Must remember that one, I thought, as I tucked it into my back pocket with a smile.

The next one was an old movie ticket. I burst out laughing as I saw the title of the film – *Fifty Shades of Grey*. Next to it in her messy scrawl she'd scribbled "hmmm…!!!!!".

I chuckled as our Fifty Shades moments flashed in my mind.

I turned another one over and my breath caught as I read "I love you, Mr Not-So-Grumpy." Oh my God. She'd said it! She loved me! Adam Wilson was loved by Molly Malahan. I had waited so long to hear that. My heart was bursting with happiness.

Next receipt: *spicy pork chops* and written "NEVER again – just like that chilli episode in Mauritius."

I laughed as I walked to the back of the car and pulled out the last few pieces of paper from under the back wiper. A receipt with *strawberries* circled and next to it: "OMG can't believe I paid $8 for a box of strawberries!!!"

Once again, I snorted with laughter. She was really one of a kind, and I wished she was here with me so that I could take her in my arms. I took out the second-to-last paper and read it, my face breaking into a big grin.

CALL ME!
NOW!

Chuckling, I unfolded the last one.

WHAT ARE YOU WAITING FOR?
CALL ME!
P.S. I love you . . . SO MUCH.

I grinned happily as I grabbed all the bits and pieces of paper and opened my car door, suddenly in a real hurry to go. I didn't want to call her, I just needed to see her, to hold her, to kiss her. Now.

74

MOLLY

I was going crazy waiting for Adam to call. I'd been back for an hour already and still nothing. Zach had gone out and so I was home alone.

Stuff this, I thought as I grabbed my keys and headed out the door. I was going for a walk by the river because I couldn't stay indoors for a minute longer. I was going crazy. The awful realisation that Adam may just not want to see me flashed in my mind, and my heart plummeted . . . Surely not. It was impossible. I tried to reassure myself as walked towards my car.

I was about to drive off when I realised that if Adam did show up here, I wouldn't be there, so I dug into my glovebox and found another old receipt and wrote:

I'M AT DEEP WATER POINT.
PLEASE HURRY!

I ran back inside to get some sticky tape, stuck the note on the front door in full view so that he had no way of missing it and finally left.

I parked my car in the main car park so that Adam would see it easily if he came, and began walking along the river.

ADAM

I stopped off at the supermarket before heading to her house. I pulled into her driveway and groaned in despair when I saw that no one was home. My gaze caught on a piece of paper stuck on the front door. I got out the car, wanting to have a look in case she had left me another one of her notes. I couldn't help grinning at the thought of my car at the Left Bank.

Oh, thank goodness.

I raced back to my car and stormed out of the driveway, impatient to see her and worried that she would leave before I got there.

I drove slowly through the long car park, looking for her car, and finally spotted it. My heart raced at the sight of it and I chuckled, thinking how ridiculous I was.

I got out the car and locked up, looking around, but there was no sign of her. At worst, I would just stay by her car until she showed up, I decided. I suddenly wondered how long she'd spent at the Left Bank earlier as she'd obviously been waiting for me for a while judging from the number of notes she'd written.

I hesitated, not knowing whether to go left or right, worried that I would choose the wrong direction. I finally turned left, thinking that she would probably walk towards that side as it overlooked Perth in the distance and was beautiful.

I strolled along the river, past the café and towards the jetty. And there she was. I stopped dead in my tracks and every molecule in my body was suddenly on high alert. I was overwhelmed with a mixture of feelings: love, happiness, anxiousness – and, okay, lust – as I observed her. She was sitting on the beach, not far from the jetty, looking out towards the river. Her long curls fell loose down her back, and I couldn't wait to run my fingers through them.

I took off towards her and approached quietly, not wanting her to hear me. My breath caught in my throat as I stood behind her, taking her in for a moment. Finally, I said quietly, "Of all of the beaches, in all of Australia, you had to be sitting on mine."

76

MOLLY

I froze at the sound of his voice, but only for a second, then I swivelled around and gazed at him in wonder.

"Adam?" I whispered, having trouble believing that he was really here.

He smiled at me, eyes full of emotion. We stared at each other for a second then I bounced up and launched myself at him, throwing my arms around his neck, entwining my legs around his waist like I had at the Left Bank, once again catching him off guard. He staggered, almost losing his balance, but laughed and grabbed me, hugging me close. After a moment, I pulled away slightly, letting go gently and sliding out of his arms. "So, want to tell me why you ran out on me this morning?

"I guess I got my wires crossed," he replied with a shrug.

"But how? What happened?" I asked, confused, reaching out and running my hand down his arm.

"Your face, when I came to give you your coffee . . ." he said, shaking his head as if wanting to get rid of the memory.

"What do you mean? I was so happy to see you!" I exclaimed, having no idea what he was talking about.

He shook his head. "You were trying to smile but your eyes look so troubled . . . I thought you wanted to tell me that you regretted what had happened."

I shook my head, totally confused. "I honestly can't remember feeling anxious," I muttered, trying to think back to this morning. "Why would I have been troubled?"

"I don't know, but I can read you like a book, and there was something worrying you . . . and I just thought it was our night together."

Suddenly I realised what must have happened. "Dr Edwards' phone call!" I exclaimed, slapping my palm against my forehead. "Of course! That must be it!"

"What do you mean?"

"Just before you walked in, Dr Edwards called to tell me that my mum had had a panic attack the previous evening, but that she was fine. It bothered me that she hadn't called me – and I'd been thinking about that just before you arrived! Oh Adam, it had nothing to do with you!"

He groaned, grimacing. "I'm an idiot for jumping to the wrong conclusion and not even letting you explain."

"No, you aren't!" I said, hugging him. "I didn't make things very easy for you and it's very understandable that you had doubts about my actions, especially after my embarrassingly drunk-ish behaviour at the Left Bank last night!"

He laughed. "You were spectacular when you jumped into my arms and told me that her boobs were fake!"

I punched him playfully. "Yeah, well, it was true. Anyway, the important thing is that you don't have to worry anymore because I'm crazy in love with you and I don't, and never did, regret being with you last night. I want to go out with you,

Adam, I want to be your girlfriend, I want to love you and be loved by you . . ."

His face broke into a smile that did at least three laps around his head and probably reflected my own smile. "Finally," he whispered, cupping my face in his hands and gently brushing his lips against mine. I kissed him back tenderly, lacing my fingers through his hair as I deepened the kiss.

77

ADAM

*a*fter a while, she pulled away and looked up at me, eyes full of love. "I read your article. It's so beautiful. Thank you."

"I see you put it to good use," I said with a wink.

She beamed at me. "Did you like my little surprise?

"You made my day," I said truthfully, kissing her softly on her forehead. "But I can't believe you paid eight dollars for a box of strawberries!" I added in mock horror.

She slapped me playfully on the arm, laughing. *"That's what you remembered out of all the rest?"* she said incredulously.

"Of course not. I also now know that you hate my deodorant!" I said, straight-faced, making her laugh.

"Zach had asked me to buy him a deodorant and I had no idea what to buy, so took that one and it was awful," she explained, eyes brimming with laughter.

I chuckled, then lifted my pointer finger. "Oh, something

else I got out of your notes . . ." I said mischievously, reaching for my back pocket and brandishing a bar of Lindt white chocolate proudly in front of her. Her eyes grew wide at the sight of it, and she beamed as she took the chocolate from me.

"You got me my chocolate!"

I nodded and grinned, stroking her cheek with my thumb. "I love you, Molly . . . so much," I whispered, repeating the words she had written on one of her notes as I pulled her into my arms, breathing deeply, just savouring her delicious Molly smell. She suddenly pushed me away slightly, narrowing her eyes at me.

"Are you smelling me," she teased, imitating my Mr McGrumpy tone.

I threw my head back and laughed, crushing her to me and holding her tight. One thing was sure: now that I had her, I had no intention of ever letting her go . . .

EPILOGUE

"So when are you getting married?" Jo asked, bursting with delight. They'd been so excited when we'd arrived at Adam's parents' house hand in hand.

"Jo! We've only just started going out!" Adam exclaimed, eyes shining with amusement.

"Yeah, well, surely you must be thinking about it?" Emma said, smiling mischievously.

"Umm, not really, no . . ." I answered, grinning at Adam, who winked back at me.

"Why? Don't you love each other?" Lily asked, her smile fading.

"Madly," we answered at the same time, beaming happily at each other.

ACKNOWLEDGMENTS

First of all, to you my lovely reader, thank you so much for reading *Stuck with Me*. I really hope you enjoyed reading it as much as I loved writing it.

So many people were involved in getting this book out there and I really need to thank each and every one of you for your help.

I have to start by thanking my sister Christine for... well everything. Thanks for reading the book 100 times and still thinking it was great. Thanks for your help, encouragement, patience and amazing organisational skills during the eighteen months that it took to get this book ready. I could never have done this without you. Merci...

Huge thanks Mame et Pape for your unending support and encouragement, for giving me feedback when needed and most of all, for being so proud of me - you're the best.

Hugs and kisses to my wonderful children, Lea, Damien and Christopher for being so proud of telling everyone that their mum has written *two* books! I can't leave out my husband, Robert, for not complaining about my unsociable behaviour when I'm writing and editing, and just giving me the time and space I need.

Merci to Patrick and Petra for your input and encouragement all along the way. Thanks also for proofreading my manuscript and making sure that we didn't leave any mistakes in there.

To my wonderful father-in-law, Jean, MERCI for always showing an interest in my 'author' life and my books. It really means the world to me. Thanks so much also for reading both my books and being so enthusiastic about them, telling me that I'd made you discover a great new genre at your ripe old age of 85 🙂 You're the best.

Thanks also to my lovely friends Josephine and Jacqueline for inspiring me to write about Little Miss Sunshine. Their smiles and never-ending optimism are both super annoying (but in a really good way 🙂) and totally inspiring.

To Vincent, for being the amazing and generous friend that he is and offering me my first printed copies of the book yet again. Merci... Thank you so much for your neverending support and encouragement and everything that you've done, and do, for me since I started out on this adventure.

A special thanks to Dany Giraud for his help and encouragement. I'm so grateful.

Many thanks also to Meredith Schorr for your wonderfully helpful and insightful manuscript critique.

Thanks to my wonderful beta readers Irene, Nicole, Sequence, Harmony, Holly and Kit. Your comments and feedback were invaluable and my book is better because of you all.

A big thanks also to my copy and line editor Katherine Trail for your great work and for helping me to get all those last little loose ends fine-tuned.

Many thanks also goes to my wonderful cover illustrator, Sue Traynor, for your gorgeous cover.

Thanks also to all my social media followers who helped me along the way. Giving feedback ranging from who Adam should look like, to which version of my prologue worked best and also giving a few of my characters their names. Amanda, Audra and Zelda were winners of *Name a Character* competitions and named Lily, Zach and Samantha.

I can't leave out the wonderful authors from Chick Lit Chat and bloggers. Thank you all so much for your support, help and advice. You're amazing.

You are all instrumental in making *Stuck with Me* the book that it is. Thank you from the bottom of my heart.

I'd really love to hear from you on Facebook, Twitter or on my blog and would really appreciate it if you would leave a review on Amazon or Goodreads whenever you have a moment. Reviews are so important to indie authors.

Thanks so much & a bientôt!

ABOUT THE AUTHOR

Cassandra Piat is a part-time English teacher and a full-time disorganised mother and housewife. Whenever she has some free time she's either with her head in a book, watching a romantic comedy or writing her own romantic comedies.

She lives in Mauritius with her husband, who prefers TV to books, and her three children who keep her on her toes and don't leave her much free time to sit down and write.

She published her first novel *What's it Gonna be?* in December 2014 and *Stuck with Me* is her second novel. She loves writing stories that take place on her beautiful tropical island of Mauritius and sharing the island life with her readers. She is currently writing her third book in her head and hopes that she will soon have time to get it down on paper.

Join her on Facebook or Twitter and sign up for her e-newsletter http://eepurl.com/bJm4Wj

ALSO BY CASSANDRA PIAT

WHAT'S IT GONNA BE? : A ROMANTIC COMEDY

With no ring in sight, Lucy Evans decides it's time to move on. Before she knows it she's off on a blind date, meets a gorgeous Englishman and finds herself with a creepy love-struck stalker! But yet she's not finding it easy to get her ex-boyfriend out of her head...

Luckily she has friends to distract her. Vic, her eccentric childhood friend, thinks her husband is playing away and her best friend, Olivia, has met a mysterious Frenchman on an internet dating site and isn't sure whether she should run off to Paris to meet him, or run for the hills?

Filled with fun, humour and a cast of zany characters, *What's it Gonna Be?* is a wonderful, sincere and light-hearted tale of friendship, growth and love - with a lovely touch of Mauritius...

WITH THANKS

I would also like to acknowledge and thank both Medine Group, owners of Casela World of Adventures, and Imatech Ltd, the pioneers in Industrial Digital Printing in Mauritius, for their generous contribution towards the publishing costs and the printing of this novel.